## The house was burning down around them

The automatic bolts clacked open and Bolan yanked the hatch upward. The air was cool and damp. Bolan had no idea how badly Brognola was injured, but there was no time to be gentle. He stuffed the big Fed down the hatch and leaped after him.

The enemy was using Thermite grenades.

Bolan pushed himself up and grabbed Brognola by his belt. He had to get down the tunnel. The sounds of the siege quickly dimmed behind them. The rifle fire had already ceased. The enemy would be dispersing as the local fire and police descended upon the scene. The local fire brigade would be totally unprepared to deal with white-phosphorous and Thermite fires.

Bolan shook his head in disbelief. He and Brognola had been ambushed.

# MACK BOLAN ®
## The Executioner

# DON PENDLETON'S
# THE EXECUTIONER®
## SAVAGE GAME

## A GOLD EAGLE BOOK FROM
# WORLDWIDE®

TORONTO • NEW YORK • LONDON
AMSTERDAM • PARIS • SYDNEY • HAMBURG
STOCKHOLM • ATHENS • TOKYO • MILAN
MADRID • WARSAW • BUDAPEST • AUCKLAND

First edition March 2003
ISBN 0-373-64292-X

Special thanks and acknowledgment to
Chuck Rogers for his contribution to this work.

SAVAGE GAME

**Printed in U.S.A.**

A sword begs to be used.

—Old Chinese proverb

They say the Sword of Vengeance has two edges:
the light and the dark. It can turn on one who
wields it, or turn on the one who wields it into
the very thing which he sought vengeance against.
The Sword of the Executioner has a single edge:
Justice.

—Mack Bolan

For my friend Charles.

*Washington, D.C.*

Grenades flew through the shattered glass doors of the office building. White smoke immediately began to fill the parking lot. More grenades, fired from launchers rather than tossed by hand, flew out at high velocity and smashed into the barricades and vehicles. The skip chasers broke apart into separate spinning and skipping bomblets that scattered throughout the parking lot. Clouds of gray tear gas mixed with billowing white marking smoke as the hissing disks spewed forth their payload. From an upstairs window, rapid semiautomatic rifle fire began systematically smashing out the lights of the parking lot. The parking area was plunged into a ghostly twilight of choking gas and smoke.

Men burst from the building with guns blazing.

They attacked without hesitation. Their faces were completely obscured by the filters of the gas masks they wore and the night-vision devices attached to them. They looked like invaders from another planet. Cones of fire blossomed from their short-barreled, highly modified M-16 carbines in rapid, controlled bursts that swept the barricaded parking lot.

ATF agents and local law-enforcement officers fell in the withering fire.

The law-enforcement officers hadn't launched the gas attack, nor had they intended to launch one until the FBI negotiators arrived, and only if they failed. The negotiators hadn't arrived yet, and the enemy had launched a gas attack of their own. The agents' and officers' masks were still in their vehicles. The killers ruthlessly fell upon the law-enforcement agents as they clawed open their car doors and fumbled for their masks with choking lungs and streaming eyes.

The butchery was short and brutal, and as economical as it was merciless.

The men broke through the police cordon like a lit match parting a spiderweb. They killed anyone in their way and ignored those who were too debilitated to fight. Any half-blinded officer or agent who tried to shoot at them was slaughtered with coordinated, two-man-team counterfire.

Nearly every kill was a head shot.

The door of the communications van slid open, and three federal marshals leaped out with their pistols blazing in their hands. The first marshal had his head blown off before his feet hit the ground. The second put two rounds into one of the men and was killed instantly as the man returned fire without flinching. The third agent desperately raised his aim against the armored killers. A round from his service 9 mm pistol punched between the lenses of one of the killers' night-vision goggles and dropped him like a stone. The agent was immediately shot by two more gunmen and fell. The agent bravely continued firing. He put a pair of rounds through one of the killers' legs and shot the legs out from under a second man. He took down another killer with a head shot as bursts of rifle fire from out of the smoke reduced his own head to a spray of gore across the fender of the communication van.

The camera angle swept across the battlefield with increasing wildness as the cameraman began to panic. The camera suddenly swung down jerkily onto a goggled, faceless gunman who was pointing his rifle straight at the lens. There was an instant's blaze of fire from the rifle muzzle that filled the lens like a camera flash.

The videotape was suddenly nothing but white noise and gray fuzz.

Bolan paused on the tape. "You say this happened an hour ago?"

He spoke to Hal Brognola without moving his eyes from the screen as he rewound the tape. The battle began playing again on the monitor for the third time. Bolan had been in a motel about to go to bed when Brognola's call in the middle of the night had him heading to a secure briefing room at the Justice Department.

"Slightly less. It's all over the news." The head Fed chewed his unlit cigar vigorously. "A friend of mine in Justice called to let me know the bust was going down. I couldn't make it on such short notice. Three marshals went down in that firefight, and I wasn't there." He punched his cigar at the screen. "I get to watch the highlight tape."

"You should count yourself lucky, Hal." Bolan watched the precision of the breakout with intense interest. "Trust me, this is ugly, but watching the reruns beats the pants off the live show. I know the marshals are your boys, but they got dominated. So did ATF and local law."

The director of the Sensitive Operations Group knew Bolan was right. There was no reason for a man at his level to have been present. It didn't matter. He should have been there. "Yeah, well, you were in town, so I called you. I wanted your input."

Bolan watched the tape again. "Why aren't there any helicopters?"

"There were. There were two."

"And?" Bolan knew the answer from the big Fed's expression even as he asked the question.

"And one was shot down. Both the pilot and copilot were lost. The other took extensive ground fire and was driven off. It was forced to make an emergency landing less than a mile away."

"And what happened to our boys?"

Brognola glared at the monitor. "They are at large in the world."

Bolan considered the carnage on the screen. "These boys aren't your regular bank robbers or jewel thieves."

"Nope," Brognola agreed. "No way in hell."

"These guys are military, Hal."

"I know, you can tell by their equipment."

"No, it's more than that." Bolan watched the men on the screen fan out of the building in a loose two-pronged formation that allowed them to put any resistance in front of them in a cross fire. "It's their tactics. This isn't an escape we're watching, it's not even a breakout. They didn't try to sneak out the back or scat-

ter. They treated this like an ambush. In an ambush, when you
are outnumbered and outgunned, your best way out is a direct
attack right down the teeth of the trap. What we're watching is
a counterattack. They used smoke to obscure their break, tear gas
to disrupt the police cordon, and they had a sharpshooter take out
the lights in the parking lot. Look at their burst control. Not one
of those guys let off more than five rounds at a time. They all
had armor, night vision and gas masks ready to go."

Bolan leaned back in his chair. "These guys are Special
Forces. The police aren't going to find them, except by dumb
luck. They've dropped off the planet. They're either already toss-
ing back their complimentary drinks on flights to international
ports of call, or if they didn't disperse, they're hiding right under
our noses, and we're talking someplace so deep we'd never suspect it. They had a back-up plan and will have had secondary escape routes. These guys are gone."

Brognola sighed. "I know."

The soldier watched the single successful exchange of fire on
the tape. "One of your boys whacked two of them before he went
down."

"Yeah, we have that. We have one body, and one prisoner."

Bolan sat up. "You have a prisoner?"

"Yeah, the guy who got it through the legs. The marshal was
armed with a 9 mm. He put two rounds through the perp's legs
and went for the head shot. His hollowpoint broke apart on the
guy's night-vision gear and slewed along the side of his head.
Our perp has a major head wound and a concussion, but he's alive
and in custody. That, and we've got the body of the one who got
popped between the eyes." Brognola shrugged. "It's kind of
strange they didn't make any attempt to drag away their dead."

"I don't think they felt they needed to." Bolan sipped some
coffee. "I don't think their fingerprints are going to show up anywhere. These guys are ghosts."

Brognola clenched his teeth around his cigar. "There's always
a clue. Someone always makes a mistake."

"You're right, but I don't think these guys are worried about
us finding one, much less being able to use it," Bolan said as he
rewound the tape again. "No, what these guys have to worry
about is a leak. There was a police cordon, marshals, ATF agents
and local law all on scene. They had to have been tipped off."

"They were. About half an hour before the shit came down."

"Anonymous call?"

"Yeah, and untraceable. That's one reason the cordon was so haphazard. No one was sure if this was for real, and even then, no one was expecting anything like this. The tip came to the Justice Department. They called in marshals and local law for backup, and the ATF arrived and tried to usurp command. Federal and local law were streaming to the scene from all directions even as this went down, and these bastards just slipped past like smoke."

"They're Special Forces, Hal. To them, escape and evasion is almost as important as firepower, and they've had extensive training." Bolan's eyes narrowed. "But someone betrayed them from the inside. Someone in the know dropped a dime on them."

"Hmm," the big Fed considered. "Maybe someone got cold feet."

"That's my bet." Bolan's eyes scanned the slaughter on the screen. "And these boys would know that, instinctively, and they'd want payback. In a big way."

"You're right." It was clear Brognola wanted some payback of his own.

Bolan watched the tape. "What was in the building that was worth all that?"

"The ATF had a temporary suite of offices in the building. They were running some kind of sting. The director is being real reticent while he gets all his ducks in a row, but it must have been something valuable."

Bolan nodded. "What happened to the agents inside?"

"Well, they were bound and gagged. Then each was shot in the head. The director is already talking 'brutal assassinations' and such."

"They bound them and gagged them for the snatch." Bolan shook his head. "They killed them only after the deal went sour."

"Yeah, that's how I figure it, too."

Bolan smiled tiredly at his friend. "So what exactly can I do for you, Hal?"

"I wouldn't mind you taking a look at the guy we have in custody, and maybe eyeballing the body we have in the morgue, if you have the time." He returned the weary smile. "I'd consider it a personal favor."

Brognola was smiling, but his eyes were hard. They'd lost

marshals on this one. Bolan knew that as far as his friend was concerned, the gauntlet was thrown.

Bolan rose. "I think I'd like to look at the body first, and all of the items taken from both men. Then I'd like to take a gander at the boy you have in custody."

*D.C. County morgue*

MACK BOLAN GAZED upon the corpse.

It was the body of a white male, approximately six feet in height and 180 pounds with the physique of a decathalete. Even in death his hardened musculature seemed to have been hammered over his bones like armor. His brown hair was short but not particularly cut in a military style. He had a long scar on one forearm that looked like a knife wound to Bolan and some ragged and shallow scars like crow's-feet on one shoulder that looked suspiciously like the results of shrapnel.

The man's mouth was opened questioningly. His pale eyes were crossed upward as if examining the path the marshal's bullet had taken between his brows to blow out his brain.

"What did you find on him and his friend?"

"The quick and dirty reports say the M-16s were Vietnam vintage, but they've been extensively modified by an unknown armorer. The serial numbers have been acid etched away. We may be able to resuscitate them with X rays, but it was a very professional job, and I'm betting they tell us nothing. There are rifles like those littering half of Asia and South America, and I'm betting our boys weren't dumb enough to have stolen them from U.S. inventory stateside."

Bolan frowned. "See if you can get one of the weapons sent to the Farm," he said, referring to the ultracovert intelligence agency known as Stony Man Farm. "We might luck out if Kissinger can recognize the armorer's handiwork."

"That'll be tough. Agents are down. I don't think the Feds will want evidence temporarily disappearing on this one."

"But, Hal," Bolan said with a grin. "You're a Fed."

"Yeah, well, I'll see what I can do."

"What else do we have?"

"Their armor and night-vision gear is American commercial manufacture, but with all identifying tags and numbers removed.

The two personal side arms we recovered are surplus, 1960s vintage, Argentine-licensed copies of 9 mm Browning Hi-Power pistols, serial numbers removed. Both had their chambers throated and their feed ramps polished to accept hollowpoints. Both men also had folding combat knifes on them. The dead guy had an Emerson, and our boy in custody was carrying a Cold Steel model with a Tanto blade. Both American knives and commercially available, but someone removed the serial numbers anyway."

Bolan sighed. Everything the perpetrators had used was surplus, commercial or of foreign manufacture. None of it was likely to lead them anywhere. "Any personal effects?"

"Both men had five thousand dollars on them. Cash, in hundreds, fifties and twenties. All well circulated and pre-U.S. Mint design change. Each man had very professional fake IDs and credit cards. They both had commercial Timex watches. The dead man had a wedding ring and a crucifix. The wounded guy had nothing. Other than that, everything else was surplus clothing and communication gear."

"Have the personals been shipped to forensics yet?"

"No, the FBI has a team on the way right now to pick it up and take the body. I used my connections to get us here first."

"I'd like to take a look at them."

"According to the report, neither article has any maker's mark or number on it."

Bolan snapped on a pair of surgical gloves and picked up a sealed manila envelope marked "personal effects." He broke the seal and upended the envelope. "Do you mind?"

"Well..." Brognola let his eyes travel up to the lighting. "You and I aren't actually here, officially."

A ring rolled into Bolan's hand. He held it up to the light and turned it around in his hand. It was thick, solid gold and heavy, but other than scratches from wear it had no markings on it. He put it back and pulled out the crucifix. It was attached to a bit of twisted leather cord.

A slow smile spread across Bolan's face.

The head Fed leaned forward. He knew that smile well. "What?"

Bolan held up the cross. "You sang in the choir, Hal, does this look Roman Catholic to you?"

Brognola peered at the silver cross. It certainly didn't. The

Savior was crucified upon it, but it had smaller arms both above and below the main cruciform, and tiny connecting panels between them. Every inch of the silver cross was crammed with miniature images of saints and angels. "Okay, so our boy is Greek Orthodox, then?"

"Close." Bolan shook his head. "This cross has three arms, with side panels."

Brognola took a stab. "He's Russian Orthodox?"

"Getting warmer."

The big Fed worked his cigar from one side of his mouth to the other. "So he's, what, I don't know, Armenian?"

"You're good." Bolan grinned. "But try about five hundred miles north by northwest."

The man from Justice frowned deeply as he consulted his mental map of the world. "Ukrainian?"

"Give the man a cigar."

He stared at the cross in Bolan's hand. "Okay, smart guy. So how do you know?"

"The side panels. The Ukrainians used the side panels attached to the cross to represent the *tryzub*."

"Okay," Brognola said with a shrug. "What's a *tryzub*?"

"A trident. The trident was the symbol of the Ukrainian Independence Movement during the Soviet era. The symbol was outlawed by the Communists, so the Ukrainians hid it all over the place in their religious architecture and icons."

Brognola simply stared. Over the years the big guy had amassed a store of useful facts that would shame most doctors of cultural anthropology and one that any intelligence agent would kill for. A frown creased Brognola's brow. It was an amazing clue, and probably one that would have taken the FBI guys days to figure out, but it didn't necessarily help them. "Okay, so maybe the guy is Ukrainian. Maybe he's an ex-Navy SEAL who had a Ukrainian grandmother. Maybe this guy's Ukrainian mailorder bride gave it to him. Maybe it's just a good-luck piece he picked up from some guy selling stuff on the street in Times Square. Either way, like you said, these guys didn't seem to care too much about dragging away their dead. This takes us nowhere in particular, not with a whole hell of a lot more corraborating evidence."

"Yeah, you're right. Some corroborating evidence would

help." A glint lit Bolan gaze. "You said we have a live one in custody?"

Brognola nodded slowly. "Yeah."

"So, where is this guy we're holding?"

"Well, he took a bullet through each leg, and he has a significant though non-life-threatening head wound. The ATF took him to D.C. General. He's under heavy guard, and the last I heard he's in stable condition. He's conscious, and he's not talking."

Bolan frowned. "They should've taken him to the U.S. Naval hospital and put a platoon of Marines around him, but that'll have to wait." He shook his head. The ATF wasn't exactly Bolan's favorite government agency, and they tended to shriek loudly when they got their toes stepped on or rank pulled on them. Wheels turned in the soldier's mind. "Hal, contact the CIA. I'm going to need a couple of things that only they can get for me at this time of night. Then I need you to get me cleared to enter the hospital, and I need it ASAP."

"You have an idea?"

"Call it a hunch."

**2**

*D.C. General*

The two men walked through the Intensive Care Unit shoulder to shoulder. Eyebrows shot up on doctors, nurses and patients as the pair passed, and people instinctively moved to get out of their way. One doctor started to raise his clipboard questioningly at the two men and then apparently thought better of it. Hal Brognola was a large and purposeful man. People often got out of his way when his eyes and his stride announced he had serious business.

The man beside Brognola walked with the commanding presence of a freight train. The force of his personality filled all available space around him. His deep, "Tsar-Green" summer parade uniform had knifelike creases and service ribbons almost completely filled the left breast of his uniform. His bill cap was a matching green with red piping. Gold braid was entwined across the bill of the cap beneath a gold two-headed eagle on the brow. A heavy gold medal suspended on a purple ribbon bounced against his chest with each stride. A holstered pistol was strapped to his uniform belt.

No one in the ICU had ever seen a full colonel of Russian Military Intelligence.

A pair of wide-eyed interns pressed themselves against the wall to make way for the two men. A nurse flushed red as the colonel briefly examined her legs and strode on.

They crossed the ICU, and a pair of men in Alcohol, Tobacco and Firearms windbreakers jumped up from chairs flanking the door to a private room. Their hands crept toward the pistols under their jackets. An immense redheaded man just under six feet tall, and looking as if he were five feet thick, rose with them. His immense proportions strained his suit jacket. A Remington 870 pump shotgun with the barrel cut down to a brutal fourteen inches hung loosely in one massive mitt. The big man stared askance at the foreign soldier, and then his eyes widened as he saw Brognola.

"Hal!"

"Hey, Marc." The big Fed nodded at his fellow marshal. "Christ, Caron, how the hell do you ever pass the physical?"

The big man grinned. "I go to the Y. I work out."

"You need to spend more time on the stair climber."

"You want to wrestle, Hal?"

"No way in hell."

The big man snorted and turned his eye on the soldier. He kept his eye on the flap holster on his belt. "Hal?"

"Yeah?"

"Who's your pal?"

"Colonel Rabskyov." Brognola made introductory hand motions. "Colonel, this fat bastard is Federal Marshal Marc Caron. He's good people. Marc, this is Colonel Dimitri Rabskyov of Russian Military Intelligence."

The Russian colonel shoved out his hand. He grinned disarmingly and spoke his English with a thick accent. "Hello, Marshal Caron. I am pleased to be making your acquaintance."

"Uhh...yeah, me too." The immense marshal pumped the Russian's hand. "Welcome to the United States."

"Thank you."

"You're welcome." Caron turned to Brognola. "I know you have lots of interesting pen pals, Hal, but what's up?"

One of the ATF agents inserted himself beside Caron. "Just who are these people, and what are they doing here?"

"This man is acting in the capacity of special observer," Brognola said. "He's here as a special favor to the Justice Department."

The soldier slid an eye over at the big Fed. Brognola's every lie was seamlessly woven with strands of the truth.

The ATF agent blinked. "What the hell is that supposed to mean?"

"It means he is here to help out with this case, as a personal favor, to me."

"And just who the hell are you, mister?" The agent was clearly unimpressed. "No one's cleared this with me."

Caron rolled his eyes toward the light fixtures. Baby-sitting ATF agents wasn't his favorite activity, and getting uppity with Brognola wasn't an activity he would recommend to anybody, even to ATF agents he didn't like.

Brognola smiled with supreme tolerance and pulled out his Justice Department ID badge. "Tell me, Agent...?"

"*Senior* Agent," insisted the agent. "Senior Agent Wakefield."

"Tell me, Senior Agent Wakefield, what do you make of this?"

The agent scrutinized Brognola's badge intently.

Several seconds passed as the significance of the pay-grade and clearance level it represented slowly manifested itself in his mind.

It suddenly dawned on the agent that the man before him stood at the right hand of God. "Uhh..."

"Yes, exactly." Brognola nodded and smiled. "My guest and I would like a moment or two with your prisoner. You're the senior ATF agent present?"

"I...yes." Wakefield cleared his throat. "Yes, I am."

"Good. I would appreciate your presence during the interview and then having your input after its conclusion."

"Uhh..."

"Thank you." Brognola smiled good-naturedly. "Your cooperation and your professionalism will be reflected in my report."

Brognola, Caron and the Russian colonel strode past the befuddled agent and opened the door. Inside the private unit, two uniformed police officers looked up from their newspapers. Both of the cops had shotguns propped close to hand.

A Caucasian male lay on the bed with heavy bandaging around his head. Both of his legs were wrapped and elevated, IVs were inserted in both arms. His wrists were held by restraints. It was clear he was heavily medicated, but his eyes flicked over to scan the intruders. His eyes went wide as dinner plates as the Russian colonel crossed the room in three strides.

His jaw dropped at the sight of the medal the colonel wore on his chest.

Mack Bolan had personally considered the Hero of the Soviet Union medal overkill, but the boys at the CIA had come through with the uniform complete with service decorations and tailoring in under ninety minutes. Bolan set his face in righteous outrage as he locked his gaze with the wounded man. He thrust out his finger like God judging from on high. Bolan barked out at parade ground decibels in perfectly inflected Russian.

"I am Colonel Dimitri Rabskyov of Military Intelligence! I am here on authority of GRU director and commander of special forces! You will cooperate fully, or you will be extradited to Russia and summarily executed! Give me your name and former rank! Immediately!"

The man on the bed went as white as a sheet. His mouth opened and closed, and he looked as if he might throw up. His jaw set in desperate silence as he broke eye contact.

He wasn't going to talk.

At least, not yet.

Bolan changed gears. He turned to Brognola and spoke in English. "He's ex-Russian. I guarantee it. So is his friend down in the morgue."

The ATF agents gaped.

The wounded man's eyes snapped back to Bolan. His jaw dropped again in utter disbelief. His shocked pallor began to redden in outrage.

Bolan nodded at Wakefield. "Don't take any crap from him. He's fluent in Russian and English, and he doesn't have diplomatic immunity, whatever he's about to start claiming to the contrary."

The suspect's lips skinned back from his teeth in a snarl of pure hatred.

Caron threw back his head and his laughter boomed. He grinned delightedly at Bolan. "Man, I like you."

He nodded happily at the man on the bed. "And you? You're going down."

The wounded man's cheek muscles flexed. His eyes burned a hole in the wall in front of him.

Brognola frowned slightly. "Looks like he's clamming up again."

"Maybe we should adjust his morphine drip a bit. That might relax him a little," Bolan suggested.

The suspect's eyes widened again in alarm.

Wakefield stammered as the interview went into uncharted waters. "Sir?" His cell phone suddenly peeped. "Uh...wait a second. I need to, uh..."

Brognola smiled benevolently. "Take your call."

Wakefield flipped open the phone with immense relief. "Wakefield."

The agent nodded and spoke in affirmative monosyllables for several seconds and then clicked his phone shut. His eyes flicked to Brognola unhappily. "Sir? The FBI is here."

"Where?"

"On the roof. They just arrived by helicopter." Wakefield cringed under Brognola's gaze. "They say they don't want anyone interacting with the prisoner without them present."

The big Fed sighed. Wakefield was clearly between a rock and a hard place. Rank had been pulled on him all night, and the last thing Brognola needed was an interdepartmental squabble. "All right, tell them to come on down. We'll let this guy stew in his own juices for a few minutes."

Caron held his shotgun loosely and smiled at the perp on the bed. "Can I adjust his drip while we wait? I say we get him high as a kite for the nice FBI boys."

Brognola grinned. "No, not just yet."

"Can I stare at him until he starts crying?"

"Yeah, you can do that."

Caron grinned and waggled his craggy brows at the man on the bed. "You're going down."

The wounded man stared stone-faced at nothing. A bead of sweat rolled down his temple from beneath his bandaging.

There was a knock at the door, and Wakefield moved to answer it. Four large men in suits and dark glasses filled the hall. "Senior Agent Wakefield?"

"Yes, sir."

Wakefield fell backward as the sound-suppressed Beretta .22 pistol spit round after round into his face.

Bolan cleared leather.

He carried a Russian 9 mm Makarov pistol as part of his disguise. The Russian weapon was small and little more than a Walther PPK on steroids. It wasn't his favorite pistol or caliber. Bolan hadn't expected a firefight. However, he believed few things were more useless than an unloaded gun. The little pistol was stoked with the hottest hollowpoint rounds the CIA had been able to acquire for him. There was a round in the chamber and a loaded spare magazine in the holster's spare magazine slot.

The Russian pistol barked in rapid fire.

Bolan's first shot cleared the shoulder of the falling ATF agent and punched into the throat of the assassin. His second and third shots walked up the killer's face and toppled him backward into his companions.

Thunder erupted as Brognola produced his .357 Magnum pistol and began firing.

There was a ping as a cotter pin sprang into the room.

Bolan roared. "Grenade!"

The grenade clattered across the floor in the wake of its safety pin.

The suits outside heaved their dead comrade backward as they slammed the heavy hospital door shut behind them.

The grenade bounced off the bedframe and spun in the middle of the floor.

Caron hurled his bulk on top of the grenade.

There was a muffled crack and the big marshal shuddered horribly as the grenade detonated beneath him. One of the cops flew backward as shrapnel tore out from under Caron's body and chopped him down at the ankles.

Bolan strode forward and put his foot into the door mechanism with all of his strength.

The door flew backward as it ripped off one hinge.

Out in the ICU ward people were screaming and crying. The two ATF agents who had been guarding the door lay sprawled dead in their chairs. The holes from a .22-caliber Beretta leaked blood from the temple of each agent. The man Bolan had shot lay on sprawled on the floor. A fourth bullet wound in the forehead had joined the three the Executioner had put into the man's throat and face. Above the cacophony of terror, Bolan could hear a man urgently shouting down the hallway.

"Encountering heavy resistance! Target confirmed! West side! Seven up! Ten right! Request immediate extraction!"

The man was shouting in English.

Bolan whipped himself around the doorjamb in a firing crouch.

A second grenade came skipping and rolling down the hall.

Up the hall, the door to the fire escape slammed shut.

The rolling grenade was a gray cylinder the size of a beer can.

The service elevator three yards down the hall to Bolan's right stood open and empty.

He took his Makarov pistol in both hands. He took a half a second to adjust his aim, then squeezed the trigger.

The bullet impacted just beneath the rolling grenade. The round shattered on the hard linoleum floor, and its fragments erupted beneath the grenade and sent it skidding off to the left. Bolan tracked it and instantly fired off another round.

The grenade went spinning into the empty elevator.

Bolan raised his aim and shot the down button.

The button exploded in a shower of sparks.

The elevator chimed as its doors started to close.

The grenade detonated with a crack, and burning white streamers streaked between the closing doors and impacted the opposite wall. Flames immediately began to kindle in the wall as the streamers set fire to everything they touched. The elevator door closed and pinched off the fountain of white fire and smoke. The emergency stop bell began hammering. Fire alarms started clamoring, and the sprinklers in the ceiling began to spin and spit into life.

For the moment, the white phosphorus grenade was partially contained.

That was the least of Bolan's worries. The enemy was willing to burn down a hospital, and he'd heard the words *Target confirmed, west side, seven up, ten right*. He knew they were about to get hammered

"Hal, get everyone out of there! Now!" Bolan roared.

Bolan turned and ran back into the room. One of the cops already has his partner over his shoulder in a fireman's carry. Bolan helped Brognola seize Caron and drag the immense agent by his shoulders. The window began to rattle with the sound of rotors. The incandescent beam of a spotlight blazed through the window and turned the world into a blinding white glare.

"What about the perp!" Brognola shouted.

"Move!" Bolan shouted.

They dragged Caron into the rain and clamor in the hall. Bolan heaved the sagging door closed. He heard the sizzling hiss over the sound of the alarms and the screaming. Bolan and Brognola threw themselves down.

Thunder rolled in the room behind them. The beleaguered door blew off its hinges and sailed across the hall on the concussion wave. Grenade fragments cracked overhead at the speed of sound and ripped into the far wall in a lethal hail.

Bolan was already up.

The Executioner's ears were ringing from the blast as he lunged into the smoke and brimstone of the devastated private room and leveled the little Makarov into the blinding searchlight. The little pistol barked in his hand on rapid semiautomatic fire.

The light flashed off. The helicopter outside veered away.

The Makarov clacked open on empty. Bolan ejected his spent magazine and slammed in his spare. The slide rammed home on a fresh round as Bolan ran to the broken window.

The helicopter was a commercial Bell 212, and it was rapidly retreating.

Bolan emptied his little pistol as fast as he could pull the trigger.

The helicopter swung around the corner of the hospital as the pistol clacked open on empty again. The sound of the rotors grew loud again overhead.

They were heading for the roof to extract their assassination team.

Bolan dropped the spent Makarov and scooped up the fallen D.C. officer's shotgun. He quickly surveyed the suspect. The Russian was dead. He lay sprawled and smoldering in the twisted wreckage of his hospital bed. He was missing most of his head. His limbs were twisted in impossible positions, except for his left leg, which lay on the other side of the room.

The RPG-7 rocket-propelled grenade had detonated like doomsday in the close confines of the private room.

Bolan strode out of the smoke into the hall. Two nurses were desperately hosing down the burning wall with chemical fire extinguishers. Choking white smoke was beginning to ooze out from between the elevator doors. The inside of the elevator itself was an inferno, and water from the sprinklers hissed and sizzled as the sprinklers struck its metal doors. The sprinklers continued to rain down, and every alarm system in the hospital rang and howled. Dead and wounded littered the hall in pools of blood that spread and ran in the puddling sprinkler water.

The ICU looked like a bad day in Bosnia.

Brognola knelt over Caron. The big marshal's face, arms and legs were smothered in blood. The front of his jacket and shirt was in shreds. Tufts of torn Kevlar pooched up out of the rags of his clothes.

Bolan knelt. "He's alive?"

"He's a mess, but he's alive," Brognola confirmed. "His armor stopped most of the fragments from entering his torso, but his arms and legs are ripped up, and he has internal injuries from the blast. But Caron's as tough as they come."

Bolan nodded. He'd been in battle on every continent on the planet. He didn't see men selflessly throw themselves on hand grenades every day.

The head Fed glanced back into the black smoke of the private room. "How's our perp?"

"His own pals whacked him." Bolan looked down the hall at the fallen man in the suit who had claimed to be FBI. He frowned at the fourth hole one of his own compatriots had put into his head. They had made damn good and sure that the same mistake of leaving wounded behind wouldn't be made again.

"Hal, these guys are badasses of the first order."

Brognola stood as a doctor and an intern took over on Caron. The big Fed broke open his .357 Magnum pistol and replaced his spent shells. He clicked the cylinder shut. "Where'd they go?"

Bolan glanced at the ceiling. "They went up. They have a helicopter on the roof, and they're extracting as we speak."

"You get a make on the chopper?"

"Make, model and markings, and I put some rounds into it for further identification." Bolan cleared his throat against the stench of burned high explosive in his lungs. "But I'm betting it's already been reported stolen, and I think we'll find it abandoned in a field someplace come dawn. These guys don't make many mistakes."

"They killed three marshals in the commission of a felony, and now they've wounded a fourth. That's the worst mistake these assholes ever made." Brognola clicked open his cell phone and punched a speed-dial button. He quirked an eyebrow at Bolan. "What have you got going on?"

"Well, actually, I was thinking of going to Costa Rica for a few days."

"Costa Rica?"

"She likes surfing."

"Do me a favor? Stick around."

*The Boneyard*

The Iceman stood with his hands in the pockets of his brown leather jacket. The predawn coastal fog crept along the ground and obscured everything at ankle level. It writhed around the tombstones and flowed over the slabs of cold marble. It seemed to swallow all sound and leave the world in a thick, threatening limbo between light and darkness. Mausoleums, crosses and markers stood out of the ground-crawling fog like islands of death in a silent undulating sea.

The thick thule fog fell like a macabre slow-motion waterfall into the hole at the Iceman's feet.

The man in the grave sniveled and shook. The casket was a cheap affair of unfinished pine, with a double-door lid. The bottom door was closed. The upper one was open, revealing the hysterical man from the waist up. Other than the manacles chaining his hands to his sides, the man showed no outward signs of any physical harm. A whimper of incoherent terror escaped his lips.

The Iceman's glacial blue eyes regarded him in the twilight.

The worthless puke had no idea what real terror was, but he was about to learn, the Iceman thought.

"All right," the Iceman said finally. "Now I'm pissed."

He didn't sound angry. The remark was almost conversational in tone.

The man in the hole shuddered.

The six men in formation around their leader radiated genuine anger. All of their professional lives they had lived by the rule that they held one another's asses in their hands. The idea of betrayal was unthinkable.

It was payback time.

"Kip?" the Iceman said with a sigh. "What *were* you thinking?"

The man shuddered again. "Please, God, I—"

"No, 'Please God' nothing." The Iceman's voice was emotionless. "You betrayed us."

"No!"

"Do you remember what I said I'd do to you if you screwed us?"

"I—"

"I said I'd put you in the Boneyard, Kip." The Iceman cocked his head slightly. "Do you know where you are?"

"Please!" The man's voice was a muffled scream coming up out of the open grave. "I didn't!"

"Yes, you did. I've run all the angles, and you keep coming up the weak link in an otherwise sound plan. The only real question that matters now is how badly you've screwed us and how much damage control I need to do." The Iceman scratched his short blond beard. "And I suppose, out of idle curiosity, I want to know why."

"I didn't!" The man in the pit was shaking uncontrollably. The manacles and shackles that held his limbs rattled and clinked against the pine box surrounding him. "I swear!"

"You know something, Kip? They say the fear of death is a thousand times worse than death itself." The Iceman nodded sympathetically. "And I realize right now you've got about as much fear going on as you think you can deal with, but let me tell you. Death? It can be real easy. I just put a round between your eyes, and bang, you turn off like a light."

"No!"

"We cover you over, and it's done. Hell, we'll even drink a whiskey to your skinny Benedict Arnold ass. We'll give you a nice marker. Marble, with a horse on it or something. I'll even give you my word, right now, that we won't go after your family."

"Please!"

"But, on the other hand, Kip," continued the Iceman, "sometimes the fear of death can be absolutely justified. Sometimes death can be real hard. For example, maybe I don't put a bullet in your head. Maybe I just close that lid, cover you over and death is hours of pitch-black, claustrophobic, asphyxiated screaming with the spiders."

The man in the grave began thrashing mindlessly against his shackles.

"You know what the problem is here, Kip? The problem is that the fear of death really is, indeed, worse than death itself. However, the flip side of that, and unfortunately for you, is that while there's life, there's hope. Even in a position like yours. Right now some part of you deep down inside really just can't believe this is happening, and that somehow you're going to get out of this."

The Iceman stared out into the fog. "Funny how that is. You know, one time, when I was in Desert Storm, we took out this Iraqi strong point. Word had just come out about Saddam had been torturing our downed pilots. We were real pissed, and to be honest, we just weren't taking any prisoners that day. Anyway, the bombers had blown open their bunker and we went in and started slaughtering these guys like sheep. I tell you, these poor bastard Iraqi militia goofs just flipped out. They threw down their rifles and went into bizarro mode. They wept, they cried, some of them crawled headfirst into their sleeping bags like they could hide from us. One poor son of a bitch actually shoved his head and shoulders into his cubby and lay there with his ass hanging out, legs flailing, while we filled his rectum full of lead. Creepy stuff, I'm telling you. I didn't know whether to laugh or cry." The Iceman suddenly quirked an eyebrow. "Kip, have I mentioned the spiders?"

"Stop! Just...stop! Please, God, just stop!"

The Iceman sighed and held out his hand. "Michael Brand?"

A very large man in a very expensive Italian suit and coat responded by reaching into his pocket and pulling out a jelly jar. He handed the Iceman the jar without taking his eyes off the man in the hole. The Iceman held the jar up in the wan light of the

predawn. There were over a dozen small shapes in the jar. Most
were tiny, unmoving clumps. A few of the small shapes tensed
or moved as he gently tilted the jar back and forth. "Know what
these are, Kip?"

The man in the grave grew quiet again. Tears streamed down
his face.

The Iceman nodded slightly now that he had the man's full
attention. "They're brown recluses, sometimes called fiddler spiders because of the violin-shaped markings on their back. You're
from back east, so you've probably never heard of them. They're
sort of America's other poisonous spider."

The man stared up in uncomprehending horror.

"Now, black widows most people have heard of. Couple of bites
from one of them, you'd most likely die. You lock as their poison
attacks your nervous system." The Iceman lazily swirled the contents of the jar. "Now, the poison of the brown recluse is more top-
ical, and it's necrotic. Do you know what necrotic means, Kip?"

"Stop, please...stop—"

"Necrotic poisons kill all tissue they come in contact with. The
spider is literally trying to turn you into soup. Leaves a horrible
wound. The bite spreads, swells up like a volcano and then col-
lapses and spreads. I've seen an untreated bite from one these little guys leave a scar three inches long and an inch deep. I swear
it looked like someone had dug a trench in the guy's arm with a
garden trowel. The poison just eats away the flesh. It's horribly
painful, from what I understand. Another interesting thing, you
know black widows? They're real lazy bitches. Nonaggressive.
But brown recluses, they don't spin webs. They're what I like to
call proactive. They're hunters, and they're aggressive. They'll
bite you again and again given the opportunity." The Iceman
blinked and looked away from the jar. He turned his attention
back to the man in the hole. "I'm sorry, Kip. Sometimes I do go
on. How are things down there, anyway?"

The man moaned piteously.

The Iceman nodded. "Yeah, feels pretty close, doesn't it? I
know that coffin's a little small, but Kip, you screwed me on such
short notice that I had to use what I had on hand."

The man's voice was a hoarse whisper. "L-listen...please..."

"Kip, I'm here to listen. As a matter of fact, I'm going to give
you my full, undivided attention. You are going to tell me every-

thing I need to know, and if you don't, I am going to upend this jar of spiders onto your face and bury you alive. Do we understand each other?"

"I—"

"Good. Now, why did you screw with us, Kip?"

The man made a gasping sound that ended in a sort of gobble.

"You're gibbering, Kip."

"You said...you said no federal agents would get hurt."

"And none would have. We had them overwhelmed and hog-tied in seconds. Except then you went behind our backs and engineered a goat screw of monumental proportions. Federal agents did die, Kip, and, I might add, you managed to get several members of one of my team killed."

"There were...ATF agents in the building."

"Yes, and there was also about ten million in unmarked bearer bonds in that building that I had my eye on."

"But I knew them. Some were...some were friends of mine, we—"

"We were your friends," corrected the Iceman. "To the tune of just under one and a half million dollars in the last two years. This was a conscious decision you made. You gave up your old friends when you decided to work with us. You betrayed your badge. That was the past, but you've also betrayed us, and this is now. So tell me what exactly did you do?"

The man whimpered.

"Kip. I'm going to speak very slowly." The Iceman unscrewed the lid of the jar. Small shapes tried to crawl up the side and slid back down the smooth glass. "What did you do?"

"I made a phone call!" The man gasped as he admitted his betrayal. "But it was anonymous! It was just a tip! I swear it! You were supposed to have detected the police activity on the radio! It was only to warn you off!"

"Well, somehow I didn't get the good word in time. Your buddies died. Good men who work for me died. You've screwed everyone, Kip, including yourself. Now tell me, who did you call?"

"The Justice Department."

"What branch of the Justice Department?"

"Th-the Marshal...Service."

The Iceman considered this for long moments.

"We met heavy resistance at the hospital. We couldn't extract our wounded man, so we had to whack him in the hospital. In the process, we lost another man." The Iceman nodded at the grim-faced men surrounding him. "He happened to be a close personal friend of ours. Part of the inner sanctum, you might say. When he went down we had to cap him to prevent leaving another leak behind. The whole hospital thing went south."

The hatred radiating out of the silent, stone-faced men was palpable.

"Now, how did that happen?"

"I—I don't know!"

"We were expecting some cops and agents in the hospital. That was factored in. They should have presented no problem. But there was a foreign military officer present. A Colonel. He had to have been Russian. That really disturbs me."

"Wh-what?"

"What was he doing there?" the Iceman continued. "How did they know that Pavel was Russian? Kip, this presents a problem of monumental proportions. One much larger than your anonymous phone call to the Marshal Service."

"I didn't—"

"There was also some kind of real high-level suit there. Someone with a lot of pull. Someone who cut right through the red tape, and both he and the colonel made like Quickdraw McGraw when my team went in. We caught them absolutely flat-footed, and we still got outshot and had to make a hot extraction. You know, Kip, because of you, I had to light up an entire hospital just to kill one of my own men."

"It was an anonymous call!" The voice of the man in the grave rose toward a shriek. "I swear it!"

The Iceman calculated the abject fear of the man in the pit. "Maybe, but something ran up a red flag with someone, and now I have a security problem. I have unwanted attention from unknown sources, and frankly, Kip, I blame you."

"No, please, listen! You don't have to do this. You don't—"

"I'm also out ten million dollars. I'm out a close personal friend. I'll give you all the credit in the world. Up until now, you were a very valuable intelligence asset, and it is going to cost me a great deal of time, money and trouble to replace you."

"Listen, I'm—"

The Iceman's blue-eyed gaze was glacial. "I'm not pleased."

"Listen, please! I can make it good! I can—"

The Iceman upended the jar over the grave.

A dozen tiny shapes fell fluttering downward, waving their legs.

The man in the grave screamed like an animal.

The Iceman tossed the empty jar to Brand and turned away. Below, the ATF agent screamed and thrashed in an agonized frenzy.

The Iceman spoke over his shoulder as he walked away. "Bury him."

*Washington, D.C.*

MACK BOLAN SAT in a booth and ate pancakes.

Hal Brognola's omelette sat untouched on his plate. He was working on his third cup of coffee. A waitress warily eyed the stub of his unlit cigar. The big Fed shook his head as Bolan poured on the syrup. "Man, how can you eat?"

Bolan looked up from his pancakes and smiled.

Brognola shifted in the booth at the stupidity of the question and nodded at the waitress to freshen his coffee. He knew the big guy could eat anything at any time of day. It didn't matter whether it was a seven-course meal in one of the finest restaurants in Paris, or some squirming thing Bolan had pulled from beneath a rock in the rain forest of Belize. He took each with equal gusto. Hard experience had taught him to take food whenever and whatever way it presented itself. Brognola was also aware that deep down, the soldier knew better than most human beings on Earth that each meal could be his last, and he treated each one as such.

The head Fed had to smile. He was the one who chewed cold cigars, pounded down colder coffee and worried. That was his job. Bolan was a breed apart.

Few people in the world could take utter satisfaction in a stack of flapjacks at three in the morning the way Bolan did.

"What are you thinking, Hal?"

"I'm thinking about what you said, about these guys being Russian special forces."

"Yeah, and?"

"I don't like it."

Bolan sipped his coffee. "Neither do I."

"I mean, I don't doubt what you're saying."

"I know that."

"But what are Russian special forces doing running an operation in D.C.?"

"Ex-Russian special forces." Bolan pushed his bite of pancakes to one side of his mouth. "And it wasn't an operation. It was a rip-off. They just ran it in—"

"A precise, military fashion."

"Exactly. Hell, Hal, you and I both know bank robbery and similar crimes are losing propositions. The bad guys almost always get caught, and even more often end up getting gunned down by the law. Most bank robbers are idiots. Yahoos off the street who think a financial institution is just a big piggy bank they can break into. It's just dumb. Even if you succeed, that much money is hard to hide. Ripping off convenience stores is easier, and given a year of steady work, almost as profitable."

"Yeah, but these guys weren't goofballs with guns all wired up on crank."

"No, they weren't. They were highly trained and highly organized. They were going for bearer bonds, not cash, and if they're using Russians, then they have an international outlet for the money. Clean as bearer bonds are, they weren't going to do anything with them stateside. They did their research and recon well ahead of the job, and even when the whole thing went south they counterattacked and pulled off a perfect extraction. Then they came back to the hospital and cleaned up the loose ends."

Brognola looked up from his coffee. "You said *using Russians.*"

"The Russians didn't plan this. They were the hired talent. The guys who came to clean up were shouting our coordinates to the chopper in English."

"You don't think the Russian *mafiya* was behind it?"

"No, I don't." Bolan considered the bite of flapjack on his fork very carefully. "Whoever was behind this had contacts in Russia. Special forces contacts. He brought in a bunch of guys who would, even if the situation went sour, be unidentifiable to U.S. law enforcement."

The big Fed smiled smugly. "You identified them."

"We're pretty sure one of them was Ukrainian. That's all we know. That's probably all we'll ever know. Even assuming we could get the Russian GRU to give us information on their operatives, getting close to whoever hired these guys will be next to impossible."

Brognola's smile fell. "We have contacts. We can work it."

"No, the big fish are here. They have international connections in the U.S. Special Forces community. They have contacts in intelligence. They have contacts in the ATF and God only knows how many other organizations."

Brognola examined Bolan's face carefully. "How would they have so many contacts?"

"Because they're all Special Forces operators and intelligence officers."

There was silence in the booth for long moments. "Is that a hunch?" Brognola asked.

"Yeah." Bolan nodded. "But an educated one. You saw the tape. These guys were experts with their weapons. They knew the building inside and out, and they knew who would be inside and where. They practiced this a dozen times before they did it. When it went sour, they broke out of the police cordon like it wasn't there and pulled the big fade. They came back and cleaned up their mess. That's not the work of criminals. That's not the work of terrorists. These guys are operators. If you're an operator long enough, you end up with very interesting friends in very interesting places. Just think about how many weird and wonderful pals you and I have accumulated over the years, Hal. Now, what if you and I decided it would be more profitable to go into business for ourselves, and I'm not talking as mercs for some banana-republic dictator or muscle for drug lords. I'm not even talking as consultants for foreign governments or business conglomerates. I'm talking you and me, Hal, going into business, for ourselves, and I'm talking big money crime."

Brognola shook his head morosely. "Terrorists and criminals are usually dim bulbs and scumbags. That's always been our advantage. What you're talking about are highly trained and highly motivated professionals, recruiting people of like mind and running operations on their own turf."

Bolan nodded. "Like I said, it's just a hunch."

The big Fed stared off into the middle distance.

Bolan knew the look. "What are you thinking, Hal?"

"I'm trying to imagine a crime syndicate made up of U.S. Special Forces and intelligence agents."

"If it's true, it's bad." Bolan leaned back in the booth. "But we've faced worse."

"Maybe."

"What's bothering you?"

"I'm imagining a group like Stony Man's Able Team or Phoenix Force going over to the dark side, Striker." His gaze filled with cold dread. "And I'm imagining a man like you leading them."

**4**

*The Clubhouse*

The Iceman walked into the rec room of the Clubhouse. Michael Brand sat in one of a number of immense leather chairs and smoked a cigar. A fire roared in the fireplace. The Clubhouse was a marvel of terraced architecture and clung to the steep mountainside by cables and struts so cleverly concealed that it looked as if it almost hovered in space. The panoramic window looked out over the redwoods and the Pacific Ocean beyond. The sky was overcast, and the morning fog hadn't burned off. The fog shrouded the ocean and skirted the trunks of the gigantic trees.

The Iceman went to the bar and poured two fingers of Macallan's eighteen-year-old single-malt whiskey into a pair of glasses. "What do you think, Jeremy?"

A slender man with wire-rimmed glasses sat at a desk with a laptop in front of him. A home entertainment system dominated the entire wall at his side. One of its tape decks slowly revolved in record mode. The man spoke without looking up. "I think that was some cold shit you pulled this morning."

"Yeah, I know. You don't like the wet stuff." The Iceman dismissed the matter. "But what do you think about the situation?"

"I don't know, Ice." The man stopped typing and folded the lid of his laptop. "I think the situation is contained, but let's emphasize the word 'think.'" He sighed gratefully as he took the whiskey. He had spent a very long night going over everything very carefully. The whole situation should simply not have happened. "I told you I didn't like screwing with the Feds."

"I know you did." The Iceman took a sip of his whiskey and suddenly grinned, revealing his startlingly white teeth. "But the deal was so sweet!"

Brand snorted in disgust and blew a smoke ring toward the ceiling. "Yeah, sweet, until Kip grew a conscience." The big man shook his head slowly. "I'm just not going to forgive him for that."

Jeremy nodded. "The deal was sweet, I'll admit it, but it went south. Shit happens and informants can be compromised. I think we can all accept that." His face tightened. "But I don't like what happened at the hospital. That was just plain odd. It's more than odd. It's anomalous, and it's indicative of a larger problem."

The Iceman looked at his drink. "Where did you put the Russians?"

"I got them out of the country and put them in Vera Cruz." Jeremy shook his head again. "And, man, are they pissed."

The Iceman could well imagine how angry they were. "Wire them each twenty grand and tell them to lay low for a while. Tell them I'll contact them personally in a week. Ask them what kind of compensation they think is adequate for the families of Pavel, Torosyan and Golik and see that it's sent. Also, tell them the traitor has been found and dealt with."

"You've got it."

The Iceman glanced at the slowly revolving reels in the tape deck. "How is our old buddy Kip doing, anyway?"

Jeremy grimaced as he leaned over and turned up the volume knob on the stereo. A ghostly mewling moan came through the gigantic surround sound speakers. The eerie sound was nearly constant and was punctuated by an occasional snuffle or gasp and the clinking of chain.

"He's been down about three hours. Half an hour ago he burst into another fit of screaming. He isn't thrashing much anymore.

It's mostly moaning and crying now, but he's got so much poison in him he can't stop shaking. I think he's tired. He screams when he gets bit, but I think even the spiders are getting weary." A despairing shriek tore through the speakers as if in answer to Jeremy's words. There was a quick thrashing, and the shriek fell into a shivering fit of crying. Jeremy turned down the volume until the sound of hellish despair was little more than background noise. He sighed distastefully. "Pine box, loose dirt, I'm thinking he'll be running out of air in another six or seven hours."

"Goddamn Feds," Brand said as he raised his bulk from his chair and went to pour himself another whiskey. "We should have buried him with some rats."

Jeremy frowned. "Rats really aren't that aggressive. You put them in a box with a thrashing hysterical human, and they're going to hide in the corner. They'd be more interested in chewing their way out than chewing on him."

"Fine, rabid hamsters, whatever. I want something going Discovery Channel on the Judas son of a bitch."

The Iceman regarded Brand dryly. "You've never seen someone after the spiders got through with them, have you?"

Brand shook his head.

The Iceman smiled. "One of these days, Michael, when we have nothing better to do, we'll disinter someone I put down. I think it might be instructive. For everyone." The Iceman swirled his Scotch whiskey. "The three of us can do Kip, tonight, if you like."

A fresh scream from the speakers punctuated the remark.

Jeremy suddenly looked very uncomfortable.

Brand took a long pull of whiskey. He met the Iceman's gaze and swallowed with difficulty. It struck the big man for the thousandth time that he could never really be sure what the Iceman was thinking. Brand was an expert at reading people, but behind the pale blue eyes, the Iceman was as close to a blank slate as he had ever encountered. He never knew when he was joking. He never knew when he was being tested.

He never knew whether he had passed or failed.

The Iceman was the scariest human being Brand had ever met in a long career of working with some of the scariest men on the planet.

Brand cleared his throat. "No, that's okay, Ice. I'll take your word for it."

The Iceman cocked his head. "You're sure?"

"Yeah, I'm sure."

The Iceman shrugged and changed the subject. "We're going to have to do a little recruiting."

The three men considered the losses they'd taken. Jeremy sipped his whiskey. "Getting more Russians should be no problem. There's a lot of disenchanted special forces guys drunk and jobless in Moscow these days."

"I'm thinking more locally." The Iceman turned his gaze upon the Pacific Ocean. "We have big things coming up. We need some upper echelon people we can trust and who add something to the pie."

The other two men considered the future.

The Iceman turned his attention to the present. "I want to know who that Russian officer was in the hospital, and I want to know who the big suit was with him."

Jeremy flipped open his laptop and his cell phone. "I'm on it. Though it's going to take some money and some time."

A muted scream tore through the speaker.

The Iceman's gaze stayed unblinkingly on the ocean. "We're still taping?"

"Oh, yeah. We've enough tape for the whole thing."

The Iceman nodded. "Send a copy to Kip's family."

"You've got it."

"Goddamn Feds." Brand suddenly sat up and grinned happily. "Hey, let's send a copy to Janet Reno."

Jeremy looked up from his computer and rolled his eyes. "Janet Reno isn't attorney general anymore, Michael."

The Iceman turned from the window. His pale eyes lit up with some inner humor. "Send her a copy anyway."

*Stony Man Farm*

MACK BOLAN SAT across from Aaron "The Bear" Kurtzman. The computer expert considered the problem that had been set before him. He had watched the videotape a dozen times and gone over both Bolan's and Brognola's reports.

"Well, I agree with your conclusions, and frankly, I don't like them at all."

Bolan nodded. He didn't like them either. "Bear, any word

from the Cowboy on those M-16s?" He referred to the Farm's armorer, John "Cowboy" Kissinger.

Kurtzman sat back wearily in his wheelchair. "Only that the workmanship is first rate. He says you could hit the butt of an ant at three hundred meters with one of them, and we're talking about a Vietnam War vintage M-16 that has seen a lot of hard use. Nothing special was done other than rebarreling. The weapons were just tuned and fitted to absolute perfection. Cowboy says they're so clean he'd be proud to let his mother eat off of the receivers."

"What about the pistols?"

"Ex-Argentine, 1970s manufacture. Like the report said. On closer inspection, the magazine wells were beveled for fast reloads, and the magazine safeties were disconnected for the same reason. The feed ramps were polished, and the barrels throated to facilitate hollowpoint rounds."

Bolan frowned. They were workingman's modifications for trained individuals expecting to go into action. "Nothing unusual? Nothing Cowboy could recognize?"

"No, nothing fancy. Just top-drawer workmanship. He says whoever these guys are they had one hell of an armorer."

It was a dead end. Bolan glanced at the vast wall map dominating the wall. "Where would you hide a bunch of ex-Russian special forces guys, Bear?"

"We'll assume some of the bad guys saw you in all of your Tsar-green glory in the hospital. They won't send their boys home to Mother Russia if they think Russian Military Intelligence is somehow onto them. We'll eliminate all of the former Soviet Republics, and that leaves, well..." Kurtzman waved his hands. "Our pals could be anywhere from the beach in Bora Bora to watching the spring roosting of the puffins in Greenland."

Bolan shook his head. "No, whoever is running this show has some major unresolved problems. He'll want these guys out of sight, but close at hand. No place where they're hard to get hold of or needing connecting flights if they need to deploy rapidly. I don't believe they'll be dispersed, but he'll have put them in a place where they won't attract a lot of notice."

"That would have to be someplace in North America. If these guys were Russian *mafiya* I'd say they'd be someplace in Canada hiding out with one of the local chapters." Kurtzman considered the map. "However, since you're assuming these guys are operators, I'd say Mexico. If these guys are ex-Russian special forces picked for a job in the States, they'll all speak English, and at least some of them have probably cross-trained with Cuban special purpose troops and have some Spanish, as well. Mexico is close by. By international standards, it's a wide-open town. It's big. Tourism tops its economy. The natives are friendly, and as long as you behave, they don't look too close or ask too many questions. Particularly when they're paid not to."

"Bear, I'm thinking about a squad of men."

"Okay. Eight to twelve great big white guys who speak Spanish with funny accents. Somewhere in all of Mexico, drinking beer. I'll get right on that then, shall I?"

"No, keep the search in the north. Mexico is still having problems with guerrilla warfare in Chiapas. Foreign mercenaries have been involved. A squad of white men with funny accents who carry themselves like soldiers could draw all the wrong kind of attention in the south. Keep it north, and narrow it to the east coast, and keep it coastal. These guys got hammered in D.C. They'll be down for some R and R. Beer, beaches and babes."

Kurtzman nodded thoughtfully. "It's still a needle in a haystack."

"I know."

The computer expert's brow creased. "They're worse than needles, Striker. They'll be cutouts. Assuming we can even find them, and hit them before they move. They won't lead us anywhere. That's why they're using the Russians in the first place. If the guys running this show are just half as good as you seem to think they are, they'll already have this base covered."

"I know, I don't want to hit them. I want to follow them, if possible, and see if they lead us to any kind of clue we can use."

"Well..." he said before letting out a long breath. "I'll put the CIA on it, and I'll call every marker we have in Mexico, but I can't promise anything."

"I know, but the Russians aren't the key to this. They're only a secondary avenue."

"What's the key, then?"

"The real operators themselves."

"How so?"

Bolan stared at the map. His eyes played over Vietnam, El Salvador, Nicaragua and Kosovo. "The top dog of this group is a guy with a dream. He'll have contacted good friends of his in special ops and intelligence and recruited them to form his core group. From there, they'll have used their contacts in other countries to pick up men and materials as needed. I suspect over the past ten years they've formed quite an interesting little cartel of crime."

Kurtzman saw where this was going. "And your primary avenue you're not telling me about?"

"We're not going to find these guys by any standard means. Only dumb luck or a real major blunder on their part will give us any kind of clue we can use to find them. However, if I'm right, these guys will always be in the market for a few good men. Particularly if they bring something to the table." Bolan sat back in his chair. "I guess I'll just have to join them."

"Really?" Kurtzman leaned back in his wheelchair. "And just how are you going to do that?"

"I'm going to need you to write me a letter of introduction."

**5**

*The Clubhouse*

The Iceman sat in his study. He wore a bathrobe against the chill of his ten kilometer morning swim in the fog-shrouded Pacific. A chamois cloth lay before him on the massive sprawl of his Brazilian heartwood desk. On the cloth lay a cleaned and oiled .44 Magnum Mateba semiautomatic revolver. The Iceman ran a brass bristle brush down the bore of a second pistol as he cleaned them after his morning shooting practice. The two semiautomatic revolvers were large and overly complicated weapons, and prohibitively expensive. However, with their semiautomatic actions and underslung barrels, they were the smoothest, least recoiling, most accurate .44 Magnum pistols in the world.

They were an absolute joy to shoot, and a work of art in the hand.

Knuckles rapped twice on his door. The Iceman spoke without looking up from oiling the gleaming revolver in his hand. "Come in, Jeremy."

Jeremy walked in with a manila folder in his hand.

The Iceman wiped down the pistol and mated a speed loader with the revolver's open cylinder. Six .240-grain .44 Magnum jacketed hollowpoint rounds slid into their chambers. The revolver's action closed with a muted click.

Jeremy eyed the enormous pistols with wary amusement. "The house howitzers?"

"Sure beats a rape whistle." The Iceman smiled as he loaded the second revolver. "Damn sight louder, too."

He placed the pair of loaded revolvers into their custom mahogany case like dueling pistols.

Jeremy laughed and slid the folder across the desk.

The Iceman regarded his chief of intelligence. He knew Jeremy didn't like wet work. However, he also knew that three times a week Jeremy went to the range with his HK-4 automatic pistol and assiduously shot five 50-round boxes of ammo. Jeremy could reliably dump the entire 10-round magazine of the little German pistol in under two seconds. He could also reliably dump those ten rounds into a playing card at ten yards. He had also earned his second-degree black belt from a very rough school of Kajukenbo. Jeremy was a very dangerous man, and his consummate skill with a pistol and his lethal ability with his hands were the least dangerous things about him.

The Iceman regarded his intelligence officer.

Jeremy's brain had killed far more people than the Iceman had ever killed with explosives, firearms, knives and his bare hands combined.

The Iceman glanced at the file without opening it. "What have you got for me?"

"Well, I've done a little poking around."

"And?"

"Well, first off, I need to tell you I had to take a million out of petty cash."

The Iceman nodded. "I know that."

Jeremy paused. As well as being the intelligence man, he handled most of the money. The Iceman was a classic Reagan-era delegator. However, unlike his favorite chief executive, the Iceman seemed to be aware of everything that happened in his organization around him down to the smallest minutiae. Oftentimes Jeremy wondered how the Iceman could know certain things. Jeremy considered himself to be in the uppermost echelon in the organization, and once again he was reminded there were aspects of business that he was unaware of. The Iceman had the habit of delegating authority and disappearing. No one knew where he went or what he did. Jeremy arranged a smile on his face. "Oh yeah, how?"

The Iceman ignored the question. "So what did you buy?"

"Well, first off, I bought a Russian."

"Really?" The Iceman quirked an eyebrow. "What kind of Russian?"

"An ex-KGB officer. He's going to look into our colonel friend at the hospital."

The Iceman took a steaming kettle from off a hotplate and poured boiling water into a silver inlaid gourd the size of a teacup. The water bubbled over a layer of greenish-looking herbs that took up two-thirds of the gourd. He took a sip from a silver-and-gold inlaid straw.

Jeremy shuddered. *"Matte?"*

The Iceman nodded and proffered the gourd. "Want some?"

"I don't know how you can drink that stuff."

"I picked up a taste for it in Argentina." The Iceman leaned back and let the warmth of the herbal drink spread through him. "It's my personal belief that our mysterious colonel is Russian special forces. Why are you buying ex-KGB officers? KGB and Russian military never got along. Ever. They had a cooperation and courtesy factor of nearly zero, and why does this ex-KGB officer cost me a million?"

Jeremy smiled and sat down. "First off, as you well know, special forces types have a code. They don't give each other up lightly. Also, the old Soviet way is long gone. This is the New Russia over a decade after the fall. Their economy is in the toilet. The entire country is in the toilet. The ruble is worthless, and half of all transactions take place in U.S. dollars." Jeremy's grin grew feral. "The other half usually take place by barter. Everyone in Moscow owes someone a favor."

The Iceman sipped his *matte*. "And?"

"As a sideline, our ex-KGB man moves a lot of Western medical supplies through Moscow. He just happens to know a Spetsnaz captain whose wife has thyroid cancer. We're sending out the latest Swiss chemotherapy drugs along with a doctor from Paris to do a proper examination and lay out a therapy regimen. The Spetsnaz captain is suitably grateful, and has expressed his willingness to cover the marker. Particularly when I had our friends languishing in Mexico drop a dime on him and tell him what good people we are."

The Iceman stared up at his hunting trophies. A boar's head was mounted on the wall. Beneath the head were crossed the broken shaft and the eighteen-inch steel blade of the spear he had taken it with. "What was the layout?"

"Four hundred thousand dollars."

The Iceman smiled. Jeremy would never have come into his study without a comprehensive plan in place. The Iceman shrugged anyway. "You're six hundred K short."

Jeremy matched the Iceman's smile. "I expect to have an answer from the Russians within two weeks."

"You're still six hundred K short."

"You know?" Jeremy said as he waved a careless hand. "There happens to be a manila envelope on your desk."

"So there is." The Iceman swiveled his chair and flipped it open. "There appears to be a personal file here."

"There are a number of personal files there."

The Iceman examined a United States Marshal Service fitness report. A redheaded Neanderthal of a man smiled from the identification photo. "Federal Marshal Marcus Caron."

Jeremy raised a finger. "Now, it starts getting good. This guy Caron was the senior marshal present at the hospital."

"Yeah, and?"

"And he threw himself on top of the grenade C.T. threw into the room. He's in serious but stable condition."

"Really." The Iceman considered that a moment. He had known a few heroes in his time. All of them were dead. This didn't mitigate his immense respect for them. However, that respect wouldn't prevent him from doing what he had to do. He flipped through several fitness reports of D.C. uniformed police officers who had been present. "How did you get all this?"

"All of the surviving agents and officers at the hospital had to give full reports to their superiors about what happened. I put about one hundred K in the right places."

"What did we find out about our Russian colonel?"

"Not much, but enough to start with. He was wearing the uniform of the Russian army and was introduced as Russian Military Intelligence. They said his name was Dimitri Rabskyov."

"He's gotta be GRU."

"Has to be. Like I said. I've put together a machine in Moscow to work on that little problem."

The Iceman came to the last file. He stared long and hard at the man staring out of the photograph. Even out of the passport quality photo the man in the picture radiated authority. He radiated trouble. "Who's this?"

Jeremy leaned back in his chair. "He is what cost five hundred thousand, and that bought just about squat. My instincts tell me seven figures may not buy much more."

"What did it buy me?"

"It bought you the name Hal Brognola."

The Iceman stared at the Justice Department fitness report. It was bare-boned in the extreme. It screamed that what the man truly represented was on a need-to-know basis. "Who is he?"

"He's the suit who was at the hospital. He arrived on the scene with our Russian colonel."

"And?"

"He used to be a Marshal. Now he works way up in the Justice Department."

"What does that mean?"

"I don't know, and that's what worries me." Jeremy frowned. "The man's a ghost. All I can find out about him is rumors."

"What kind of rumors?"

"Only one that really interests me."

"What's that?"

"Rumors like he's had direct access to the last three Presidents of the United States."

The Iceman stared long and hard at the man in the photo. The Marshal Service didn't play games with Russian intelligence colonels. That was the provenance of the FBI and the CIA. The Iceman's instincts spoke to him. "We won't be able to find out anything more about him through normal channels."

"No." Jeremy saw what was coming. "I don't think so, either."

"I think an attempt at a wiretap or standard surveillance would only expose us further. I think any probe would get us discovered before we ever find anything."

"I think you're right. My gut tells me this guy is real trouble," Jeremy said, nodding unhappily. "So what do you want to do?"

"A soft probe won't work."

"So we—"

"Go in hard. It's the one thing this guy won't expect."

"But—"

"Bring the Russians back up from Mexico. Tell them they're going back to D.C. Get them all the equipment they need. Pay them double if you have to. Bring in this captain from Moscow and some of his pals to fill the holes in the ranks. He owes us."

"But we—"

"We're going to pull a snatch."

Jeremy's eyes went wide.

The Iceman nodded. "I want the Russians broken into two teams, with C.T. and Hertzog in command, respectively."

"I don't know if a D.C. operation so soon is such a good idea."

"And send Brand to make sure it gets done right." The Iceman rose from his chair. "I want him, Jeremy. I want Hal Brognola. Him and Marshal Marcus Caron. I want them in holes. I want them in the Boneyard with spiders on their faces."

The Iceman's terrible gaze was unblinking. "Then I want this Russian colonel."

## Norfolk, Virginia

MACK BOLAN STRODE into the bar and was assaulted by a wall of music.

Calvin James walked beside him.

It wasn't a particularly nice bar or in a particularly nice part of town. The bar was lined with off-duty sailors and the locals who wanted to meet them. It was Friday night, and a local band was massacring the Doors' "Roadhouse Blues" with enthusiasm. A number of wanna-be bikers lounged around wearing their colors and watched the working girls dance with each other. Their faces hardened as they noticed James and the color of his skin. The way the African American carried himself seemed to prevent any stupid remarks from coming out of their mouths.

James smiled and nudged Bolan. "Ain't no trash like white trash."

"We try," the big guy responded.

They moved through the crowd toward a booth in the back. A hanging lamp spilled a pool of light in the murky dimness behind the jukebox. A solitary man sat in the booth, his back to the wall. He wore a leather biker jacket. Over it he'd put on a denim jacket with the sleeves torn off, like a vest. His mustache and beard were gray, and long lanky gray hair spilled out onto his shoulders from underneath the olive-drab bandanna he wore on his head. He looked to be in his late fifties. His skin had the saddle-leather look of a man who'd had a tan for most of his life. Deep lines marked his face, and where there weren't lines there were scars.

He raised a cigarette to his mouth and took a long drag. He held the cigarette with the pincering double-hook of a stainless-steel prosthesis. A pint of something sat by his left hand. Bolan noticed it was untouched. His body language as he sat in the booth made it clear to all that he owned it. The man looked up from beneath thick salt-and-pepper brows as he became aware of the two men approaching him.

James grinned. "Captain Hook."

"Calvin James." The man spoke with a thick Southern accent. "What brings your monkey ass in here?"

The Stony Man warrior shrugged. "White women, what else?"

The man in the booth threw back his head and laughed.

Bolan waited while the two men shared a SEAL moment.

"Don't shit me, Calvin."

"What makes you think I'm shitting you?"

The man laughed again and looked Bolan up and down. "Who's he?"

"A friend."

"Really." The man examined Bolan with calculating eyes. "He ain't one of us. He looks like one badass dude, but he ain't one of us."

"No, he isn't," James responded. "But he's a close personal friend of mine."

"Well, that don't comfort me none." The man smiled and raised his hook to take another long drag on his cigarette. "But it don't create any sense of moral obligation on my part, neither."

"Yeah, Hook, I know, but the man needs a job."

The man regarded James long and hard. "I haven't seen you at a SEAL meet in a while, Calvin. Talk is you've got some other kind of gig going on. And no one has any idea what that might be." He peered up at him unblinkingly. "Why don't *you* give the man a job?"

"Now, I have love in my heart for this man," James answered.

"But, like you said, he ain't one of us, and unfortunately, when it comes to my extracurricular activities, well—" James leaned forward conspiratorially "—he just ain't a brother. Know what I'm saying?"

The man in the booth considered this long and hard. "Are you shitting me, Calvin? You wouldn't be shitting me, would you?"

The two former SEALs regarded each other. Calvin shook his head slowly and spoke with utter conviction. "Hook, this man is the most crackerjack operator you are going to meet in this lifetime. And he is a close personal friend of mine."

Hook raised an eyebrow at Bolan. "You a spook?"

"I've been spooky." Bolan grimaced slightly. "But spooky didn't pay my bills, and I did not feel the love."

Hook nodded at the wisdom of the statement. "How you know Calvin?"

Bolan smiled. "Some spooky shit."

"Ah." Hook took a sip of his beer. "Well, what kind of work you looking for, friend?"

"Anything that pays." Bolan's face became stone. "But I won't run drugs, I don't pimp little girls and I frown upon those who do." The Executioner suddenly smiled disarmingly. "Other than that, I'm currently open to suggestions."

"Yeah." The corner of Hook's mouth turned up slightly. "You're a friend of Calvin's, all right." He took another drag on his cigarette. "Why don't you boys sit down."

Hook motioned at the cocktail waitress. "So what are you looking for exactly, friend?"

"Calvin says you can find a man work."

Hook nodded. "Well, I ain't exactly Executive Outcomes, but I made a few connections in my day, and I can sometimes find work for friends. Mostly in Central and South America. How's your Spanish."

"Not bad. What kind of work?"

"Well, you know," Hook said with a shrug, "everyone needs muscle down there. Anyone would hire Calvin just so they can say they have a U.S. Navy SEAL as a bodyguard. It's got prestige to it. Organizing and training the local scumbag's goon squad pays a little more than bodyguarding. If you can get into security and operational consultation, that takes you up another pay grade. Course, like I said, you'd be working for scumbags, mostly. You might not be handling the drugs or selling twelve-year-old girls on street corners, personally, but you'd be working for people who do. Of course, if you don't dig that, there's working for the local governments down there. The job descriptions are almost exactly the same, bodyguarding important people, training the local soldiers or acting as a security consultant. They usually don't pay quite as well, and, frankly, the line between the scumbags and the freely elected government can get pretty goddamn thin where you'd be going."

Hook leaned back and took a long drag on his cigarette. "Of course, you know all that, don't you."

"Yeah."

"Course you do."

James leaned forward. "You got anything else, Hook?"

Hook's cigarette stopped halfway to his mouth. "What do you mean, Calvin?"

"I mean you got anything else for a close personal friend of mine."

"Anything else. For a close personal friend of Calvin James," repeated Hook. He took another long look at Bolan. "You know, Calvin, I have love for you in my heart. Love from back in the day. So I can tell you what I got."

"What's that?"

Hook reached his left hand into the inside pocket of his leather jacket. His hand came out with a very expensive, titanium-bodied cell phone. "I got this."

"That's a nice phone," James said. "And?"

Hook held up the phone to the light and regarded it as it gleamed. "And I don't know where it came from. I don't know who sent it to me. I never asked for it. I never put in the requisition form, know what I'm saying? I'm saying it just appeared in my mailbox some years back, along with a big old wad of cash."

"And?"

Hook smiled at the phone in bemusement. "And sometimes, from right out the blue, without rhyme or reason, this phone? It rings."

The three of them fell silent as the waitress brought a pitcher of beer and two mugs for Bolan and James. The waitress was a redhead whose more obvious charms had obviously undergone a startling miracle of science. She eyed the men in the booth with smiling suspicion. "Hook, you getting into trouble?"

"No way, baby, you know me," he said, grinning. "I don't get into trouble. I get other people in trouble."

The waitress rolled her eyes. "Oh, I know you, Hook."

The three of them leaned in closer as she walked back to the bar. James took a long sip of his beer. "So what happens when the phone rings?"

"Same thing every time. A voice asks me if I know anybody who might like a job. Usually SEALs preferred. Sometimes asking for particular skills. Sometimes asking if I have any pen pals in certain exotic locales. Sometimes if I just know anybody reliable. Then they hang up. If I have someone or can find them, I give that individual the phone, and in about a week it rings, and they set up a meet. The phone comes back to me in the mail, with a finder's fee."

Bolan poured himself another beer. "And you got no idea who these people are?"

"No, I don't." Hook shook his head. "And I don't want to. I'm a simple man. I've got simple needs. The arrangement helps keep my yacht afloat and all my hogs in chrome." His eyes slid to the waitress's behind as she walked by. "Like I just told Peg, I don't get into trouble. I get other people into trouble. And I sleep like a baby. I want to keep it that way."

"I can respect that, but can't you tell me anything? I don't like the idea of stepping out into thin air. You never heard from any of your inductees again?"

"I don't induct. I just introduce. Man, I'm a cutout, and I know it." Hook stubbed out his cigarette. "I got some thank-you notes. They didn't tell me anything. Just thanks for the introduction, and they sent me a little cut of whatever they were getting out of respect. The rest I sent along, I never heard from again."

Bolan tossed back his beer. "So you've sent friends up this pipeline?"

"I have, and I would again. Hell, I wish they would offer me a job. Whatever it is." Hook held up his prosthesis. "But what the hell, I had my fun, and my beer tab is covered."

"You need references?" Bolan asked.

"I don't need shit. If you're a friend of Calvin's, you're good as gold as far as I'm concerned." Hook lit another cigarette and placed it in his claw. "Whatever they want to know is between you and them. Like I said, I don't set up the meet. You'll make all the arrangements among yourselves." Hook polished off his beer and leaned in close. "But I'll tell you, I suspect they got significant filters, and I think the interview is a stone-cold pass-fail situation. You know what I'm saying?"

"You're saying if I don't pass the screen test, Calvin here is most likely to be out one close personal friend."

"That's exactly what I'm saying. I'm glad we understand each other. I don't want no bad blood with you, or with Calvin if you don't live up to your hype." Hook leaned back in his seat. "Now, this phone just happened to ring two days ago."

"Really."

"Oh yeah, really."

"What'd they ask for?"

"Someone reliable. Someone with skills. Someone who's looking for employment options."

James smiled. "I think you just read the man his résumé."

"So," Hook said as he grinned at Bolan like a wolf, "you want the phone?"

"Oh yeah," Bolan answered. "I want the phone."

Hook vised the phone in the pincers of his prosthesis and held it out. *"Vaya con Dios, amigo."*

**6**

*Jug Bay, Maryland*

Hal Brognola looked up from the file in front of him as Mack Bolan walked into the room. The house was one of several outside the District of Columbia that Brognola worked out of when there was a hot operation going and he didn't want to go to the Farm. The flat roof was reinforced to accept a helicopter landing, and the neighbors were few and far between. There was an empty field behind the house and beyond that a bit of woods and a creek. A one hundred yard tunnel led beneath the field to the creek. The creek end of the tunnel looked like a barred drainage pipe. Bolan had taken a Jeep along the creek and come in through the tunnel. A series of entrance codes he had entered at several points had prevented the trip up the tunnel from being fatal.

Brognola held up a photo. "You trust this Hook character?"

"Calvin does, to a point. They knew each other when they were both active SEALs. Hook was a good soldier approaching retirement before a land mine in Nicaragua tore him up. According to the Bear, he was involved in cross-training the special forces groups of other countries, particularly South America.

He appears also to have been involved in some of the CIA's less savory activities down there, until he got blown up and earned his nickname." Bolan shrugged. "Hook doesn't smell like lilacs, but I wouldn't call him dirty either. He's treading the line."

Brognola nodded. It was how he figured it as well. "So what are you going to do?"

Bolan held up the gleaming phone. "I'm going to sit tight and hope someone drops a dime on me."

The big Fed leaned back in his chair. "I don't exactly like sitting around lonely by the phone waiting for a date to the prom."

"It's the only lead we have at the moment."

"Yeah, and meantime who knows what these guys do next."

"Hal, we—"

Something smashed against the window and made a loud, secondary thump. The bulletproof glass was spiderwebbed with cracks and smeared with gray. Whatever had struck fell clattering to the porch outside. Metal scrabbled out on the wood decking, and loud multiple hissings made a noise like angry cobras. Billowing gray ghost shapes rose before the cracked window.

"That was fast," Bolan stated. "Looks like your invitation to the dance came early." The hissing noise grew louder. "That was a barricade-breaching munition. I'm thinking CS gas, with multiple skip-chasing bomblets."

"Yeah, we're getting hit." Brognola picked up the television remote control from the coffee table and punched a button. Steel shutters fell across the cracked window and across every window in the house. Each shutter had an observation-firing slit with a steel shutter that locked from the inside. Glass shattered mutely behind the shutter, and gray wisps oozed around the steel shield.

"Goddamn it! That thing is supposed to be airtight!" Brognola clicked another button on the remote. The large flat-screen television clicked into life. The screen was divided into eight screen-within-screen images that showed the entire perimeter of the house. In the eerie gray-green world of the hidden infrared cameras, figures were moving.

Bolan rose from the couch. "Where're the guns, Hal?"

Brognola pressed another button.

The liquor cabinet swung open soundlessly, taking the whiskey, port and the decanters with it. Behind the liquor was a recessed rack of weapons. Bolan smiled. Hanging from a hook was a web belt with a .44 Magnum Desert Eagle, a Beretta 93-R and an assortment of spare magazines. Not that Bolan hadn't brought his own with him, but it was nice to know that Brognola was prepared.

Bolan ignored the pistols and went to the racked Stoner light machine guns.

A 100-round plastic ammo box was already in the feed well. Four more ammo packs were enclosed in canvas pouches on a bandolier. Each belt held a pair of grenade pouches. The Stoner's twin brother was racked next to it. Bolan took the weapon and a pair of three-inch .357 Magnum Smith & Wesson revolvers on a pistol belt and tossed the hardware onto the couch. On a shelf below the weapons were several pairs of night-vision goggles. Bolan lobbed one to the sofa and perched another on top of his head. He took out the remaining Stoner and ammo packs for himself.

Brognola returned from the closet with two sets of body armor in his hands. "Here, take thi——Jesus!"

He flinched as one of the window shields blackened and a ten-foot jet of superheated gas and molten metal shot across the room between him and Bolan, igniting the armchair he had previously been sitting in.

Bolan leaned away as heat from the armor-piercing jet washed across his face. "They're coming in hard!"

Smoke alarms chirped into life inside the house, their lights strobing in every room.

Bolan shrugged into the armor Brognola threw him and felt the reassuring weight of Threat Level III ceramic inserts wedged between the woven Kevlar. He slung the Stoner and glanced at the huge screen of the television. Bulky figures in goggles and gas masks were charging the house from all sides.

"Those guys are armored, Hal!" Bolan racked the Stoner's bolt and chambered a round. The action was as slick as oiled glass. Bolan knew Kissinger had gotten his hands on the weapons before they had been passed on to Brognola. "What are you feeding these ladies?"

"I've got .60-grain steel-core, spoon-tip, armor-piercing incendiary!" The big Fed held up the remote. "You ready?"

Bolan nodded. Brognola pushed a button. The smoke alarms

went off and their strobes cut. Every light in the house went out, and the interior was plunged into blackness except for the torch of the burning armchair.

Brognola looked down at the chirping noise on his belt as his phone rang. He scooped it off its clip and flicked it open. "This is Brognola! What?"

Booted feet were thudding on the porch.

"Dammit!" His face split into a snarl at what he was hearing. "All right! I need backup! Jug Bay location! ASAP! By helicopter! Expect heavy resistance! We are extracting by the creek!"

He clicked the phone shut angrily. "The bastards hit the hospital Marcus was in. They killed the two marshals guarding his door. Witnesses say they tried to take him alive. Marcus had his piece with him. We've got two perps dead."

"What about Marcus?"

"They couldn't take him alive, so they capped him." His face was a mask of rage. "The cavalry is coming, but it's going to take a few minutes. We need—"

The house shuddered down to its foundation. Orange fire filled the rear of the house as the back door failed. The stench of burned high-explosive sheared through the house on a hot wind as the blast wave funneled down the hall and nearly took Bolan and Brognola off their feet.

"Jesus Christ!"

"We're breached, Hal! They'll hit the front next! We're out of here!" Bolan moved to the hallway. Feet thudded in the back of the burning house. Bursts of automatic rifle fire preceded the invaders as they stormed in.

Bolan and Brognola were cut off from the tunnel.

The Executioner knelt beside the doorway to the hall and held up his fist, and Brognola took the other side to create a cross fire. The Executioner waited two seconds as the sound of running men shouting into their radios filled the hallway.

They were shouting in Russian.

Bolan rolled onto the floor in front of the hall doorway. Brognola brought his muzzle around the doorjamb, firing at hip level. The two light machine guns ripped into lethal life in their hands. Both weapons were set at their maximum cyclic rate.

Within three seconds, two hundred rounds of armor-piercing incendiary ammunition filled the narrow confines of the hallway.

Bolan and Brognola held down their triggers until the Stoners clacked open on smoking empty chambers. The killers shuddered and fell in the withering hail. The hallway was a hellstorm of smoking tracer trails that hung in the air. The five men lying in the hallway had each taken nearly twenty hits apiece. Wisps like cigarette smoke drifted upward from the incendiary bullet strikes in their defeated armor.

Bolan ejected his spent ammo pack and clicked a fresh one into place. "We've got to move! They weren't expecting two of us! Or this kind of resistance! They'll regroup and hit us again any second!"

"Cover me!" Brognola racked his action on a fresh ammo pack and moved at a crouch along the hallway. Bolan sent a series of short bursts over Brognola's head to keep the enemy down. They needed to reach the bedroom. The master closet was where the tunnel entrance was located, and the master closet itself was a steel-walled strong room that would take shaped charges to breach.

Bolan didn't put it past the bad guys to have brought flexible shaped charges with them.

The Executioner moved as Brognola crouched and sent bursts through the smoke to cover him.

The kitchen was on fire. The enemy had used at least a twenty-pound satchel charge to breach the reinforced walls and steel back door. The area of the house from the crumpled back door to the shattered double sinks of the kitchen was open to the night. Tracers streamed back at them from outside. The head Fed reached into his bandolier and pulled out a pair of hand grenades. He tossed one to Bolan. Both were white phosphorus.

The two men pulled the pins, and the cotter levers pinged out into the smoke. They hurled the grenades through the besieged kitchen. The grenades detonated, and streamers of burning phosphorus erupted into what remained of the back porch.

"All right!" Brognola said as he rose. "That should hold them up for a second or—Jesus!"

Bolan threw himself down as a rocket hissed through the burning white-and-yellow phosphorus and the black smoke of the burning kitchen and porch. The rocket sizzled overhead and shot down the hallway. It flew into the living room and detonated behind them.

The house was going up like a torch.

Brognola scrambled up. "We—"

Bolan roared. "Hal!"

A second rocket hissed into the house and struck the big Fed full in the chest.

Brognola was lifted off his feet as the RPG-7 rocket-propelled grenade hit him at four hundred feet per second. He flew fifteen feet down the hallway and bounced off of the doorjamb with bone-breaking force. Orange light flared as the five-pound warhead detonated against him.

"Hal!" Bolan burned half of his 100-round ammo pack as he swept his weapon in an arc out into the night. He ran down the hallway as automatic rifles fired back. His friend lay smoldering on the floor. His Stoner light machine gun was slagged in two. The Kevlar and nylon fabric of his armor had been burned away in an almost perfect dinner-plate shape in the middle of his chest. The shaped charge of the warhead had been designed to send a jet of superheated gas and molten metal burning through the milled steel or aluminum of a light-armored vehicle.

The ceramic laminate of Brognola's Threat Level III armor trauma plate had stopped the HEAT warhead cold.

Bolan grimaced as he quickly checked his friend. Brognola was a mess. He was unconscious, and blood bubbled between his lips with each ragged breath. His eyebrows were gone, and flash burns blistered his face and hands. Blood caked the back of his head where he had bounced off the door frame.

The house buckled as a second satchel charge breached the front. The blast shoved Bolan against the wall. He took a Willie Pete from his web gear and flung it back into the living room. It detonated with a crack, and choking white smoke and burning phosphorus filled the breach in the front.

Bolan kicked away the melted halves of Brognola's weapon and seized him by his web belt. He dragged him and fired one-handed bursts from the hip as he staggered down the hall.

The house was turning into an inferno.

Bolan raised a disbelieving eyebrow as the titanium phone in his pocket rang.

Tracers streaked into the hallway through the flames and the smoke filling the kitchen spilled out into the hall in choking clouds. Bolan crouched beneath the incoming tracers and clicked the phone open. "Hello!"

"Hi," a friendly voice spoke. "I see you took the phone."

"Yeah!" Bolan fired off another burst from his weapon and glanced back at Brognola. His lips moved as he drew a ragged breath. "I'm kind of busy right now!"

The voice on the line paused and listened as automatic rifle fire sought out Bolan through the flames. "Are you all right?"

"No!" snarled Bolan. "I need a job!"

"It sounds like you have a job."

"Yeah, I do!" Bolan answered as he fired off a burst. Something was making a smashing noise against the side of the house.

"Where are you?"

Bolan crouched as the rifle fire raked lower and said the first thing that came into his head. "Kamchatka!"

The voice paused. "Really."

"Yeah! Really!" Bolan held the phone up as the rifles cracked outside. "What does that sound like to you?"

"They sound like AK-47s."

"Yeah! Can I call you back?"

"No. You can't. Can you get out of there?"

Bolan did desperate math in his head. "I got a flight for Unalaska Island in eight hours! There are people there who owe me money! You know where that is?"

"Don't lose the phone. Someone will meet you. Good luck." The line went dead.

"Who...?" Brognola's voice was a ragged gasp. "Who was that?"

"Hook's friends. I've got a date to the prom." Bolan shoved the phone back in his pocket. "Hal, can you walk? I need you to—"

The big Fed's eyes rolled as his head slumped.

"Damn it." Bolan grabbed him by his belt and tried to manage a light machine gun and his friend at the same time as he crawled down the hallway. The house was full of choking smoke and the brimstone stench of explosive. Bolan abandoned the Stoner and groaned as he crawled toward the master bedroom, pulling Brognola behind him.

He heaved Brognola through the doorway and kicked shut the reinforced door. The house shook as something made a thumping noise on the roof. Several more thumps followed. The enemy was no longer trying to assault the house. They weren't going to try to brave burning white phosphorus in an assault.

They were going to burn them out.

Bolan dragged his friend toward the closet door. The steel shield covering the bedroom window buckled and blackened as something struck it. A white-hot plume blossomed, hissing and shrieking into the room, and splashed against the far wall. The wall instantly caught fire. Bolan flinched and desperately punched the key code into the closet door as a second antiarmor round penetrated the sagging shield and the air in the room became too hot to breathe. The bed and the lamp shades were burning.

Sirens wailed in the distance.

The airtight closet door hissed open, and cool air blew in Bolan's face. He hooked Brognola under his arms and pulled him in. The soldier booted the door shut behind him, and it automatically locked. The sounds of the burning and dying house were muted behind the armored walls of the strong room. Bolan took a deep breath and knelt on the floor. He pulled up a flap of carpeting to expose the hatch to the tunnel.

Bolan's head snapped up at the scent of scorching wood.

The wood paneling in the roof above was smoldering and turning black.

The soldier quickly punched in another code on the keypad.

He glanced up as the ceiling flared into life. The stench of burning metal overcame the smell of wood smoke. The heat in the strong room was quickly becoming unbearable. Bolan leaped to one side as flame dripped from the ceiling. The exposed steel sheathing was white-hot. Bits of it began flowing down like a molten metal fountain. The carpet instantly caught fire.

They were being slagged.

The automatic bolts on the hatch clacked open, and Bolan yanked the hatch upward. The air that sucked upward was cool and damp. The entire ceiling was on fire. The carpet was flaring up all around him, and black smoke filled the tiny chamber. Bolan had no idea how badly his friend was injured, but there was no time to be gentle. He stuffed Brognola down the hatch and leaped after him.

Something spattered against Bolan's back as he went down the hatch, and heat flared against his shoulder blades.

Bolan rolled on the tunnel floor, but the heat didn't smother. It grew in intensity against his back. The Executioner tore at the tabs of his armor and ripped it away from himself as he rolled up. He flung the armor to the floor of the tunnel with singed hands.

The vest flared up like newspaper thrown into a fireplace.

Bolan seized Brognola and desperately dragged him backward down the tunnel.

The Kevlar and nylon of his discarded armor congealed and burned around the central trauma plate. Bolan squeezed his eyes shut as something dripped through the open hatch. Bits of rock ricocheted down the tunnel with the intensity of the heat differential. Bolan fell as a piece of rock snapped away and cracked into his forehead. He kept his grip on Brognola and kept shoving them both backward as blood poured into his left eye.

Bolan pushed himself up and grabbed Brognola by his bandolier.

The tunnel was little more than four-foot-diameter concrete tubing with a light every ten yards. There were two checkpoints with keypads imbedded in the walls. He punched in numbers with a burned finger and dragged Brognola farther along.

A steel shutter slid down from the tunnel roof.

Bolan sagged backward.

The sounds of the siege quickly dimmed behind them. The rifle fire had already ceased. The enemy would be dispersing as the local fire department and police descended upon the scene. Bolan shook his head. The local fire brigade would be totally unprepared to deal with white phosphorus and thermite fires. The only thing they would be able to do would be to cordon off the house and wait for the incendiaries to burn themselves out. There would be nothing left of the house except possibly the fireplace. Bolan hacked and winced as he pulled the cool fetid air of the tunnel into his smoke-filled lungs.

He and Brognola had gotten mauled.

Marshal Marcus Caron had been murdered in his hospital bed. The bodies above would be burned beyond all recognition. The enemy's tracks would be covered. They had left no clues, and the only lead he had was a disembodied voice on a cell phone. Bolan wondered if the two events were connected. Definitely.

Bolan checked his watch. He had to be in the Aleutian Islands in twelve hours to shore up an alibi he had made up off the top of his head two minutes ago.

Brognola's voice was a croak from the floor of the tunnel. "Mack..."

"Yeah, Hal?"

"These...bastards..." Brognola said as he drew a gurgling breath. "They go down."

"Oh yeah." Bolan took hold of Brognola's web belt and wearily began hauling him down the tunnel again. "They're going down."

**7**

*The Clubhouse*

"Hertzog is dead."

The Iceman was silent as he considered the news. "What happened?"

Brand's voice was bitter over the phone. "They encountered heavy resistance. The house was fortified, and Brognola was heavily armed."

The Iceman leaned back in his chair. "And?"

"Hertzog used satchel charges to breach the house. He led the initial assault. Brognola had a light machine gun, and they ran right into it. He didn't make it. Neither did his entry team. Temirkov was preparing a second assault when Brognola used Willie Petes to seal the breaches. Temirkov called me asking for instructions. I told him to burn the place to the ground and that Brognola asshole with it."

"And?"

"And the Russians painted that place red. Temirkov fired RPGs into the interior to set more fires and fragged the roof with Willie Petes of his own. Then he lobbed in thermite to make sure the fire burned completely out of control."

"Well?"

"The place burned down to its foundation."

"Bodies?"

"They came out pretty fused and twisted. I'm waiting to find out how many are officially tallied."

The Iceman's voice was more conversational than accusing. "So, you don't know if Brognola is dead."

Brand swallowed uncomfortably. "No, not yet. But surviving inside that inferno would take divine intervention. Like I said, it burned down to its foundation, and he didn't break out."

"Maintain surveillance on his house and his office." The Iceman peered at the map of Washington, D.C., on his computer. "What happened with Caron?"

"C.T. took a team in to snatch him. He took out the two marshals who were baby-sitting him, but the bastard was awake and lucid and had a .45 under his pillow. C.T. lost two Russians. He capped Caron and called for extraction.

"I wanted him alive." The Iceman's tone was neutral. "I wanted them both alive."

Brand hardened his voice. "Things went FUBAR, Ice. Both teams met unexpected resistance. Hertzog's dead. He was a friend of ours. I made a decision. So did C.T."

"I see."

There was no indication in the Iceman's voice whether he approved, disapproved or was about to have someone killed.

Brand quickly changed the subject. "How is the recruiting campaign going?"

The Iceman allowed the conversation to shift. They had lost a lot of operators and valuable intelligence assets. They had also lost two of their own. The ranks needed refilling, and warm bodies wouldn't do. They needed real talent. "There may be a couple of likely lads down the coast. I'm checking their references."

"How about old Hook?" Brand asked. "He come up with anything for us?"

The Iceman smiled slightly as he stared at the cell phone sitting on his desk. His eye turned back to the map on his computer. His finger went to the mouse and he tracked the arrow westward from Washington across the continental United States. It swung up the West Coast and through British Columbia. He tracked the arrow to Alaska and the screen shifted as he went westward. The mouse swung out into the Pacific and stopped.

The Iceman looked upon the long finger of the Aleutian Islands. He put the arrow on Unalaska Island and right-clicked. The flat-screen monitor began streaming information. The Iceman stared unblinkingly upon the windswept island just south of the Arctic Circle.

"I made a phone call. It seems our friend Hook may have found a live one."

### Gulf of Alaska

MACK BOLAN SAT in the copilot's seat of the streaking F-15E Strike Eagle fighter jet. "How's Hal?"

The gray waters of the gulf passed beneath him. Bolan had dragged Brognola down the tunnel and piled him into the Jeep he had parked by the creek. He drove straight to Andrews Air Force Base. A waiting helicopter had taken him to Walter Reed Hospital under a false name. Half a platoon of U.S. Marshals in plain clothes had taken over an entire floor of the hospital.

Jack Grimaldi had been waiting for Bolan at Andrews Air Force Base. Barbara Price, Stony Man's mission controller, had cleared them a flight path, and within the hour they had commandeered a Strike Eagle and were on their way.

They were now soaring across the Gulf of Alaska toward the long chain of the Aleutian Islands. Adak Naval Air Facility on Adak Island overshot their destination, but it was the only nearby island with an airstrip long enough to accept the takeoff and landing of a supersonic jet fighter. Price would be burning up the airwaves to try to arrange some sort of private aircraft to be on Adak airfield fueled and ready to go. From Adak Island they still had a four hundred mile hop back up the island chain to Unalaska.

It was one hell of a long trip to go wait for a phone call.

Kurtzman spoke over the F-15E's satellite uplink. "Well, considering he took a hit from a rocket propelled antitank grenade center body mass, it could be one hell of a lot worse."

"How bad is it?"

"He's pretty beat up, but he'll live. The ceramic plate took the armor-piercing jet, but he has second-degree burns on his face and hands. The ballistic Kevlar distributed the energy of the blow itself as best it could, but he still has four broken ribs and a hairline fracture of the sternum. His right lung got punctured and deflated on him. He also has a minor concussion. Other than that, he's suffering from smoke inhalation and massive contusions all over his body."

"Yeah, but how's he, otherwise?"

"Lucid," Kurtzman answered. "And extremely agitated."

Bolan could understand Brognola's anger. The big Fed had lost a friend, and Bolan knew what that felt like from personal experience. It never got easy. He also knew from personal experience that the need for payback was always a little more passionate when someone tried to burn him alive. "Evacuate him to the Farm as soon as you can get a doctor to sign him out. The bad guys found both Hal and Marcus and hit them within forty-eight hours. Marcus is dead, and Hal probably would be, too, if I hadn't been there. I think it would be best if Hal dropped off the planet for a couple of days."

"I'm way ahead of you. I've already seen to getting his family out of town."

"Good."

"What about you?"

Bolan took a deep breath and coughed. He could still feel the smoke in the bottom of his lungs. "Barring a change in the weather or a screwup at Adak Airfield, I should be on Unalaska Island within my timetable."

Kurtzman made an impatient noise. "Couldn't you have said El Salvador or something? It's a hell of a lot closer."

"Kamchatka was the first thing that popped into my head, and it puts me light-years away from the scene in Jug Bay. Whoever we're dealing with doesn't know I was there, but they called while it was going down, and I don't want them putting two and two together."

"I did a little research, Striker. Unalaska Island has three industries. One is fishing. Two is processing fish. Three is a port of call for Alaskan cruise ships in summer. It's pretty damn desolate. You fly in on a private plane, and you're going to stick out like a sore thumb."

Bolan watched the whitecaps on the gray waters of the gulf far below. "I know, but so will the bad guys. We had to scramble on this one, and I'm betting our resources are better than theirs. I think they'll have had to scramble even harder to get people here. Besides, I've got Jack."

"Damn straight." Grimaldi craned his head around and grinned.

Kurtzman made a bemused noise. He couldn't decide which of the two men got the other into more trouble. "Barbara's seeing about requisitioning whatever weapons and gear we can lay our hands on for you at Adak, but it is probably going to be a very basic kit. Probably M-16s and very low-tech surveillance equipment. We're talking maybe a pair of binoculars and a 35 mm camera."

"Don't worry, I've worked with less. Besides, this is supposed to be a job interview, not a showdown in the streets."

"You be careful," Kurtzman cautioned. "I have a feeling it's going to get real interesting, real fast, whichever way this goes down."

**8**

*The Elbow Room, Unalaska Island*

Warm air rushed against Bolan's face as the bitter cold outside tried to suck the heat out of the bar. The windchill outside brought the late-afternoon temperature to only slightly above freezing. He pushed back the hood of his parka and reconnoitered the bar. The establishment was about half full. Johnny Cash played on the jukebox. The fish-processing plant hadn't changed shifts yet. The men in the bar had the look of commercial fishermen rather than factory workers. They wore boots that had seen hard service, and denim or flannel shirts. They had put in on Unalaska to get paid, get laid, get drunk and then go out on another run. The serious drinking hadn't begun yet, and most of them sat together over their pitchers of beer watching baseball on the big screen TV.

Bolan went to the bar.

The man behind it was large, powerful, bald and smiling. "Hi! How you doing? I'm Mike."

"Doin' good, Mike." Bolan peered around again. "How about one of whatever's on tap?"

"Coming up." Mike poured the beer and slid it across the bar. He peered at Bolan astutely. "Haven't seen you around. You aren't a fisherman, and you don't look factory, either."

"I'm just passing through."

"Passing through? Here? This is Unalaska Island." The bartender snorted disbelievingly. "Like, passing through from where to where?"

"Kamchatka." Bolan smiled and took a drink of his beer. "To anywhere."

The bartender looked Bolan up and down again and gave this weighty consideration. "Okay, then."

The man went down the bar and grabbed a couple of bottles for another customer.

The door opened again and a blast of chill air swept through the bar. Grimaldi came into the bar grinning like an idiot. "Sure is cold!" The pilot took a chair with his back to the wall and began wolfing down pretzels and watching television. At Adak, Bolan and Grimaldi had availed themselves of the armory. They had left the two commandeered M-16s on the plane. The pilot had taken an ancient-looking Thompson M-1 submachine gun and removed its buttstock. The weapon was strapped to his chest and concealed beneath his voluminous parka.

The bartender came back down the bar and glanced up at the game. The Giants and the Padres were working their way through the sixth inning of a no-hitter. "Who do you like?"

"The Pirates."

"Ah." The bartender considered this. "So, Kamchatka to anywhere, huh?"

Bolan nodded and sipped his beer. "That's about the size of it."

The man's voice dropped low. "Well, maybe you should just go there, then."

"Go?" Bolan kept his face pleasant. "Where?"

"To anywhere. Pittsburgh, maybe. Go catch a home game. But you don't want to hang around here."

"What?" Bolan asked as he sipped his beer. "Is it my cologne?"

"No," the bartender said, sighing. "It's just that you seem like a nice guy."

"I am," Bolan responded. "And?"

The man's voice dropped to a warning whisper. "And you are about to get stomped if you don't move."

One of the two phones Bolan was carrying rang.

"Hold that thought, Mike." Bolan took out the cell phone he had acquired on Adak and concealed it in front of his body as he opened the line. He glanced up at the mirror over the bar and could see Grimaldi's face was turned toward the wall. The pilot's voice came across the receiver. "Striker, I think you're about to get your ass kicked. Six o'clock."

"Thanks." Bolan looked into the mirror and scanned behind him. Near the back of the bar three men were staring at him. A woman sat with them, but her face was obscured by the frosting on the edge of the mirror. Bolan examined the men as their eyes burned holes in his back. One was the size and shape of a refrigerator in overalls. The other was a lanky blond-haired man in jeans and a jean jacket. The third was a short Asian male with a bodybuilder's physique straining his white thermal sweatshirt.

Bolan slid the phone discreetly back into his parka and spoke quietly to the bartender. "And who are those fellas?"

"That is Nikolai, Stubing and Chimpy, and you are in a world of hurt. I don't know who the hotty is."

"They're bad news, then?"

"Mister, they are bad everything. I can't count the number of fights they've started around here."

Bolan shrugged and finished his beer. "Why don't you eighty-six them?"

The bartender blinked. "Mister, this is Unalaska Island. We don't eighty-six fishermen. Know what I'm saying?"

Bolan nodded respectfully. "I understand."

The Army Colt .45 pistol Bolan had taken from the armory on Adak was a reassuring weight in the small of his back, but a shooting and the resulting trip to the police station could screw up the one lead he had. "Any suggestions?"

"I'd suggest you get your— Here we go. I'm calling the cops, but it'll be a few minutes before they get here. Forgive me, but I ain't jumpin' in without serious backup."

"I understand completely." Bolan turned slowly on his bar stool.

Nikolai, Stubing and Chimpy had stood up from their chairs.

Bolan raised an eyebrow as his other phone rang.

He kept his eye on the three men as he reached into his parka pocket. The men tensed and halted warily as Bolan's hand disappeared inside his coat. They relaxed and sneered as Bolan's hand came out holding the cell phone.

"Faggot," muttered one of them.

Bolan clicked on the phone. "Hello?"

A woman's amused voice spoke. "Good luck."

The line went dead.

Bolan's eyes flicked past the men to the table behind them. A stunningly beautiful Oriental woman in a spectacular sable coat clicked a cell phone shut. She folded her hands and smiled demurely at Bolan.

The three men moved forward in a phalanx.

"Oh shit," Mike snarled.

"Hey, you! Faggot!" Nikolai shouted. The big man spoke with a thick Russian accent as he came in at the point of the formation. His huge fists were red and scarred from years of working knives and nets. He leaned toward Bolan. "Yeah, you! I'm—"

Bolan lunged from his bar stool like an Olympic fencing champion. His thumb sat wedged on top of his fist. The tip slid between Nikolai's collarbones and punched into the base of the big man's throat. The Russian's eyes bugged wide, and his mouth opened as his trachea was compressed against his spine.

Nikolai went as white as a sheet and collapsed to the floor with a sickened wheeze.

Bolan's hand had already retracted. He shook his head in disgust. "Can't you assholes see I'm on the phone?"

Chimpy's eyes narrowed. His hand moved like a man performing a magic trick. Steel glittered in the light as the butterfly knife opened intricately in his hand.

Bolan's hand blurred into a short windup, and he hurled the cell phone into Chimpy's face. The blow was only a distraction. Chimpy involuntarily pulled his head back as he was struck between the eyes.

Bolan seized the man by the wrist and yanked his knife-arm straight. He slid to one side to keep Chimpy between himself and Stubing. Bolan's forearm swung up like a sledgehammer against the back of Chimpy's elbow.

The man screamed as the joint hyperextended and broke.

Bolan held on to the hardman's wrist as the knife fell from his nerveless fingers. The Executioner cupped his right hand and slapped it concussively over Chimpy's ear. The man screamed again as his eardrum ruptured.

Bolan allowed him to fall. Stubing hadn't pressed in. He had stepped back and picked up a bar stool. He raised it above his head. "You motherf—"

The Executioner lunged, seized Stubing's elbows and shoved. Stubing staggered back off balance, and Bolan swung his boot brutally between the man's legs.

Stubing made a choked sound of agony, and Bolan ripped the stool out of his palsied hands. His opponent took one step back as his knees buckled beneath him.

Bolan swung the stool down and skimmed the ground with it like a great golf club.

Stubing pinwheeled ninety degrees as his ankles were scythed out from under him. He fell out of control to the floor and didn't move. Bolan tossed away the stool and turned to the bar. He had to raise his voice above the sound of Chimpy screaming. "Yo, Mike! You okay with this?"

"What? Yeah, oh, hell, yeah! And that beer's on me." Mike shook his head in disbelief. "You stick around, and the citizens committee will probably pin a medal on you."

"Thanks." Bolan smiled. "Now watch this."

Mike blinked. "What?"

"Now I leave with their girlfriend."

Mike gaped as Bolan scooped up his fallen phone and walked across the bar to the table in the back. The Asian woman smiled at him sunnily. Her hair was so black it had an almost blue sheen under the light, and it fell to her waist. Bolan set the phone on the table.

"Hi, my name's Belasko."

"My name is Cisasthmi Pukulan Anggun. My friends call me Pooky."

"Well, do I pass?"

The woman's brow furrowed ever so slightly. "Let's talk about it."

Bolan jerked his head. "Let's get out of here."

Anggun nodded. "How about the restaurant in the hotel? You hungry?"

"Sounds good to me."

The woman stood and slid her arm into Bolan's. He waggled

his eyebrows at Mike in passing. The bartender stared in awe as the big man stepped over the moaning bodies littering the floor and took the woman with him.

*Unisea Hotel, Unalaska*

THE WOMAN WATCHED the Executioner eat with appreciation. Bolan had eaten bear meat before, and it could be tough and stringy. The patrons of the hotel were almost all people who had landed from the cruise ships that plied the spectacular Alaskan coastline. They expected to be fed well, and the chef had to compete with the chefs on the cruise ships. The chef had obviously put a lot of time and care into the piece of grizzly on the table before Bolan. The soldier ate grilled bear steak and drank five-year-old cabernet from the Napa Valley with gusto.

The woman smiled. She spoke her English with a slight accent. "You seem to enjoy your food."

"A man's strength can be measured by his appetites." Bolan sopped bear grease with a piece of bread and shoved it into his mouth. "Indeed, a man's strength flows from his appetites."

Anggun stared at Bolan with great seriousness. *"Enter the Dragon."*

"You know, I like a girl with good taste in movies." Bolan met the woman's luminous dark eyes. She didn't look Chinese, Japanese or Korean. Bolan pegged her for Southeast Asian. Her name could well be a cover, but Bolan was willing to bet she was Indonesian, probably by way of Java. "So, what did you say to those guys back in the bar?"

The woman lowered her eyelashes at Bolan demurely. "I told them you were my boyfriend."

Bolan smiled. "Sounds okay to me."

The woman made an amused noise. "I also told them you were an asshole."

Bolan shrugged. "Uh...well, yeah, sometimes."

"I told them they could take me to my room in the hotel and gang-bang me if they wiped the floor with you."

"Really? Wow." Bolan sipped his wine. "What if I'd lost?"

Her nose wrinkled delightfully. "I'm glad you won."

"So," Bolan said as he refilled her wineglass. "How'd I do?"

The woman's face grew serious. "You survived an attack by three brutal men. You incapacitated all three without killing them, and they didn't lay a finger on you. You ingratiated yourself with the locals and extracted before security forces arrived and without anyone knowing your identity." Anggun examined the ruby red depths of the cabernet in the candlelight and then locked gazes with Bolan. "You can tell a lot about a man by how he handles himself before, during and after a brawl."

Bolan acknowledged the compliment with a grin. "You're not the voice I first heard on the phone."

"No." She sipped her wine but didn't elaborate further.

"Are you the boss?"

"No."

"Oh." Bolan let a slight frown crease his brow. "But you have pull. If you didn't, you wouldn't be here."

"Hook liked your attitude." Her eyes drifted across the breadth of Bolan's shoulders. "So do I."

"I like you, too." Bolan smiled winningly. "A lot."

The woman raised an amused eyebrow.

Bolan's face hardened. "But in Kamchatka I lost some good friends and just about all of my investments. I'm currently stranded here shit out of luck and without a ride."

"Your luck may have changed." She shrugged. "Or maybe not, but I can guarantee you some pocket money and a plane ticket to wherever you want to go. We owe you that much for the interview." Bolan could see the wheels turning behind the dark eyes, but he could pick up no clue about what she was thinking. "What were you doing in Kamchatka?"

Bolan broke eye contact. "We don't know each other well enough."

The woman nodded.

He pressed a little. "Do you have the pull to get me a job?"

She regarded him seriously. "I already have a job for you."

"Where?"

"Los Angeles."

"When?"

The woman's face set into an exquisite look of inscrutability. "Forty-eight hours. My plane leaves in forty-five minutes."

"What kind of job?"

The corners of the woman's lips turned up "You're going to Hollywood, baby. You're going to get your big audition." She leaned closer and swirled the wine in her glass. "You game?"

Bolan leaned back and emptied his wineglass in a gulp. "Baby, I am the game."

## 9

*Men's room, Los Angeles International Airport*

Bolan stood in the stall and dialed a number on his cell phone. He had called Stony Man Farm from the men's room in Anchorage and given Kurtzman what little he knew. The computer genius had been given a good eight hours in which to work some magic.

The line clicked on with the first ring. "Striker."

"What have you got for me, Bear?"

"Not much. We have no records of a Cisasthmi Pukulan Anggun. Neither does the CIA or Interpol. Cisasthmi Anggun is an Indonesian name, just like you pegged it. But we have no reason to believe it's her real name."

Bolan recognized the sound of smugness in Kurtzman's voice. "But?"

"But the Pukulan part adds some flavor, but I'm not sure it's anything we can pin down."

Bolan frowned and looked at his watch. "Make it quick, Bear. If I'm in here more than two minutes, it's going to look suspicious, and I don't think she's going to buy any excuses about irritable bowel syndrome."

"Just this. Pukulan is not an Indonesian given name. It's a martial art."

"Really."

"Indonesia has about a million martial arts, almost all regional. Pukulan is practiced strictly in East Java. Saying Pukulan is like saying karate. It's an umbrella term with a fairly large number of substyles."

"Why would she use Pukulan as a middle name, then?"

"I don't know, Striker. People in Southeast Asia can have one name or twenty, depending on their region, tribe, clan, religion or employment status. Almost all of their names are dripping with meaning. Of course, it could be an alias, and she figures most round-eyes she meets are too dumb to notice or care."

"I don't know. I'm thinking it's a personal name. She likes the nickname Pooky. It's a hunch, but I think Pukulan may be a name she earned and is proud of."

"I think you may be right." Kurtzman's tone lowered in warning. "But listen, Striker, they take their martial arts seriously over there. They're often wound up in the local religion, as well. Her people wouldn't hang a moniker like that on her unless she was a real badass."

Bolan considered the combination of the woman's utterly perfect posture, the totally relaxed way she carried herself and her absolute lack of visible concern before, during and after the brawl. "Bear, I'm thinking badass."

"Yeah, and I've had another thought, as well."

"What?"

"If you're right, and we're dealing with a group of ex-Special Forces and intelligence types, she could be an ex-Dutch Intelligence agent."

"What kind of pull do we have with Dutch Intelligence?"

"I'm working on it, but it could take time. Lots of red tape to cut through."

"Bear, if you have 'Pukulan' up on your computer, E-mail me every style you have listed."

"I'm way ahead of you. I've got you the top ten nastiest, from the most well known to least. I'm sending now."

Bolan watched Indonesian words with English translations

scroll across the tiny LED screen on the phone. Each style had a one sentence description. He memorized the first five and then erased the message. "Bear, I've gotta go."

"I know. Listen, when you took off with Miss Anggun, Jack got in his plane and went back to Adak. He took the F-15E you two liberated, and when we knew you were headed to Los Angeles, he went on afterburners and flew to China Lake. He beat you to L.A. by about five hours. He's in LAX right now. Have you cleared customs?"

"No, I was hoping you'd have something for me before I step out of the airport and step into whatever I've gotten myself into. What's the scoop on Jack?"

"He'll be blonde, mirrored sunglasses, grinning like an idiot. We have a plane or helicopter with your name on it on every landing strip in the greater L.A. Basin, under the name Belasko. If you have to bail out, pick any airfield and go. Jack has a car. A silver Saab convertible. Do you want him to shadow you?"

Bolan considered that. Grimaldi was a beautiful ace in the hole, and he was loathe to give up what little backup he had. "No, these guys are giving me an audition. If they even catch a hint of tail, I think my ass will be smoked immediately and without warning."

"All right." Kurtzman clearly wasn't pleased. "But I'd be happier if—"

"Bear, I've got a date."

"Okay." The computer ace paused. "You think these are the people we're looking for? Hal's been asking."

Bolan considered the question. They had no proof of anything. But his instincts were speaking to him. "I'm starting to get a feeling."

"What kind of feeling?"

"That these are some very scary people."

Kurtzman was silent.

"Bear, I'll contact you when the situation permits."

Bolan clicked off the phone and went to his audition.

*Hollywood*

THE CONVERTIBLE Honda 2000SE slipped through the traffic like a silver dream. The wind of the sports car's passage sent the woman's dark hair flying behind her like a raven cloak and drew looks from every car around them. Anggun clearly had extensive offensive driving skills and even more clearly enjoyed driving fast cars.

Bolan watched La-La Land fly by. "What style are you?"

Her head turned as she spoke over the rush of the wind. "What?"

"I asked what style you practice." Bolan held up a fist. "Whip-style? Tiger? Big-Heart? What?"

The woman's dark eyes regarded Bolan with keen interest. *"Klipap."*

Bolan shrugged. "Never heard of it."

"Thunder style." The woman slid the car up into the Hollywood hills.

Bolan filed that away. He had lied. The Bear's E-mail had told him that in English *Klipap* meant thunder style, and specialized in nerve-center attacks. "So what's the job?"

"Wait." The woman took the car up into the hills. They passed the palatial estates of Hollywood's wealthiest. The hot desert wind blew across them and then cooled as they dipped into the shade of the canyons. The canyon roads twisted and wound, and Anggun took them at breakneck speed.

She pulled into the shade of a stand of pilatnon pines. A corral fence separated a field from the road. She pulled a pair of small, rubber-armored folding binoculars from the bag between her feet and handed them to Bolan. "You see that guy riding out there?"

Bolan brought the glasses to his eyes and scanned the field. A man in polo gear was riding a magnificent black Arabian. "Yeah."

"Open the glove box."

Bolan popped the glove box and stared at the contents.

On top of several folded maps and a leather license and registration folio lay a pistol. It looked like a .45 Colt automatic pistol, but the lack of a grip safety and its flatter, more graceful lines identified it as a Spanish Star Model A. It was a pre-WWII pistol. The grips showed a great deal of holster wear. Most of its original deep blue finish was gone. Bolan noted with interest the short, fat, cylindrical length of a sound suppressor screwed onto the muzzle.

An eyebrow rose slightly as he noticed the extra lever mounted on the slide.

It wasn't a Star Model A. It was a model M.

M was for machine pistol.

Bolan leaned closer without putting his hand on the gun. The stamping on the side said Cal .38 Super-Automatic.

It was a ridiculous weapon. It would be uncontrollable on full-auto, and with its 8-round pistol magazine it would shoot itself empty in a fraction of a second. The powerful .38 super rounds would rip the sound suppressor's baffles to shreds, and would fail to hide the supersonic crack of the high velocity ammo as it left the muzzle. Such a weapon was useful for only one thing, and that was assassinating someone at spitting distance.

Bolan regarded the pistol. He'd been forced to dump the pistol he'd taken from Adak before he'd hit the metal detectors at the Anchorage terminal.

"And?"

Anggun pointed out into the field. "Kill him."

Bolan turned and regarded Anggun.

A MAC-11 submachine gun had appeared in her hand like a magician's slight of hand. The weapon was pointed at Bolan's head. The weapon was hardly bigger than a large pistol and fired .380 ACP rounds. As a combat weapon, it was almost as useless as the Star machine pistol in the glove box. But it was suitable for exactly the same purpose. There was no room to dodge and no cover to be found in the two-seat cockpit of the Honda, and the little machine pistol would tear its 30-round magazine into Bolan and leave him headless in about two seconds.

The woman was no longer smiling. "This is a pass-fail situation."

Bolan sighed. He reached for the Spanish pistol with his left hand. The muzzle was pointing away from Anggun and he kept it that way as he took the pistol into his hand. "So, you want me to kill that guy?"

"Yeah," she said, nodding very slowly. Her huge dark eyes never blinked. The black muzzle of the MAC-11 never wavered from Bolan's temple. "I do."

Time seemed to compress as Bolan blurred into motion.

The muzzle of the Star met the MAC-11's as Bolan whipped his weapon backward. The MAC-11 was momentarily pinned against the passenger seat. Bolan leaned forward violently as the submachine gun exploded in Anggun's hand and a 3-round burst tore into the leather of the passenger door with a sound like meat being cut.

Bolan ignored the gun. It wasn't his most immediate problem.

The first two fingers of the woman's left hand had branched open into twin spears that shot toward Bolan's eyes with liquid speed.

There was almost no time to block, and blocking the blow of a nerve-style martial artist only offered him or her the opportunity to do something unthinkable to the limb that was offered. Bolan didn't attempt to block. He didn't yank his body back and offer it to the submachine gun.

He flicked his right wrist and brought up the binoculars between his face and her hand.

Anggun's fingers punched through the lenses.

Bolan twisted the binoculars and shoved down with all of his weight.

Her eyes flared wide. Both of her hands were pinned beneath Bolan's. Her submachine gun was pointed uselessly at the passenger door. The bleeding fingers of her right hand were twisted into the body of the miniature binoculars like some terrible Chinese finger trap. Her eyes flicked down to the muzzle of the Star pistol that pinned her own weapon.

It was pointed at her chin.

Bolan spoke conversationally. "I wonder if this is loaded?"

The woman's eyes were unreadable.

Bolan slitted his eyes for the spit and the head-butt attempt, but they didn't come. "I think we'd both feel a lot better if you put on the safety."

The safety of the MAC-11 flicked on with a click.

"Drop it."

Anggun's hand opened and the machine pistol slid down the seat to rest against the small of Bolan's back.

The soldier dropped the Star and released both of her hands. "Do I pass?"

The woman slowly withdrew her fingers from the broken binoculars. Blood welled up out of the deep cuts the shattered optical glass had left. She didn't look at her injured hand. Instead, she regarded Bolan with profound inscrutability.

"Should you?"

"Well, you take me into totally unfamiliar territory, no situation report, no reconnaissance, issue me a totally unfamiliar weapon and tell me to go and whack a target. I don't know who he is, I don't know if he's armed, if there's security on the premises, I have no idea of the premises at all, much less a secondary escape route or how to extract if things go south. I'd have to be one hell of a nut to go and do it, and I'm thinking if I'd taken the gun and stepped out of the car, you would've whacked me on general principle." Bolan leaned back in his seat and ejected the Star's magazine.

The copper gleam of a jacketed wadcutter solid sat at the top of the feed-lips. Bolan slid the magazine back into the gun.

"Do I pass?"

The cell phone in Bolan's pocket rang.

The barest hint of a smile crossed the woman's face.

Bolan kept his eyes on her and slowly took out the phone. "Hello?"

The voice he had first heard on the phone spoke. "Let's talk."

"HOOK SEEMS TO LIKE YOU." The man sat across from Bolan drinking orange juice. His eyes were as blue as Bolan's own. "So does Pooky."

Bolan looked into the man's eyes but could read nothing. The man had blond hair and a short blond beard. He had large white teeth. He was utterly relaxed. The soldier could only discern one thing from the man: he was utterly dangerous.

Bolan smiled. "I like Hook. He seems like good people." He drank the beer he was offered and raised a leering eyebrow. "And I'm fond of Pooky, too."

"Everyone's fond of Pooky." The man raised a bemused eyebrow of his own. "But she doesn't like everyone, if you know what I mean. You impressed her. That means you impressed me."

"Thanks." Bolan looked out across the veranda at the massive ranch houses that peeked out of the pines lining the canyon. "I thought she might be mad."

"No, she likes a man who can handle himself." The man smiled. "But I wouldn't spar with her anytime soon if I were you. She just might feel she has to put you back in your place."

"It might be worth it."

The man snorted. "So tell me a little something about yourself, Belasko."

Bolan knew the man had run what little info he'd been able to glean through every channel he had. Bolan didn't need to lie, and the best lies were always seamlessly woven with truth. "Not much to tell. I made sergeant back in the day, made sniper specialist, then I got into some heavy shit, with some very bad people."

The man seemed to file sniper specialist in his mind. "What kind of heavy shit?"

"I don't want to be rude, but I don't know you well enough, yet."

"Okay. And?"

Bolan was surprised that the man didn't seem to mind his reticence. "And then I got an offer."

The man nodded knowingly. "Uncle Sam called back his own."

"He did."

"And?"

Bolan didn't need to lie about that either. The truth of his life was enough "The hours were long, the work was hard and the pay sucked. I did a lot of things I'm not proud of, and I saw a lot of good people die, and die for nothing."

"You got any family?"

"I got a brother, someplace." He thought of April Rose and a bitter breeze blew through him. "I had a woman, a while back, but my job screwed it up. The rest of my family is gone."

The man nodded. "I did some research. This friend of yours, Calvin James, was a rock-solid SEAL. Hook says he served with him. Hook says if Calvin recommends you, it's good as gold."

"Calvin and I have worked together on occasion. I saved his life. He thinks he owes me."

The man steepled his fingers. "There were some big chunks of Calvin's past service, and current activities, that I can't get into, at least, not yet."

The casual way he said "not yet" set off alarms in Bolan's head, but he kept it off his face as the man continued.

"But, I know Hook, and within limits of his uses, I trust his judgment. My question to you is, if Calvin James is involved in black operations, why couldn't he get you a job?"

"Calvin was a decorated SEAL. He put himself through UCLA and got a degree. He doesn't have any black marks on his record. He's always been in the right place at the right time. He's a crackerjack. He can get a job doing anything he wants anywhere he wants. Me..." Bolan deliberately broke eye contact and looked away as he spoke the truth. "I don't have that kind of pedigree."

The man leaned back in his chair and waited for more.

Bolan sighed bitterly and put anger and resentment into his voice. "Listen, I'm too young to retire and too old to start over. I never went to college, and there's nothing I've done in the past ten years I could put on a résumé. You know what I'm saying?"

"I know exactly what you're saying." The man's glacial blue eyes locked with Bolan's. "Tell me, Belasko, how do you feel about America?"

Bolan took a long sip of his beer and considered his response. He finally rolled his eyes in disgust. "I don't know, love my country, fear my government?"

The man considered that for a moment.

"And that's your attitude?"

Bolan put the bottle down on the table hard. "That is a goddamn fact."

"Indeed." The man nodded. "It is." He cocked his head slightly. "Tell me about Kamchatka."

Bolan let out a weary breath. "More lies. More mistakes. Like I said, it's hard to start over. I've made a lot of contacts over the years, but almost everyone I trust is either dead, retired or moved on to better things. It's hard to carve yourself a new niche in this world without backup or people you can trust."

The man nodded at the wisdom of the statement. "You have any money?"

Bolan let his face fall. "I am dead busted."

The man nodded unconcernedly. "Pooky will take care of you here in L.A. for the next day or two. I need to make some phone calls. We'll talk again."

The man rose, and Bolan took his cue to leave. The man suddenly turned and smiled disarmingly. "Belasko?"

"Yeah?"

"I hear you won't sell drugs or pimp little girls."

"No." Bolan set his chin defiantly. "I won't."

The man's smile widened. "You have any problem taking down people who do?"

Bolan smiled back. "Not in the slightest."

**10**

*The Clubhouse*

The Iceman picked up the phone. "What have you got for me Jeremy?"

Jeremy's voice was excited over the phone. "I found some interesting anomalies in our attack on Brognola."

"Oh?"

"A lot of details are on a need-to-know basis. I'm working on those, but there are things that got mentioned in the police and fire reports."

"Like what?"

"Like they only pulled five bodies out of the ruins."

The Iceman nodded. "Hertzog led in the initial four-man assault team, personally."

"That's right, and all five bodies are John Does, not identified."

The Iceman's voice grew speculative. "Hal Brognola is still alive."

"That's my guess, too," agreed Jeremy. "Question is how.

Another interesting side note is about the weapons the local authorities pulled out of the wreckage."

"What about them?" the Iceman asked. "Those are guaranteed sterile."

"Yeah, but there were seven of them."

"Seven." The Iceman's eyes widened slightly. "By my math that means there was an extra."

"Yeah, five were AK-47s."

"Those belonged to Hertzog and the Russians. What were other two?"

"Get this. Stoner light machine guns."

The Iceman's eyes narrowed. The Stoner light machine gun was one of the best weapons ever made in its class. The Navy SEALs had wreaked havoc with them in Vietnam. The Iceman was intimately familiar with them. "How many?"

"A pair of them. One of them was nearly melted in half. The second was pulled out of the rubble, scorched but intact. So, I'm thinking either our pal Brognola carries one on each hip, or—"

"Or Mr. Brognola had some help," interrupted the Iceman. His fingers drummed once on the desktop. "I'm thinking our mysterious Russian colonel has made another appearance. It would explain a lot about how Hertzog failed to take the house. Neither he nor the Russians were expecting multiple targets with heavy weapons."

"Yeah, okay, then." Jeremy was clearly perturbed. He didn't like random factors that couldn't be accounted for. "But how did the Russian colonel get into the house? And more to the point, how did he and Brognola get out? They didn't come out through the thermite and white-phosphorus fires. Nothing came out."

"They had a tunnel. It's the only explanation. Brognola and the Russian extracted clean and are at large." The Iceman peered up at his map of the world. "So, tell me Jeremy, what have you learned about our Colonel Dimitri Rabskyov?"

"Only one thing."

"What's that?"

"There is no Colonel Dimitri Rabskyov."

The Iceman smiled. "Really."

Jeremy's voice grew excited. "My Russian contact came through in spades. The captain who owes him a favor pulled in markers of his own within Russian Military Intelligence. There is no Colonel Dimitri Rabskyov currently in the GRU, nor has there ever been a GRU colonel by that name. He was able to run a detailed check through service records kept by Russian Military Intelligence. There have been several hundred Dimitri Rabskyovs who have served in the Russian military since WWII. All are dead or accounted for. The ex-KGB boy we bought was able to do a fairly extensive search of KGB files, and they came up empty, as well. As for this being an alias for some other Russian agent, I can find no evidence at all to suspect that Russian Military Intelligence has any close ties to the Justice Department or been running a joint operation with them. All GRU and ex-KGB operators in D.C. are accounted for during the attack on the hospital. How this Brognola character could show up at the hospital with one in tow, much less even know to bring one, is a major anomaly."

The Iceman smiled slightly. "He didn't."

It was Jeremy's turn to be surprised. "He didn't?"

"No."

"Then who was he?"

"I don't know, but I have been considering the matter, and I think you've confirmed my suspicions. If the Feds thought they had a Russian agent, they wouldn't bring in a Russian colonel. They wouldn't want the Russians to even know they had the guy until they had done a thorough interrogation of their own. They would have brought along a CIA linguist or an interpreter. Instead, our boy Hal shows up unannounced with a Russian special forces colonel in his back pocket. A CIA interpreter or a Fed who spoke Russian would get nothing out of Pavel. He was a rock." The Iceman smiled slightly in appreciation at the beauty of the enemy ploy. "But Pavel was captured, wounded and heavily sedated. Suddenly seeing a colonel from his own unit in full dress uniform, in the hospital and demanding answers would have rattled him. It was a clever move."

Jeremy was silent a moment. "How did you figure that out?"

"Because it's what I would have done."

Jeremy paused a moment. There wasn't any bragging in the Iceman's tone. It was simply a statement of fact. "So how do we play it?"

"Jeremy, I want you to take as much money as you need and get a couple of your best infiltrators, but make sure they're expendable and know nothing in case they get caught."

"What kind of infiltration?"

"I want a couple of men in suits and acting like Feds. I want you to get a list of every person on the hospital's seventh floor, as well as the identity of as many of the surviving D.C. cops who were present in particular. Then I want your boys to very quietly interview these people. Use any pretense, I don't care, but I want every description we can get of the Russian colonel, and then I want a composite sketch made up."

Jeremy let out a breath between his teeth. "That could take a little time. It could also be dangerous. We could easily set off alarm bells with the wrong people, and I don't know if it could lead anyplace."

"Maybe it won't lead anywhere." The Iceman shrugged slightly. "But do it anyway."

"I'm on it." Jeremy's tone lightened. "So how is the recruiting going on your end?"

"One of those two guys C.T. found in Southern California may work out. The young guy, Del Carpio, doesn't have a whole lot of experience, but he's got sand, and his records and ratings are immaculate. I think we can mold him."

"Really?" Jeremy's interest peaked. "What about that live one Hook was talking about?"

The Iceman was silent for a moment. "If he pans out, I think he could go all the way."

"He's that good?" Jeremy was clearly somewhat suspicious. "We still know almost nothing about this guy."

"I know. I also know this. This guy isn't a cop, and he sure as hell isn't a Fed. He walks with big medicine. He's an operator."

"You trust him?"

"I didn't say I trusted him. I said he's got the vibe. I don't know about him for sure, yet, but we're going to find out real quick."

"Where is he now?"

"Los Angeles."

"L.A.?" Jeremy's voice grew concerned.

"I'm sending Brand and C.T."

"Yeah, and who's watching him now?"

"Pooky's taking care of him."

"Pooky's a bitch."

The Iceman smiled at the tone in Jeremy's voice. "Jeremy, do you know the difference between a bitch and a slut?"

Jeremy paused. "No."

"A slut sleeps with everyone."

Jeremy's voice grew cautious. "And?"

"A bitch sleeps with everyone except you."

*Los Angeles*

BOLAN'S HAND CLOSED around the grips of the .38-caliber pistol as his eyes flicked open.

Anggun made a small noise as Bolan shifted his weight and extricated his arm from beneath her head.

The day before they had ditched the bullet-riddled car and rented another. Then they had gone shopping. Bolan had stopped at a gun store and bought all six boxes of .38-caliber jacketed solids they had in stock, as well as a folding Buck hunting knife with a pocket clip. He'd asked the owner if he had any Star magazines. The man had said he could order them. Bolan had ordered them overnight express. Then the woman had taken him clothes shopping on Rodeo Drive. After lunch, they had gone and shot four of the boxes of ammo at the Hollywood range while they waited for his three new Armani suits to be altered. The Star functioned flawlessly. They had eaten dinner at an even more expensive restaurant, gone dancing at an invite-only nightclub, played pool in a bar on the worst side of town, then picked up a twelve pack of beer, rented Kung-fu movies and checked into a hotel.

There was a noise outside the door.

Bolan flicked the selector lever on the Spanish pistol to full-auto as he leveled the muzzle at the entrance.

Anggun spoke sleepily. "You won't need that."

A moment later there was a knock.

Bolan kept the muzzle of the pistol where it was. "Who is it?"

"You decent?"

"Give us a minute." Bolan rolled out of bed. The woman's two bandaged fingers trailed down his back as he did. He pulled on a pair of jeans and shoved the pistol into the small of his back.

"You decent yet?"

"Yeah, we're—"

A key turned in the lock and the door opened. Two large men stood just outside. One was half a head taller than Bolan and a good forty pounds heavier. He didn't have the physique of a bodybuilder, he was just big. His shoulders looked as if they'd barely fit through the door. Beside him stood a man who could have been an Asian copy of Bolan himself.

The Executioner needed to take only one look at the two men. The way they carried themselves and the look in their eyes told him all he needed to know. The men were armed, and they were operators.

Bolan smiled. "Morning."

"Morning." The big man looked over to where Anggun sat on the bed and grinned. She had draped a blue-black kimono that matched her hair across her shoulders. "Morning, Pook."

The big man looked Bolan up and down calculatingly. "So you're the guy everyone is talking about."

"Who's talking?" Bolan asked.

The man grinned. "All the best people." He held up a small express package. "Here's your mail."

Bolan pulled the knife from his back pocket and flicked it open one handed. He cut open the box, and there were four blue-steel pistol magazines inside. Bolan closed the knife and put it away. He took out the Star and ejected the full magazine and the round in the chamber onto the bed. He slid in a spare magazine, cycled the action, then ejected it.

The big man jerked his head at the pistol while Bolan tested the new magazines. He peered a moment at the rubber bands Bolan had wrapped around the grip to make the gun ride securely in his waistband. "You okay with that?"

Bolan nodded as the last magazine ejected and fell away cleanly. He reloaded the pistol and sat on the bed as he started loading the spares. "It'll do."

"We figured we'd let you hold on to it until we can arrange something more to your taste."

"Thanks. I appreciate it." Bolan put the loaded magazines into the pocket of the leather jacket he had bought. "So what's on the agenda for the day?"

The big man smiled again. "I heard you went shooting yesterday."

Bolan nodded.

"Heard you're pretty good."

"Yeah."

"Well, let's go see how good you really are," the big man started. "You have a meeting with the man."

*San Gabriel Mountains*

THE BLOND MAN TURNED and waved as the convertible 5.0 Mustang pulled up and parked beside a Jeep and a Land Rover. The gleaming black plastic and steel length of a military Joint Service Combat Shotgun hung from the crook of his elbow like a duck gun. In the Jeep, a pair of German shepherd dogs sat tethered to the roll bar, wagging their tails and peering at Bolan inquisitively. Four other men stood around a makeshift firing line. Weapons were carefully laid out on a pair of gun benches. Bolan's eyes stared at the weapons from behind his sunglasses. The vast majority of them were 9 mm Beretta Model 12 submachine guns with attached sound suppressors. The shooting area formed an L alongside the mountain. The road continued another twenty-five yards and ran into a dirt embankment. A half dozen silhouette targets mounted on plywood frames stood in front of the packed earth. Ten yards past the side of the road, the mountainside fell away into a narrow valley. Three spring-loaded traps to throw clay pigeons were arranged in an arc of shooting circles spaced seven yards apart.

Sandwiches and beers in ice buckets were piled high on a folding table. Each man, except one, had a pistol strapped to his belt. A young Hispanic male of about twenty-eight years of age stood off to one side, drinking a beer. He had a slightly uncertain look on his face.

The blonde walked up and stuck out his hand. "How you doing?"

Bolan took the hand and shook it. "Good."

"You know Pooky, and you've met Michael Brand and C.T."

"Yup. Real friendly fellas. Thanks."

The leader gestured to the young man standing to one side. "That's Del Carpio. He's the other new boot. He's been showing us what he can do."

Bolan nodded at the young man. "How you doing?"

"Good, man." The young man nodded earnestly. "Real good."

Bolan shrugged at the blonde. "So, what do I call you? Boss?"

"Well, I generally prefer *El Supremo*." The man smiled. "But you can call me Iceman or Ice. Everyone does."

"Okay, Ice."

"Listen, Belasko. You seem like a nice guy."

"Thanks."

"But recently I've run into some reliability problems." The muzzle of the Iceman's semiautomatic shotgun swiveled around and didn't quite point at Bolan's knees. "I've developed an initial good impression of Del Carpio, here. But there's a small chance that you, however, may not walk out of here alive. So, what I would like for you to do right now, is to take the machine pistol we sent along to you, and, with the first two fingers of your left hand, take it from the back of your pants and slowly set it on the table there with the sandwiches."

Seven heavily armed men watched Bolan unblinkingly. Del Carpio's eyes went to the table covered with weapons and then scanned the men around him uncomfortably. C.T. smiled at him. The Asian's hand rested on the 9 mm Walther pistol he carried at his hip.

Bolan took out his pistol and set it slowly on the table.

The Iceman nodded. "And the knife."

Bolan slid the knife out of his back pocket and put it next to the pistol. He considered his options.

He didn't have any.

Bolan raised his hands. "So what's up, Ice?"

"Listen, when Pooky told you to kill me, she told you it was a pass-fail situation. So is this. We're going to run a little operation tonight. You and Del Carpio are both invited. He's already made up his mind. What about you? You in or you out?"

Bolan glanced around at the semicircle of men surrounding him. No weapon was pointed directly at him. But each man had a weapon at hand, and Bolan had each man's undivided attention.

"Can I think about it?"

"Sure." The Iceman glanced at his watch. "How long do you need?"

Bolan shrugged. "A beer?"

Seven extremely dangerous men stood staring at Bolan without blinking. The Iceman regarded Bolan with a smile that didn't reach his eyes. "C.T., give the man a beer, to think about it."

The Asian stared at Bolan with eyes that hooded like a hawk's as he reached into the bucket and pulled out a can of Mexican Modelo beer. He made a show of brushing the water and ice off it.

The beer rolled off his fingers in a spinning left-handed line drive while his right hand went back to the Walther holstered on his hip.

The beer smacked into Bolan's open left hand.

Seven heavily armed men waited for Bolan to open the can and spew beer all over himself.

Bolan very slowly reached into the pocket of his shirt and took out the ballpoint pen he had taken from the hotel. It was now a question of saving face. He had drunk the venom sacks of cobras swimming in cognac in Thailand. He'd had rice wine in Okinawa that'd had pit vipers fermenting in it for twenty years. He'd drunk fermented mare's milk in Mongolia.

Shotgunning a beer wasn't much of a problem.

Bolan suddenly punched the pen into the bottom edge of the can and tilted his head back as he cracked the tab. He opened his throat and didn't bother swallowing as the pressurized beer shot down his gullet.

The semicircle of men stared in slight surprise.

Bolan took the empty can from his lips and with a single short motion crushed it.

"Okay," Bolan belched. He smiled happily as he tossed the crumpled can over his shoulder. "I've thought about it. Count me in."

Michael Brand threw back his head and laughed. "You know, I like him!"

C.T. smiled and shook his head ruefully as he pulled out another beer.

Del Carpio sighed with obvious relief.

Even the Iceman seemed vaguely amused.

The big man's hand thudded on Bolan's shoulder. "Yeah, well, now we know you can drink beer and beat up girls in sports cars. Question is, can you shoot?"

Bolan shrugged and took the beer C.T. offered him. "I don't know, can you?"

"Here we go!" Brand threw back his head again. "Ice, let me see that kidney buster again."

The Iceman tossed him the military assault shotgun. The big man checked the weapon's loaded chamber indicator and nodded at C.T. "Load three."

The Asian grinned and put three clay pigeons into the trap's arm.

Brand stepped into the shooting circle. "Pull!"

The weapon was instantly shouldered and booming on rapid semiauto. The first pigeon flew almost directly down into the valley below. It broke apart with the first shot. He was already turning like a turret and shot the second. The third was already almost out of shotgun range, but it smashed apart with the third shot.

Bolan nodded to himself. Shooting a triple was a neat trick, but not that hard. Most people could do it with a little practice. But the big man was using buckshot, not birdshot, and he had controlled the big shotgun on semiauto with a blinding speed and assurance that rivaled Carl Lyons, Able Team's leader.

"Not bad." The Iceman stepped to the shooting table and picked up one of the Beretta submachine guns. "Load three."

The big man loaded three pigeons and stepped back by Bolan. "Watch this. It's goddamn unnatural."

Bolan watched with keen interest.

The Iceman unlocked the single steel strut of the Beretta's folding stock and clicked it into place. He racked the action and stood holding the twin pistol grips of the submachine gun casually. "Pull."

C.T. pulled the trigger on the trap.

The arm swung and launched the three clay pigeons off in three different directions.

The sound-suppressed submachine gun coughed three times in the space of a second.

The three pigeons spun and broke apart almost simultaneously with the tinkling sound of cracking clay.

"Goddamn!" Brand roared. "I get goose bumps when he does that!"

Both Bolan and Del Carpio shook their heads slowly.

The Iceman was an extremely dangerous individual.

He turned as if he had read Bolan's thoughts and held out the Italian submachine gun. He nodded at C.T. while he smiled at Bolan. "C.T., load three."

"Naw." Bolan shook his head. "Load one."

The men looked at Bolan in disappointment.

Bolan cracked the beer C.T. had given him and went to the shooting table. Eyebrows rose as he picked up the Star machine pistol and unscrewed the sound suppressor. Bolan walked to the shooting circle as the Asian loaded the trap. He took a long pull of the beer in his left hand and stared out across the narrow valley. The Star was of pre-WWII manufacture, and like most military guns of the time, its sights could be charitably described as rudimentary. However, Bolan had taken the weapon shooting the other day. He knew that it shot about two inches low and to the left of the point of aim, and he had painted the front sight white with Liquid Paper.

Bolan finished the beer. He crumpled the can in his fist and tossed it behind him. He shoved the pistol's selector lever to full-auto, he took a long deep breath and then slowly let out half of it. "Pull."

The trap sent the single pigeon spinning into the air over the valley like a discus.

Bolan's took one step forward and turned his body sideways like a fencer. He extended the machine pistol to eye level and took a half second to track the clay pigeon's arc. Both of his eyes remained open as he indexed on the bright white lump of front sight.

The pigeon seemed to spin almost suspended out over the valley.

Bolan slowly squeezed the trigger.

The pistol snarled on full-auto. Wild recoil immediately yanked the muzzle skyward as the pistol violently cycled all nine rounds. The pistol clacked open almost instantly on an empty chamber.

The clay pigeon split and tumbled apart into two pieces as a .38-caliber bullet punched it in two.

Bolan lowered the smoking pistol. He regarded it for a moment and then grinned at C.T. "Give me a week. Then you can load three."

"Damn!"

"Wow..." Del Carpio stared in awe.

Bolan ejected his spent magazine and turned to the Iceman. The Iceman's eyes were unreadable.

Bolan grinned good-naturedly as he reloaded. "So where's this party tonight, and who's the guest of honor?"

**11**

*Gulf of California, altitude 14,000 feet*

Bolan deployed from the Grumman Gulfstream and plunged into the darkness.

He had very little choice. He was out of contact with Stony Man Farm. He could attempt to contact the police, and have the people he'd met brought up on weapons charges, but that would be an act of futility. The only names he had were Michael Brand, Pooky, C.T. and Iceman. Even if they were arrested, Bolan knew these were the kind of people who would make bail and then disappear like smoke. He also knew he would very likely die in the attempt, and he had nothing at all to connect these men to the dead U.S. marshals.

But they sure as hell had the vibe.

It was a clear night. Below him, Bolan saw the stars reflected in the still waters of the Sea of Cortez. They were far from the tourist capital of Cabo San Lucas, and beneath him the long thin arm of the Baja Peninsula was only sparsely dotted with the lights of villages and ranchos. Bolan plunged through space with seven other men, all as heavily armed as he was. Whatever the night's true objective, he knew full well what was expected of him. He had to prove to these men that he wasn't a cop or a Fed.

He had to get himself a body.

Bolan vaguely wondered if his parachute would open. If they had doubts about him, dropping him into the drink at thirteen hundred feet per second would solve any liability problems. He would be just one more unidentified body in the Sea of Cortez. That was if the Humboldt squids that rose from the depths at night to feed left anything worth trying to identify. Bolan had been in Baja before. The local fishermen preferred being eaten by sharks. The sharks were swift; one hit, and a man was done for. The squids were six to eight feet long, and frequently engaged in feeding frenzies. A dozen of them could grapple over a man all at once as they tugged him down into the depths. Their horned tentacles heaved, and twisted a man apart even while the squids ate him alive, one horrid beakfull at a time. Bolan considered the dark waters rushing up at him. The luminous dial of his altimeter said ten thousand feet.

If his chute didn't open, he would never feel the cold embrace of the squids.

Their target was in Mexico. He had been assured the target was legitimate, and was told they had alternate extraction routes if things went wrong. He would be taking the same risks as everyone else. The pay was ten thousand dollars, with possible membership privileges in "the Club," based on performance. There was no mention made of Bolan's balking at the last moment or failure to perform. The Iceman's smiling omission of any such possibilities left it very clear what would happen to Bolan if they occurred.

The soldier checked his altimeter. He was at six thousand feet.

Brand plunged next to Bolan only a few feet away. He gave Bolan the thumbs-up and seemed to yank back upward into the sky like a giant yo-yo as his chute deployed.

Bolan pulled his own rip cord and felt the heave of his harness tightening against him as the chute filled with air and slowed his descent. He took his steering handles and swung the airfoil toward land. They took a steep descent angle and aimed for a strip of beach and the lights of a large seaside hacienda.

Details became clearer as Bolan swiftly soared downward. A lighted pier thrust out into the water, and the dock attached to it had a shed and a gas pump. A huge pleasure yacht was moored to the pier. Bolan noted the yacht had an orange landing circle on a roof big enough to hold a decent-sized helicopter. Beyond the beach, a gravel path led up to a double iron gate. High adobe walls surrounded the hacienda. As Bolan flew toward the beach, the harsh glare of the floodlights revealed a pair of men in civilian clothing lounging by the gate smoking cigarettes. Both men were carrying automatic rifles slung over their shoulders.

The men at the gate ducked out of view as Bolan pulled his chute into a stall and his boots crunched into the sand of the beach at a run. He flicked off the safety of the Beretta Model 12. Bolan considered his weapon as he released his harness. He and Del Carpio carried the same submachine gun as the rest of the team. He had seen the other team members loading armor-piercing rounds. All of them were wearing Threat Level III body armor, but Bolan and Del Carpio's weapons were loaded with subsonic hollowpoint rounds. The ammo the two of them had been issued wouldn't defeat their teammates' armor. If Bolan tried to shoot his way out, he would have to take out all seven men with head shots.

They would have no such problems with him.

Bolan and Del Carpio didn't have tactical radios. Bolan had been told to stay by Brand's side, and C.T. was baby-sitting Del Carpio. The Executioner knew there would always be a pair of eyes on them, and they wouldn't hear what was being said.

Brand, C.T. and Del Carpio landed beside him seconds apart. The other four men landed behind them, and Bolan heard the muted clicks of safeties being flicked off weapons.

The big man kneeled beside Bolan in the sand.

Bolan glanced toward the hacienda. "So what happens now?"

"You're having your doubts," Brand said. "That's to be expected. You're wondering what the mission is, and you're thinking about what you're going to do when I tell you to whack someone you don't know. I don't blame you. So I'll tell you what the deal is. We're going up to that hacienda, we're going to do some serious damage and take what we came for."

The muzzle of Bolan's submachine gun didn't move, but his finger was on the trigger. The selector switch was on full-auto.

"But first," he said, "me, you and C.T. are going to take a little field trip."

"What about Del Carpio?"

"He'll stay here with the rest of the boys, for the moment."

"Okay." Bolan could feel the muzzles of the men behind him aimed at his back. "Where're we going?"

"The yacht," C.T. said. "There's something we want you to see before we hit the house."

"All right." Bolan followed Brand as he rose, and they moved out along the edge of the surf. The Asian fell in behind him. The sound of the surf covered them as they took cover under the pilings of the pier. Brand moved into the shallow water and began to heave his massive frame up one of the pilings. He leaped out, and his hand seized the yacht's railing. The crepe sole of his boot made no noise as he pressed it against the hull and yanked himself aboard.

Bolan swiftly followed him over the rail. The Executioner crouched, and C.T. instantly dropped behind him. The sound of classical music came from somewhere in the yacht's interior. Out on the foredeck beneath the bridge stood a man in a black watchman's sweater and cap carrying an Uzi.

The big man went to a door and quickly slid inside.

Bolan followed him into an empty lounge filled with plush couches. One wall was dominated by a massive entertainment center, and on the wall opposite was a small but well-stocked wet bar. Brand stood listening at the opposite door for a moment and then opened it a crack. He peered out and then motioned Bolan to follow as he slid out of the lounge. The corridor was narrow but plushly paneled and carpeted. Bolan noted it was also soundproofed as the classical music disappeared.

The big man halted and pulled back his sleeve. He wore a diagram of the yacht's layout beneath a clear plastic panel in a waterproof armband. He nodded to himself and proceeded down the corridor. Bolan still felt C.T.'s muzzle pointed at his back. He weighed his chances of head-shooting both men before one of them could cut him in two and decided to go along a little further and see what developed.

They came to a door and stopped. Brand went inside and Bolan followed. The room was Spartan, with a large sink and a tile floor with a drain. Bolan's eyebrow rose as he noticed a spot of blood on one of the sink's spigots. Brand pushed past through the next door and stopped.

"Here you go."

As Bolan entered the room, Brand flicked on the light.

Bright overhead fluorescent fixtures lit up the room. Inside was an operating table. Shelves folded out of the walls and were lined with surgical instruments. An anesthesia rig and a bank of refrigeration units sat in a corner. In another corner sat a table with a desktop computer and a monitor.

Brand spoke very softly. "You know what this is, Belasko?"

Bolan's instincts whispered to him. What they whispered was too horrible to speak of. Bolan went frosty even as he played dumb. "Looks like a surgery."

"It's a chop shop." Brand moved to a filing cabinet. He took out a multibladed lock pick and swiftly defeated the filing cabinet's lock. He slid out the drawer. Inside were numerous files. He pulled out a three-ring binder and opened it up. His face set in a grimace. "Take a look at this."

Bolan knew what he would see as he took the binder. Inside were medical files. Each file had a photograph attached to it. Bolan flipped pages. Each photograph was of a boy or girl of teenage years or younger. Beneath each one were descriptions of the medical check-up they had received and what of interest was noted.

Beneath was a list of which internal organs had been harvested from each of them.

The big man spoke low. "It's understandable, you know. If I had the money, and my wife or my kid was dying, I wouldn't ask any questions. I'd pay up, and I'd be grateful. I don't blame the parents. Hell, in a way, I can even accept some poor bastard who has it done to save himself. No one wants to die. But only the very wealthy can afford this kind of service, and it's the best kind of gig in the world for the asshole running it. No one wants you to get caught. They'll go out of their way to see that you don't. They'll bend over backward to see you get paid in ways that can't get traced, and see to it that the local and even international law leaves you alone. Presidents, politicians, CEOs, this is the kind of thing they don't talk about, but it's something they keep in their back pocket in case things go wrong for them. Like I said, I can understand it."

Brand's jaw set beneath the black greasepaint that camouflaged his face. "But for someone to get saved, someone else has to die." His finger tapped down on the face of a smiling girl who couldn't have been more than sixteen. "The scumbags who kidnap, chop and run the business? Them, I have a problem with."

There was a moment of profound silence in the surgery.

"You understand what we're all about, Belasko?" Brand's

eyes blazed out of his greasepaint. "We're the top of the food chain. We're the predators who prey upon predators."

"Oh, I understand." Bolan's voice was as cold as the grave. "I understand perfectly."

"You got a problem with that?"

C.T. spoke from the scrub room. "Someone's coming."

Bolan pushed past C.T. and stepped into the corridor.

A pair of men were coming down the hallway. One wore a lab coat and spoke animatedly in Spanish. The other man wore a suit and carried a laptop under his arm. He nodded thoughtfully at what the medic was saying.

Bolan knew exactly what was happening. It was a perfect recruitment. A beautiful woman, a righteous cause and a big payoff somewhere at the end of it. The next few operations would be exactly the same, and then, somewhere down the line, the missions would cross the line.

And by then he would be in too deep, and probably beyond caring anymore.

None of that mattered at the moment. The Club didn't matter at the moment.

Bolan had seen the brand of evil standing in front of him before.

They all went down. No matter the cost.

The man in the lab coat suddenly stopped as Bolan appeared in the corridor. He was aghast as he took in Bolan's blackened face and tombstone eyes.

The medic shuddered as the sound-suppressed Beretta fired from Bolan's hands. The man sagged as the 5-round burst walked up his chest. The man in the suit flung his laptop and turned to run. Bolan jerked his head aside from the flying computer. He put his first burst into the target's back and staggered him. The second burst put him down.

"Jesus!" C.T. snarled. "We are a go!"

Bolan stepped over the bodies and went to the next door down. "C.T., go kill the sentry on deck!"

The Executioner's voice brooked no argument. C.T. slid past him down the hallway.

Bolan began kicking doors. Most of the staterooms were empty. He kicked a door, and his lip curled. Within was a thickly carpeted floor. Toys, stuffed animals and beanbag chairs were strewed around the room along with two sets of bunk beds. There was a TV and a VCR with several videotapes of cartoons scattered about. Bolan was thankful that the room was empty and moved on. Bolan kicked a door and shot a man who rose from his bed with a pistol in his hand.

Brand followed, covering his every move.

They swept the boat from stem to stern. The first mate died in his bed. Bolan put a burst into his brain before he even woke up.

C.T. appeared at the landing to the bridge. "The sentry is down. I think we're clean. Most everybody is up at the hacienda." He glanced through the massive arc of the bridge window out into the dark of the beach. "The boys are ready and waiting." He looked at Brand. "It's your call."

The big man turned and looked meaningfully at Bolan. "What do you say, Belasko?"

Bolan spoke over his shoulder as he strode out of the bridge. "I say we burn the bastards to the ground."

*The hacienda*

THEY SWEPT DOWN like wolves. From out of the darkness they fell upon the hacienda. The two men at the gate shuddered and fell as multiple bursts from the sound-suppressed weapons took them from the shadows. It was a matter of moments to overcome the lock and disable the alarm on the gate.

Brand spoke quickly. "The scumbag up in the house is Eddie Alejandro. He was a pimp and pusher in Tijuana, then in the mid-90s he got involved in pushing Mexican steroids into Los Angeles. He made connections in the underground medical community on both sides of the border. Someone realized Alejandro could acquire kids and runaways easily. They made him an offer, and he's been in the body-parts business ever since."

Brand glared up at the hacienda on the hill. Bolan followed his gaze.

"The chop jobs are done on the yacht, in international waters right off the coast. A helicopter takes the organs straight to L.A., where a waiting Learjet takes it to the buyer on standby. Once they've been harvested, the kids go over the side, and about three thousand fathoms of Cedros Oceanic Trench does the rest. It's usually kidneys and livers, but I hear they're even harvesting corneas these days." The big man shook his head. "It's gotta suck to be twelve years old and wake up out of anesthesia blind and drowning in the Pacific."

"You don't have to stroke me." Bolan turned and slowly regarded Brand. "We're righteous on this one."

The big man almost took a step back from Bolan's burning gaze. "Eddie thinks he's protected and everybody loves him, but he likes to keep a lot of bodyguards around him, anyway. He's developed a thing for big guns and cocaine. Our latest intelligence as of an hour ago says he has about ten men with him tonight. He's not expecting any kind of trouble, but they say all the coke he's snorting is turning him into a real yahoo. Things could go hot quick with this guy."

"So let's drop him and get out of here." Bolan glanced at the Jeep parked outside the gate. "Let's take that with us."

Brand smiled and waved his hand in a circle to the rest of the men waiting in the dark. "Okay."

Bolan put down the windshield and secured it as men piled into the Jeep until the roll bars were dripping with warriors. He put the vehicle in gear and began driving up the little hill. The hacienda was a modern nightmare of pastel pink and blue adobe. The driveway was a circle of paved white stones with a fountain in the middle. As they approached the floodlights of the house, men dropped off of the side of the Jeep like outriders.

"How do you want to play it?" Brand asked.

Bolan considered the Jeep. It had a steel bumper with a winch, as well as a full off-road roll cage. "Let's go knock on the door."

The big man made a cutting motion with his hand, and the last two men in the back leaped out of the vehicle.

The V-8 engine roared as Bolan floored the gas pedal.

The Jeep shot stones in all directions as the huge off-road tires bit into the gravel circle of the driveway. Bolan shoved it into first gear and the chassis bounced and rocked with bone-jarring force as they hit the long shallow steps.

The great double oak door smashed off its hinges as the Jeep hit it at thirty miles per hour.

A man armed with an M-16 was knocked off his feet as a flying oak door scythed into him. Bolan stepped on the brakes, and the tires screeched and spun on the tile flooring of the cavernous foyer. The foyer opened onto a cathedral-sized central room dominated by a central fireplace big enough to barbecue an entire cow. When the wheels finally gripped the floor, Bolan drove into the central room. Brand was already shooting.

A man with an AK-47 came out of a side hallway, and bullets ripped into the Jeep's front fender. Bolan extended his submachine gun in his left hand and walked a burst up the man's chest.

Behind the Jeep, C.T. and the rest of the team streamed into the house.

A pair of balustraded stairways bracketed the vast room and arced upward to an open balcony that overlooked the central room. The balcony was girded along its length with a thick marble railing.

Armed men suddenly appeared on the balcony and began firing.

Bolan's team began engaging from the foyer entrance, and two of the bodyguards fell instantly. The hacienda's interior echoed with the snarl of gunfire and the roar of the Jeep's engine. The big man sat next to Bolan firing short controlled bursts. He was capping each man who appeared over the balcony as though he were in a shooting gallery at the county fair. His weapon clacked open on empty, and he ripped the spent magazine free.

Bolan fired another one-handed burst and aimed the vehicle toward the steps leading to the balcony.

A half-naked man appeared at the railing holding a rifle bigger than he was.

Eddie Alejandro.

The weapon hammered into life. The hood of the Jeep blew off. The engine made horrible noises as things broke apart and flew about the engine compartment. The glass of the lowered windshield shattered, and chunks of foam and black tape spewed away as bullets tore into the roll bar.

"Jesus!" Bolan spun the wheel and leaped from the dying vehicle. "Jump!"

Bolan hit the floor with bruising force but rolled to his feet. He put the stonework of the central fireplace between himself and the bullets seeking him. The Jeep continued forward and rammed into the wall beneath the balcony.

The huge weapon above hammered, and chunks of stone and

clay flew away as the gun chewed away the fireplace. Brand rolled beside Bolan and cringed as bullets tore away stone above his head. "What the hell is that!"

"I only got a quick look!" Bolan snarled. "But I think Eddie's got a Mendoza light machine gun!"

"That's no goddamn light machine gun!" The big man's face split into a visage of hatred as the weapon hammered. The clay wall of the foyer erupted, and one of his team staggered backward and fell motionless to the tiles.

"It's a machine rifle, .30-06!" Bolan whipped his Beretta over the fireplace and fired a burst toward the balcony. "I think he's shooting steel-jacketed bullets!"

"Come on!" screamed the man on the balcony. "I'll kill you all!"

The automatic rifle came into life again, and stonework flew. Beside him, men poured fire down into the central room and the foyer with their assault rifles.

"I kill you all! You hear me?" Alejandro screamed.

Bolan slid a fresh magazine into his weapon.

"Asshole thinks he's Scarface!" Brand snarled.

"Eddie's got 20-round magazines," Bolan observed. "And him and the boys aren't observing any kind of coordinated fire protocols."

The iron hood of the fireplace sagged on its bolts above them. Sparks flew as it was chewed apart. There was a sudden silence as the men on the balcony all ran dry.

Bolan and Brand popped up. Behind them C.T., Del Carpio and the rest of the team had the same idea. Four men with M-16s fell as they were riddled in the middle of reloading. Alejandro had prudently stepped back. His weapon ripped back into life.

"Come on!" he yelled. Marble flew as he fired through the balcony railing. "You are cowards! I spit on you!"

The Mendoza automatic rifle chewed up everything in its line of fire. C.T. and the other men were forced to retreat deeper into the foyer, where it took a foot of wall thickness to stop the steel-jacketed bullets.

Bolan spun the sound suppressor from the barrel of his weapon. "Tell me you have men flanking!"

"I've got two working their way around the back! They had to take out dogs! Eddie had four guys out back. Three are down."

Brand put a hand to his earpiece. "They're flanking him now. They say they'll be inside and behind Eddie ETA two minutes!"

Both men flinched as the iron hood failed and collapsed with a clang on top of the crumbling fireplace.

Bolan shook his head at the jagged iron inches in front of his face. "We don't have the time!"

"We're not charging down the muzzle of that thing!" Brand roared. "I've already lost a man!"

Bolan popped up as the machine rifle upstairs ran dry. His submachine gun ripped into life, and another of Alejandro's men collapsed.

"Come on, Rico! You and me! We kill them! We kill them all!" Alejandro screamed.

The man was down to his last bodyguard.

Bolan grimaced. Alejandro also seemed to have every round of steel-jacketed .30-06 ammo in North America. Bolan peered around the edge of the fireplace. He considered the stricken Jeep below the balcony and vainly wished for a hand grenade.

He would have to do this the hard way.

"No! No charge! Have your men remove their sound suppressors! I need Eddie and Rico's heads down for two seconds!"

Brand stared at Bolan and then spoke quickly into his throat mike. He nodded at the response and back to Bolan. "All right, it's your funeral! C.T. and the boys are going to give you covering fire on three! One! Two! Three!"

The big man's team all popped out and fired their Berettas on full-auto. The hacienda echoed with the sound of the concentrated firepower.

Bolan vaulted over the fireplace and ran for the balcony. He waited for the big automatic rifle to chop him to pieces. The half-dozen submachine guns of Brand's team ran dry, and they ducked back behind cover.

Bolan dived under the shelter of the balcony.

"You think I don't see you? Huh?" Alejandro's voice rose to a hysterical shriek.

Bolan heaved himself flat against the wall as bullets tore down through the balcony. He squinted and jerked his head aside as floor tiles exploded upward as Alejandro dumped his entire magazine down at him.

"How you like that, huh?" Alejandro screamed. "Stick your head out!"

Bolan stared at the perforations above him. The 9 mm hollowpoint rounds in his Beretta wouldn't tear through wood flooring and marble like the Mendoza machine rifle above. He could hear the man reloading. His buddy Rico's M-16 streamed fire down into the room and the foyer beyond alternately.

Bolan dropped the Beretta and drew the Star .38 super machine pistol. He glanced back at the fireplace. The frontal arc of it was gone. Broken stone and ash littered the floor. The iron hood lay crumpled across it. It would only take one or two more bursts before Brand was hit.

"Come on, Rico! We gonna—"

Brand popped up from behind his failing cover. He took a suicidal half second to shoulder his weapon and take careful aim. He squeezed off a single round and ducked back.

"Rico!"

Rico tumbled over the edge of the balcony and fell to the tiles three feet away from Bolan. Brand's head shot had traveled temple to temple through the front of Rico's brain and crossed his eyes.

"Rico!" Alejandro screamed.

The Mendoza hammered into life.

The fireplace collapsed under the assault. Brand was either dead or on his belly.

Bolan stepped into the Jeep and climbed up the roll cage. He perched on top of it and judged the angle. He wasn't quite in line with the balcony. It was going to be an ugly jump. Bolan switched the Star to his left hand.

The soldier distinctly heard the clack of the Mendoza racking open on an empty chamber.

Bolan leaped.

He flung himself at the edge of the balcony. His hand slipped along smooth marble and then closed around a rail. Bolan twisted his body upward and his left boot heel hooked the edge of the balcony.

Bolan yanked himself up, clinging to the balcony like a spider as he thrust the Spanish machine pistol between two of the rails.

A short, scrawny little man stood a few feet from the edge of the balcony. He wore nothing but purple bikini underwear and a pair of canvas magazine bandoliers crossed over his chest. A massive automatic rifle was cradled in his hands. The wood around the red-hot barrel popped and ticked with the heat. Spent magazines and brass shell casings littered the balcony in a sea of spent firepower. Alejandro fumbled a fresh magazine into the top of the rifle's smoking breech while he screamed at Brand.

"You, out of the fireplace, asshole! You hear me? I'm gonna roast you in the rubble!"

Alejandro blinked in confusion as he suddenly noticed Bolan on the rail below him. The hardman's eyes were wide open, as his pupils dialed to pinholes. White powder dusted his left nostril and the left half of his pencil-thin mustache. He sniffed violently and blinked at the .38-caliber muzzle pointing at him and then at Bolan.

"Hey," Alejandro said, "what's up?"

The Star machine pistol ripped into life with a sound like tearing canvas. The 9 mm round burst walked up Alejandro's torso and face as it took him between his eyebrows.

His body went rigid. The machine rifle fell from his hands. He rocked back on his heels and slowly toppled like a falling tree into the sea of spent shells that littered the balcony like confetti.

The hacienda was suddenly silent.

Bolan vaulted over the rail. He ejected his spent magazine and slapped in a fresh one as he flicked the Star back to semiauto. "Eddie's down!" He glanced back over the rail quickly while he covered the upstairs. "Brand! You all right?"

Broken stone and shattered mortar shifted as the big man did a push-up out of the rubble of the fireplace. A section of the iron hood fell away from him with a clang. He shook himself as he put his earpiece back in place. His face was white beneath the blood and ash on his face. He nodded shakily up at Bolan as he spoke into his tactical radio.

Bolan lowered his pistol as the two-man flanking team appeared from different sides of the staircase. They gave Bolan the thumbs-up.

"Clear!"

"Clear!"

Brand stood. "All right. Come on. We've got work to do. C.T., what's the status on Shpagin?"

Bolan cocked an ear at the name.

C.T. knelt in the foyer by the fallen man. Del Carpio stood beside C.T., and his eyes continued to sweep the hacienda. The Asian shook his head. "Shpagin took three in the chest. He's gone."

Brand sighed. "Take four men. Make sure the rest of the house is clear. Then put in the call for extraction."

He nodded at Del Carpio. "Good work."

Brand suddenly grinned at Bolan. "You, Spider-man. Follow me."

Bolan walked downstairs and retrieved his submachine gun. He followed Brand down a hallway, watching as the big man checked the notes on his wrist and came to a door. Brand put a burst into the jamb and kicked it in. Beyond the door was a small study that resembled a drawing room out of the English Victorian era. Brand went to a bookcase and examined it for long moments. He reached into a canvas pouch of his web gear and pulled out a coiled length of adhesive flexible charge.

Brand fitted a length of charge along the joint of the wall and the bookcase, pressed a detonator and stepped back. He elbowed Bolan in the ribs knowingly. "Here's where it gets fun."

He pulled a small remote from his pouch and pushed the red button. The flexible charge hissed and made a noise like a whip crack. Orange flame jetted around the seam, and the whole bookcase swung out on a concealed hinge. Brand waved away acrid smoke as he walked through the hidden door. "Check this."

He flicked a light switch in the hidden chamber.

Bolan let out a breath. Eddie Alejandro had put his faith in immense automatic weapons.

He had put his financial resources into gold.

The room was a bare, ten-by-ten-foot cube, and empty, except for a pallet stacked high with one kilogram gold bars. Bolan did a quick eyeball of the gleaming pyramid of bullion before him. There had to be fifteen million dollars' worth of gold in the pile.

"Oh, man!" said Brand appreciatively. "They say virtue is its own reward, but damn, does that shine."

Bolan nodded slowly. "Righteousness pays."

"It pays handsomely," Brand answered. "All you have to do is keep the faith, and then God helps those who help themselves."

Bolan nodded in agreement. "How are we extracting? The yacht?"

"No. That butcher shop goes to the bottom. We'll do a minimal cleanup. We leave the blood and damage, but the bodies go on the yacht and we scuttle it over the Cedros Trench."

"So," Bolan said as he looked long and hard on the gold. "We send Eddie and his friends down to the squids."

"Damn right. They deserve each other."

"What about us?" Bolan asked. "I didn't see an airstrip."

"The Russians are bringing in a boat for us right now. A commercial deepsea sport fisher. They'll be pissed about Shpagin. They've been taking a lot of losses lately. They should be here any minute. We load the gold, and C.T. will follow us in the yacht and sink her at sea."

Russians. Taking losses lately.

Bolan filed that away. He suddenly grinned at the gold. "Brand, we're going to need a wheelbarrow."

**12**

*San Diego Bay*

"Yeeeeeee-haw-yes!" Michael Brand howled. He tossed back the shot of tequila in his right hand and poured down half the beer in his left to chase it. He squeezed his eyes shut and shook his head. His eyes flared wide as the liquor settled. "Oh, hell, yes!"

The big man pointed his shotglass at Bolan. "I love this guy!"

Bolan shrugged and slid down his tequila. The ten-year-old Maduro Silver was exceptionally smooth. The very hull of the houseboat vibrated as every album the Rolling Stones had ever recorded blared out of gigantic speakers on continuous rotation. It seemed like every stripper in San Diego had been invited to the party. The houseboat was full of drunken half-naked women hanging on grinning, drunken dangerous men. Tri-tips sizzled on the grill, and swordfish steaks were on standby for the second course.

"I was dead!" Brand roared. "I'm telling you, I was maggot meat! Prone and stone cold in the crosshairs! Then Belasko caps Eddie between the eyes! I love this bastard!"

Bolan nodded modestly and took a sip of his beer. "Someone

## The Gold Eagle Reader Service™ — Here's how it works:

Accepting your 2 free books and gift places you under no obligation to buy anything. You may keep the books and gift and return the shipping statement marked "cancel." If you do not cancel, about a month later we'll send you 6 additional books and bill you just $29.94* — that's a saving of 10% off the cover price of all 6 books! And there's no extra charge for shipping! You may cancel at any time, but if you choose to continue, every other month we'll send you 6 more books, which you may either purchase at the discount price or return to us and cancel your subscription.

*Terms and prices subject to change without notice. Sales tax applicable in N.Y. Canadian residents will be charged applicable provincial taxes and GST. Credit or Debit balances in a customer's account(s) may be offset by any other outstanding balance owed by or to the customer.

NO POSTAGE
NECESSARY
IF MAILED
IN THE
UNITED STATES

# BUSINESS REPLY MAIL
FIRST-CLASS MAIL    PERMIT NO. 717-003    BUFFALO, NY

POSTAGE WILL BE PAID BY ADDRESSEE

**GOLD EAGLE READER SERVICE**
**3010 WALDEN AVE**
**PO BOX 1867**
**BUFFALO NY 14240-9952**

If offer card is missing write to: Gold Eagle Reader Service, 3010 Walden Ave., P.O. Box 1867, Buffalo NY 14240-1867

# Get FREE BOOKS and a FREE GIFT when you play the...

# LAS VEGAS GAME

*Just scratch off the gold box with a coin. Then check below to see the gifts you get!*

## YES!
I have scratched off the gold Box. Please send me my **2 FREE BOOKS** and **gift for which I qualify**. I understand that I am under no obligation to purchase any books as explained on the back of this card.

**366 ADL DRSL**

**166 ADL DRSK**
(MB-03/03)

FIRST NAME

LAST NAME

ADDRESS

APT.#

CITY

STATE/PROV.

ZIP/POSTAL CODE

| 7 | 7 | 7 | Worth TWO FREE BOOKS plus a BONUS Mystery Gift! |
|---|---|---|---|
| 🍒 | 🍒 | 🍒 | Worth TWO FREE BOOKS! |
| 🔔 | 🔔 | ♣ | TRY AGAIN! |

Offer limited to one per household and not valid to current Gold Eagle® subscribers. All orders subject to approval.

had to pull your ass out of the fireplace before you got buried under it."

C.T. leaned back on the rail, wearing nothing but a towel. The pair of spectacular redheads he had just taken a shower with hung on each arm. "No way man, I saw it. I saw you take that balcony the hard way. It rocked. The Bulgarian judge gave you a 9.9."

Bolan raised an eyebrow. "I was expecting a ten."

"Yeah," C.T. shrugged as his hands wandered on his women, "but you walked back down the stairs. Your dismount sucked."

"Next time I'll do a back flip."

"I love this guy!" Brand repeated. The big man had been drinking since noon. "Love him, love him, love him!"

Bolan glanced around. The houseboat was just short of palatial. It belonged to Brand. He had to admit it, the big man knew how to throw a party. They had loaded the gold and scuttled the yacht, then traveled at good speed up the Baja Peninsula with no incidents. The fishing along the way had been spectacular. At no time had Bolan ever been left alone. The soldier knew any attempt at privacy would have been met with grave suspicion, despite his exploits. They had come to dock beside the big man's floating frat house. The party had already started, and they were greeted like conquering heroes of Valhalla. Whooping women had flung beers and their bikini tops between the boats, and the party had begun in earnest.

Del Carpio stood with a stunned look on his face while a stunning blonde whispered in his ear.

Even the surly Russians had brightened when they found what was awaiting them.

Bolan looked up as he felt eyes on him. The Iceman relaxed on a lawn chair on the roof of the houseboat. He saluted Bolan with his whiskey and motioned him up to join him. Bolan polished off his beer and clambered up the ladder to the roof.

Anggun reclined on the roof near him. Her utterly graceful body was stretched out topless upon a towel. Her cinnamon skin seemed to drink in the rays of the late-afternoon Southern California sun. Her huge dark eyes opened, and her perfect lips spread in a lazy smile as she propped herself up on her elbows.

The Iceman motioned to an empty deck chair. "Have a seat."

Bolan took the offered seat. Anggun rose and went to the bar. She poured Bolan a whiskey and then went back to sunbathing. Bolan took a sip and recognized the peaty taste of single malt from the Hebrides Islands. He grinned over his glass. "What's up, Ice?"

"I hear you did good." The Iceman's eyes were hidden behind his sunglasses. "Real good."

Bolan put a scowl on his face. "Eddie was a scumbag. Hell, I would have done him for free."

"Yeah, but we still give out points for style." The Iceman set down his glass. "You and I agreed on ten thousand for the job. I know you'd like a piece of all that gold, but it's spoken for. But I'm going to up your pay to fifteen thousand. Every member of the team said you were a hard charger, and Michael says you saved his life."

"Yeah, and if he slobbers on me any more, I'm going to start getting worried."

"Get worried. I'm a grateful kind of guy." Brand appeared at the top of the ladder. He took a seat at the Iceman's right hand. The big man didn't seem quite as drunk as he had a few minutes ago. He reached into the pocket of his khaki shorts and pulled out a thick wad of hundred-dollar bills. "I want to up it to twenty."

Bolan took the offered money and looked at it earnestly.

Brand nodded at the cash. "That'll pay some bills, won't it brother?"

"Yeah, it will." Bolan let out a long breath.

"Ice told me you'd hit some hard times." Brand clapped Bolan on the back with bone-jarring force. "Well, now you're on the gravy train, brother, and it's got biscuit wheels."

"Well, I don't know what to say, except thanks." Bolan pushed the wad of cash into his pocket. "Do you mind if I give Calvin a cut of this? I owe him."

There was nothing to be detected behind the mirrors of the Iceman's shades. "No, not at all. It's the right thing to do."

"Thanks. I mean, thanks a lot." Bolan looked around and smiled uncertainly. "Jeez, you guys really know how to live."

"Fight hard, party hard." Brand rose from the chair to his full height. "Be hard."

The Iceman rose and took his whiskey with him. "We'll talk later," he said to Bolan.

A chorus of women's voices called up from the deck below. Four women raised their hands to their mouths and pantomimed an oral obscenity in perfect synchronization. "Michael, are you coming down or what?"

"Oh, I'm coming down, all right."

The big man grinned at Bolan. "You don't have to worry about me slobbering on you. I'll leave that to Pooky."

"I never slobber, Michael." Anggun rose upon her elbows again. Her eyes were deadly serious. "I never spill a drop."

"Goddamn!" Brand said, shaking his head at Bolan. "You be careful, brother. A girl like Pooky can teach you things about yourself."

The Iceman and Brand descended to the debauchery below.

Anggun reclined back on her towel. "I need tanning butter."

Bolan sipped his whiskey. The ship was jammed from stem to stern with strippers and Special Forces soldiers. There was no way he was going to sneak away or find any way to get out a message. He let his eyes drift across the woman's body as he reached for a jar of coconut-scented tanning lotion.

He was just going to have to maintain his cover.

THE ICEMAN LOCKED HIS GAZE with Michael Brand's. The two men stood alone in the big man's cabin while the party raged on in every other inch of space on the boat.

"What do you think, Michael?"

"Del Carpio's a trooper. He'll do."

"Yeah, he's going to work out." He looked at the big man pointedly. "What about Belasko?"

"He can't be a cop. No way in hell. When we took the hacienda, he didn't hesitate. I'm telling you, he didn't even blink. You should have seen him cap Eddie. He unloaded an entire magazine into the sorry son of a bitch, left-handed, hanging from the banister. And it wasn't cowboy bullshit. He did it because it was the only way to bring Eddie down in time to save my ass, and like I said, he didn't hesitate. He didn't even blink." Brand shook his head at the memory. "It was beautiful."

"Yes, but killing Eddie was righteous."

"Goddamn right, it was. You should have seen the little shit, standing there in his underwear hosing down Shpagin with a machine rifle bigger than he was. Baby-butchering son of a bitch." The big man's tone sobered. "I saw the yacht. It was exactly like you said. And when Belasko saw it, let me tell you, he got real frosty. I'm talking cold. Boneyard cold, Ice. It was scary. Even C.T. was surprised, and you know C.T. He doesn't surprise easy.

I'm telling you, I wouldn't want to be on the wrong end of this Belasko guy."

"No, he's not a cop," the Iceman agreed, "but that doesn't mean that he's kosher."

"Hey, Ice, I hear you. We don't know anything about this guy, but I'm telling you, he's as tough as they come, and you can tell, he's got a code." Brand's eyes narrowed. "You know, he almost reminds me of you."

"Where is he now?"

Brand rolled his eyes up toward the ceiling. "Him and Pooky have been up on the roof for about four hours now. Guy must do yoga or something." Brand lowered his gaze again. "What does Pooky say about him?"

The Iceman smiled wryly. "She seems to like him."

Brand gazed up at the ceiling again. "Yeah, I can see why. But what does she say about him?"

"About the same as you. He's fast as lightning. He doesn't hesitate, he walks with big medicine and there's no way in hell he's a cop."

"So—" the big man's eyes narrowed again "—you buy his story?"

"I buy every single thing he's told me, Michael." The Iceman's eyes traveled toward the ceiling. "But he's told me almost nothing."

"Nature of the business, Ice. You know that. Trust is hard to come by these days. It has to be earned, and it works both ways."

"I know."

Brand folded his massive arms across his chest. If someone held an inscrutability contest, the Iceman and Anggun would be neck and neck. "Well, I like him. He earned my respect last night."

"I know."

"I know you know, Ice, but you're the man." Brand stared meaningfully at the California legal pre-ban M-14 semiautomatic rifle on wall over his bed. "Do we bring him in or do we put him down?"

"I haven't made up my mind." The Iceman pulled a pair of Cuban cigars from his shirt pocket. "I've got Jeremy doing some research for me on a couple of fronts."

Brand's face lit up at the sight of the cigars, and he dug into his shorts for his lighter. "You know, Ice, if this guy pans out, he's going to be one hell of an addition to the Club. He could be final mission material."

"Oh, I agree. He is a very interesting prospect." He let Brand light his cigar, and the two men took deep draws of the contraband tobacco. "Listen, I want you, C.T. and Pooky to keep an eye on our friend while we see what Jeremy comes up with. Buddy him up with Del Carpio. For now, I don't want him alone for a second. I want to see if he gets itchy to call anybody."

"You got it. We wine him, dine him and he goes nowhere without an armed escort." The big man laughed. "All in the name of good camaraderie of course."

The Iceman and Brand looked up at the ceiling again and blew smoke into the mirrored ceiling over the bed. The Iceman examined his cigar. "Where's Lawrence?"

The big man looked at Ice warily. "Lawrence?"

"Yes." The Iceman nodded. "Lawrence."

Brand scratched his head. "Last I heard, he was taking some R and R up in Yosemite, climbing Half-Dome with some of his rock rat buddies."

"Get his butt off the granite and get him down here. I think I want him around for a while. I like his instincts, and I want his gut feeling on the latest developments."

"You got it." Brand smiled knowingly at the ceiling. "And meantime?"

"Meantime?" The Iceman smiled around his cigar. "I've got another test or two in mind for the new boy."

**13**

## Stony Man Farm

Calvin James walked into the Computer Room. Aaron Kurtzman's stern look of concentration brightened as he looked up from three computer screens scrolling information simultaneously. "Calvin!"

"Bear."

Kurtzman gestured expansively toward the coffee station. "Want some coffee?"

James leaned away instinctively as he looked at the stained and battle-damaged coffeemaker. "No, thanks."

Kurtzman nodded absently. "You sure?"

James shuddered as he looked at the black brew in the stained urn. God only knew how long that coffee had been boiling away while the computer expert had been working. James changed the subject. "I got a message from Striker today."

"What!" Kurtzman shot upright in his wheelchair. "When?"

"Got a package." James reached into the inner pocket of his suit and pulled out a small overnight express package. His PO box was block printed on the front. There was no return address. James reached inside the thick package and pulled out a stack of hundred-dollar bills held together by a rubber band. "Ten K, Fed Ex from the big guy."

Kurtzman riffled the thick wad. "Well, now, I know he's fond of you..."

"No, man, look close. Look real close. Go down five presidents and tell me what you see. It would take a man of your intellect to notice." James shrugged modestly. "Or mine."

Kurtzman peeled off the top five bills and glanced at the sixth. He held it up to the light. His eyebrows rose as he held up another note and then another. "It's Morse code."

The computer expert admired Bolan's skill. Each bill had one or, at most, two words in Morse code on it. The dots and dashes were scrawled across each note in dents, tears, folds in the corner, fingernail scratches or pinhole perforations. Bolan had made use of numerals, stains and preexisting damage on the bills, as well. It wouldn't slip past military intelligence or stand up to close scrutiny, but no one who quickly riffled the wad or examined only a couple of the bills would notice, particularly if they didn't know what they were looking for.

Kurtzman grinned. "He's under close watch. I suspect he can't get to a phone or a radio without raising suspicion."

"Yeah, that's what I'm thinking, too. He put a note in with the money. All it says is 'Thanks, C.J.,' He probably put it past the bad guys as a commission fee for me for setting him up with Hook."

Kurtzman nodded anxiously. Bolan had been incommunicado for a week and a half. Grimaldi had been ghosting Los Angeles with a plane ready at every airstrip in the L.A. basin. Brognola was climbing the walls of the sick bed they had set up for him on the Farm. Even Kurtzman had been starting to feel a little antsy about things. He raised an eyebrow at James. "I'm assuming you've already read the message?"

James put a hand to his chest in vague offence. "It was addressed to me, wasn't it?"

"Yeah, yeah, all right. You win." Kurtzman rolled his eyes. "And?"

James pulled a folded piece of paper with the translation on it from his jacket. He quoted from memory as he handed it over to Kurtzman. "He says *Russian involvement confirmed. Stop. Illegal ops confirmed. Stop. Cannot confirm involvement ATF raid, hospital. Stop. Suspicion high on all three. Stop. Check out*

*USSF names.* I'm assuming that he means United States Special Forces. *Iceman, C.T., Michael Brand, Del Carpio. Stop. Target Eddie Alejandro terminated, Mexico, drugs, organ harvest, check specs. Stop. Will communicate again ASAP. Stop.* The last thing is an address in San Diego, California. He either ran out of money or had nothing else solid to report."

Kurtzman picked up the note and reread it. "I'll start running this immediately. You want to run a copy of this up to Hal? He's heading back into Washington against doctor's orders later tonight. Oh, and give him this."

The computer expert held out a double cassette tape and a sheaf of reports.

James took the tape. The label said Smalls: Presumed Execution.

"What's this?"

His face hardened. "The stuff nightmares are made of."

James eyed the tape warily. "What's on it?"

"Eight hours of a guy dying the hard way. There's strong evidence to suggest that it's ATF Agent Kip Smalls."

"Eight hours?" James's eyes widened, and he unconsciously held the tape a little farther from himself. "From what?"

"We don't know. Audio experts have run the sounds. They've identified the sounds of chains clinking, wood scraping, whimpering, begging, screams of pain and finally what sounds like asphyxiation or strangulation." Kurtzman shuddered. "Some kind of torture tomb is all we can figure. They tortured the living hell out of him before he died. Whoever did it to him never said a word."

"How did you ID him?"

"The tape was sent to Smalls's family," Kurtzman said with a sigh. "His wife identified his voice. She had to sit through the whole thing."

"Damn." James shook his head. "That is cold."

"Whoever did it also sent a copy to the former attorney general. Why, we don't know. Needless to say, she was appalled. The FBI is guarding her around the clock."

James tapped the tape in his hand. "How's it connect with Hal and Striker?"

"That's the interesting part." Kurtzman pointed at the sheaf of reports. "We're tying it to the D.C. hit, because Smalls worked on the same team as some of the ATF agents who died in the raid."

"Let me guess," said James. "Smalls went missing the very next day."

"That's right. There's been an APB out on him, but I don't think we're going to turn him up anytime soon."

The Stony Man warrior stared at the tape uncomfortably. "All right. I'll give it to Hal and tell him you want him to give it a listen and read the report."

"Good." Kurtzman leaned back wearily in his wheelchair. "Maybe it'll stop him from hobbling down here every half hour and wheezing at me."

"Not a problem." James sheafed the files and picked up the message money Bolan had sent. He folded the stack of cash into a massive wad and shoved it into his pocket.

The computer expert looked askance at the former SEAL.

James shrugged innocently "It was addressed to me, wasn't it? There was even a thank-you note. Don't worry. I'll find something positive to do with it."

*San Diego*

THE MACHINE PISTOL'S slide clacked into battery. George Del Carpio watched as Bolan reloaded the cleaned and oiled pistol. "A .38 Super, huh?"

Bolan nodded as he flicked on the Spanish pistol's safety. "Yeah, it's what they gave me. I decided to hold on to it."

"My father had one. His was a Colt, though. Nickel-plated with ivory grips"

Bolan smiled. "Let me guess. He was a cop. Mexico City."

The young man grinned. "Man, you are good."

The soldier put the cocked and locked pistol into the back of his belt. Anggun was out shopping, and when she wasn't around Del Carpio was constantly at his side. As new recruits, it was natural, and it also kept Bolan from ever having a moment alone. The soldier was positive the phones on the houseboat were bugged, as were all the rooms. "A lot of guys south of the border used to carry those. Lots still do. Your father was a cop. What about you?"

"Well, he was, and when I was little I wanted to be one, too."

"What happened?"

Del Carpio's face fell. "He got shot. When he died, my mother took me and my sisters to San Diego to live with my aunt. Then we moved to L.A."

Bolan nodded. "And you? What got you tapped for all this?"

Del Carpio looked away in embarrassment. "I got into some trouble when I was a kid. Got in with the gangs. My dream of being a cop was long gone. I hated 'em. By the time I was eighteen, I was looking at doing time or getting dead. Some really bad stuff went down my senior year. I lost almost all my friends to drugs, guns and jail."

The young man's eyes grew faraway in memory.

"And then I was walking down the street and I saw the recruiting poster. You know, 'The Few, the Proud.' I know, it sounds stupid, but I was eighteen, I had no money, a 9 mm in my pocket and I wasn't going to graduate high school. Suddenly the Marines sounded real good. I stared at that poster for an hour until a guy came out to talk to me. I signed up right then. As a boot, I scored in the top percentiles. My sergeant rode me like a mule until I got my High School Equivalency. Then he rode me right into Green Beret training, and I made it. Top of my class. At graduation he told me my ass was going to Officer Candidate School, and if he wasn't saluting me within the year he was going to have me busted back to private. He was the first person who ever believed in me. He taught me to believe in myself."

Bolan gazed intently at the young man. "And then?"

"You know how the nineties went. The military kind of went to hell. Readiness went to hell, morale went to hell. Political correctness became the norm. I got deployed to Yugoslavia. Saw some real ugly shit going down." Del Carpio's voice grew bitter as his eyes looked out into the past. "Women and children. Massacres and mass graves. I saw it all. I thought I was a tough little gang-banger in my day, but I never knew what the word atrocity meant. We sat on our asses for months while the government dicked around bombing the civilians in Serbia's capital when we should have been cleaning house on the ground in Kosovo. All political bullshit with no objective and no end in sight. We accomplished nothing. We just switched who was terrorizing who. It was all...I don't know.... You know what I'm saying?"

"Oh yeah." Bolan spoke from more experience than he cared to think about. "I know exactly what you're saying."

"Yeah, well..." Del Carpio said with a sigh. "So I got out, and then I had nothing to do. There I am living with my sister and her husband, working in an auto-parts store and taking a few junior college classes in accounting, going nowhere, when suddenly this guy shows up with my service record in hand and asking me if I wanted a job. You know, at first I thought he was CIA."

Del Carpio grinned and waved his hand around the opulent cabin of the houseboat. "These guys, they ain't CIA."

"No, they're not."

"I was nervous at first, deploying with no idea what was going on, but capping Eddie? Don't get me wrong, but it felt...." The young man suddenly looked nervous. It was clear he looked up to Bolan. "How did you feel about it?"

Bolan smiled. "How did you feel about it?"

The young man's eyes lit up. "Man, we had an objective. Clear-cut. A scumbag was chopping up kids. So we took him down hard. For the first time in my life, I felt like I was using my training, using the skills I'd busted my ass for, and for something worthwhile. I was doing the right thing. Like the Big Man said, the predators that feed on the predators. It was...."

Del Carpio sought for a word.

Bolan nodded slowly. "Righteous."

"Yeah, man, righteous." Del Carpio shook his head wonderingly. "And did you see all that gold? Oh man! This gig pays! I mean, look at these guys! They fight the good fight, and they ain't choirboys. They live large, I'm talking 2XXL!"

Bolan watched the stars in the young man's eyes. An operation like this would be any disillusioned young soldier's dream. A knock on the door suddenly interrupted them. C.T.'s voice came through the door. "You two lovebirds decent?"

The door swung open, and C.T. came in. "Got a little job tonight. You boys interested?"

Del Carpio shot up out of his chair. "Hell, yes!"

Bolan raised an eyebrow. "What's the plunder like this time?"

"Nope." C.T. shook his head. "No plunder, not this time. This one's personal. But you clear twenty grand, up front, right now."

"Hell, yes!" Del Carpio repeated. He looked pleadingly at Bolan. Bolan and C.T. looked at each other and rolled their eyes at the young man's earnestness.

Bolan shrugged. "Now how the hell am I supposed to say no to that?"

C.T. grinned. "Just say yes." He produced two stacks of bills and tossed them to Bolan and Del Carpio.

"Jesus." The young man stared in awe at the two-inch-thick stack of bills in his hand.

C.T. smiled and nodded. "Listen, you should both talk to Pooky when you get back about starting an offshore account. She's got some connections, and a man walking around with that many hundred-dollar bills can start the wrong people asking questions."

Del Carpio stared at the money. "Oh, yeah, definitely."

Bolan put his money in the drawer of the nightstand. "What are we doing?"

"Things are moving pretty quickly, changing by the moment. You're both on a need-to-know basis at the moment. But don't worry, you'll be fully briefed before game time, and it's righteous."

Bolan nodded. "Anything we need to do?"

"If I were you," C.T. said, shrugging, "I'd get some beauty sleep. It's going to be a long night."

Del Carpio grinned at Bolan as the Asian closed the door. "I need to start thinking about starting an offshore bank account. Can you believe that?" The young man shook his head in disbelief. He looked like a little kid at Christmas. "This just gets better and better."

Bolan considered the money and C.T.'s advice. Anggun was Indonesian and had offshore financial connections. That meant the Caribbean. The Dutch ran major offshore banking facilities on a number of their possessions in the Caribbean Sea. Bolan drew the Star and slid it under his pillow as he flopped back on his bed.

It was time to have a serious conversation with Anggun.

If he survived the evening's festivities.

**14**

*At 18,000 feet*

The Learjet tore across the sky. Bolan didn't know their destination, but he knew the compass on his watch told him they were heading east, and by the hours they'd flown he knew they were close to the coast. By Eastern Standard Time it was just past 10:00 p.m. He sat beside C.T. and Del Carpio near the cockpit. Seven Russians filled the rest of the cabin. C.T. was clearly in command on this operation.

Bolan put down the magazine he was reading. "So, how did you end up in all this?"

C.T. stared at Bolan for a moment. "What do you mean?"

Bolan allowed an embarrassed look to cross his face. He made a vague gesture around them. "Well, Learjets, party boats, I mean..."

The Asian's expression didn't change. "You mean how did I become part of the Club?"

"Yeah, I guess."

C.T. cracked his knuckles. Bolan observed his hands. They were heavily callused. The thick tissue covering his fists spoke of endless hours of grueling martial-arts training. The man's eyes relented slightly. "Well, you know, Ice gets around. I had the training and I had a job, but it wasn't particularly rewarding, if you know what I mean. Ice made me a better offer. Same as you, only I know him personally, from back in the days when he started the Club. I was one of the charter members."

Bolan smiled. C.T.'s English was perfect, but to someone with training, he had tiny, detectable, inflections in some of his words. English was his second or possibly third language. His first was probably Mandarin.

"Let me guess," asked Bolan. "Assault commando?"

"Close." The man smiled but his eyes grew guarded again. "Combat swimmer. How did you know?"

"I did some cross-training with the commandos on Quemoy Island with Colonel Lu."

C.T. half smiled as he accepted the information Bolan had deliberately let slip. He would undoubtedly check it, but the Executioner had worked with Taiwanese special forces operatives before, and he could make the story stick. C.T. smiled in memory. "Yeah, I knew Colonel Lu. He was a real ball breaker. Course I was a cadet back then. I hear he retired and moved to Australia some years back."

"Well, I am an old fart," conceded Bolan. "So what's the story on the party tonight?"

"Half paycheck, half payback."

"Mixing business with pleasure." Bolan raised an eyebrow. "Is that smart?"

"Not usually, but this guy is a real asshole. He betrayed us and got some of our guys killed. We don't let that slide."

"So who is he?"

"He works deep in the federal government. This idiot has friends in high places, and he thinks he's untouchable."

C.T. smiled unpleasantly. "He's about to find out how wrong he is."

Bolan considered that very carefully. Someone on the inside had to have let something slip about the ATF massacre and the subsequent battle at the hospital. Now it was payback time for the man who had done it. Whoever the Judas was, he wanted him, too, but alive. Bolan wanted him in shape for a very thorough interrogation. Whoever the weasel was, he could prove vital in bringing down the Club, much less proving that they were the ones involved in the attacks and trying to assassinate Brognola. Bolan had to try and keep the man alive.

Bolan yawned and looked around the cabin. He knew C.T. and the Russians would execute him in a heartbeat if he made one false step. Del Carpio sat two seats down and grinned at Bolan. The young man was a wild card, and Bolan had serious reservations about taking him down. The soldier took a long breath and let it out slowly. It would take less than an eye blink for the whole situation to go critical in his face.

C.T. handed Bolan a photograph. "This is our boy."

The pilot's voice spoke over the intercom. "ETA five minutes."

"All right!" C.T. called out. "Everything has been prescoped out for us. Observers are on-site to let us know of any change. This should be a turkey shoot, but we're going to brief the new boys, and I want you all to pay attention. I want to be locked, loaded and frosty in forty-five minutes after touchdown!"

The Russians nodded and began buckling up for landing.

Bolan stared at the face in the photo.

Del Carpio leaned over and peered at the photo in Bolan's hand. "What do you think? He look dangerous to you?"

Bolan shook his head in contempt. "He looks like a real asshole."

"Oh, he is." C.T. nodded. "And we take him down tonight."

Bolan handed back the photograph of Hal Brognola.

Things had just gone critical.

*District of Columbia*

THE HELICOPTER THUMPED across the sky. The lights of the capital swept past below. Eleven heavily armed men sat in the belly of the bird. Each man wore a blue windbreaker over his body armor. Across the back of the jacket the words Marshal Service were printed in block letters. They all wore marshal's badges openly around their necks. Bolan cradled the 9 mm Colt 635 submachine gun in his hands. It was one of the standard heavy weapons issued to United States marshals when they engaged in an interdiction or went to capture suspects who were believed to be heavily armed.

C.T. and two of the Russians also carried cut-down M-79 grenade launchers under their windbreakers. Their barrels had been shortened to fourteen inches, and the stocks had been sawed down and shaped into the rudiments of a pistol grip. The cut-down grenade launchers would be totally inaccurate and recoil with wrist-breaking force, but at short range they would deliver their 40 mm munitions through windows and breach barricades.

They were more than suitable as concealable, close-range as-sassination tools, as well.

Bolan hadn't been issued one. Once again, he had been issued subsonic 9 mm hollowpoint rounds in his submachine gun. The rest of the team's weapons were loaded with high-velocity armor-piercing ammo. However, as a sign of their increasing faith in the soldier, he had been issued a tactical radio.

"All right!" called out C.T. over the rotor noise. "Just like we rehearsed it! I want two five-man sections! I'll lead the front!" He nodded at a wiry looking Russian. "Daniil, you're taking the rear! We should be able to walk right up. There is a marshal's in-terdiction team leader named Jow in Texas. Our intelligence tells us that this Brognola has never worked with him. Intelligence is dropping a dime on Brognola right about now to tell him to ex-pect us. He opens the door, we blow his head off and extract. We think he's alone, but he surprised us before. Expect him to be heavily armed. Expect possible reinforcement. If things go sour and we cannot extract by helicopter, head east two klicks to the river. We have extraction positioned there. Any questions?"

The men in the helicopter shook their heads. They had already put a great deal of research and practice into the scenario. The Russians clearly wanted some payback.

C.T. tapped Bolan on the chest. "Belasko, you're with me! You and I are the ones with nonaccented English! If for some reason we have to talk our way in, or out, you back me up. Just agree with anything I say. Don't get creative and don't shoot until I do."

Bolan nodded. "You got it!"

"Del Carpio!" C.T. pointed at the young man and then the Russian commander. "You go with Daniil. You stick to him like glue. His English is fair, but his Spanish is better. He's in com-mand of your group. You do whatever he says. You got it?"

Del Carpio grinned and saluted the Russian sharply. "Yes, sir!"

Daniil smiled against his will and saluted back. The rest of the grim-faced Russians smiled in spite of themselves. The young man's good humor was infectious.

The helicopter began a swift descent as they passed beyond the lights of the city and the suburbs. C.T. pulled on a black baseball cap marked Marshals, and everyone followed suit. He gave Daniil the thumbs-up. "Go!"

The helicopter's skids brushed the tops of a bit of thin woodland, and Daniil and his team locked in their rapeling harnesses and dropped out of the helicopter. The rest of the Russians reeled in the ropes, and the helicopter skimmed the trees for half a klick. They passed over a small house and dropped into the acre of fenced field in front of it.

"All right!" called out C.T. "Here we go! Just like we planned it. Straight in, like we own the place!"

The lights of the house were on. C.T. leaped to the ground, and Bolan followed. Four Russians jumped behind Bolan. They made no attempt to take cover or disperse. Security floodlights popped on, and the team trotted straight across the field and into the glare. They went straight for the front door.

Brognola's voice spoke over the intercom beside the door before C.T. could knock. "That's far enough."

C.T. held his badge up to the camera mounted over the door. "Mr. Brognola? I'm Tom Jow. My superiors should have contacted you. I was instructed to bring my team here ASAP." The hardman shrugged convincingly up at the video camera. "Can you tell us what's going on here, sir?"

"I got the call, Marshal. Just a second, and we'll talk."

Locks turned on the door. Light from inside poured out as it cracked open.

C.T. dropped his badge, and his finger slid around his submachine gun's trigger.

Bolan roared. "Gun! He's got a gun!"

C.T. started in surprise.

The Executioner raised his muzzle and fired a point-blank burst into the side of C.T.'s head. Blood and brains sprayed into the face of the Russian flanking him. Bolan whirled and brought the telescoping stock of his weapon into the face of the Russian standing behind him. He smashed the butt into his face and whipped the muzzle around. He touched off a 3-round burst into the Russian's smashed face and brought the weapon to his shoulder as he put another burst into the skull of the man wiping brains out of his eyes.

"What is happening!" Daniil's voice shouted in alarm in Bolan's earpiece.

The two remaining Russians whirled their weapons on Bolan.

The Executioner's burst took one Russian in the forehead. The soldier jerked to one side as the muzzle of the last Russian's weapon swung onto him. The hardman began shouting into his radio, and Bolan bellowed over him to drown him out over the tac-com. The two men stood four feet apart and exchanged bursts. Bolan felt the searing kiss of the steel-cored, armor-piercing bullets. Fire sliced under his right arm as he held his weapon at the shoulder and returned fire. The Russian's burst walked upward and tore across the top of Bolan's shoulder.

The strobing muzzle-flash was the end of the world as it climbed toward Bolan's face.

The soldier squeezed his eyes shut and held down his trigger as Armageddon erupted.

The world went bright orange behind Bolan's eyelids. An ice pick drove through his eardrum and into his brain as the supersonic armor-piercing bullet cracked the sound barrier inches from his ear. Superheated gas seared the side of Bolan's face and unburned bits of gunpowder sprayed into his cheek and jaw.

Bolan's submachine gun clacked open on a smoking, empty chamber.

Thunder rolled through his skull and dazzling afterimages flashed across his vision. Bolan blinked and yawned to try to clear his head.

The Russian stood before him. What had been a human head and shoulder had been reduced to red ruin.

The corpse fell through the porch rail and onto the lawn.

Bolan's knee buckled. He was hit, and he didn't know how bad. He couldn't hear anything and his face was on fire. He gasped and shouted into his throat mike. His words sounded distant and underwater in his own head. "C.T.'s down! We're taking massive fire! Brognola is not alone! Repeat, Brognola is not alone!" Bolan dropped his submachine gun on its sling and tried to shake the blood out of his eye as he rose. He drew the Star machine pistol and took it in both hands as he turned on the helicopter. It sat about fifty yards away with its rotors threshing the night air. Bolan put his front sight on the pilot's side of the canopy. He squeezed off all nine rounds into the helicopter's windscreen on rapid semiautomatic.

"The chopper's hit! We have mulitple casualties, we are—"

Bolan ripped the throat mike away from his neck to end the transmission. He hammered his fist on the door and glared up into the security camera. "Hal! It's me!"

The door swung open, and Bolan found himself staring down a .357 Magnum N-frame Smith & Wesson revolver. Brognola stood in his slacks and a T-shirt. His eyes flared wide at the sight of Bolan's face. "Mack! You're—"

Bolan put a hand on the door frame to steady himself. He could barely hear the big Fed. "There's another team coming up from behind the house. Is this place armored like the last one?"

"No, this is a regular federal safehouse. Damn it Mack, your face is—"

"They have incendiary grenades, Hal," Bolan interrupted. The soldier felt a wave of nausea pass through him. "You're about to get torched."

The muted thumps of the M-79s spoke in answer. Glass crashed on the far side of the house.

Brognola looked hard at Bolan "Mack, you are hit! You're bleeding."

"Grab a jacket and cap! Get a gun!"

Brognola shoved his revolver in the front of his waistband and stripped a dead Russian of his jacket and submachine gun. He grabbed a Marshal's cap and pulled the bill low over his eyes. Bolan held up his microphone again. "Daniil! I'm hit! Shpitalny's hit bad! We are—"

"Extract!" Daniil's voice shouted back dimly through the taccom. "Extract! We extract for the river!"

Bolan reloaded the Star and threw Brognola's arm over his wounded shoulder as he stopped transmitting. "Listen, we have to take them out when we join up. They're all wearing armor. Go for the head shot."

"I got it! Come on!"

Bolan leaned on the big Fed as they hobbled around the side of the house and made for the trees. Grenade launchers thumped at the edge of the woods and grenades looped over them. The back of the house was already burning. Bolan and Brognola made for the muzzle-flashes in the tree line.

The big Fed let his head hang and kept his face concealed beneath the bill of his stolen cap.

Bolan staggered into the scrub oak. Del Carpio and the Russians clustered toward them. Del Carpio's eyes went wide when he saw Bolan's face. "Jesus, man! You're—"

Bolan brutally pistol-whipped the young man with a backhanded blow. Del Carpio's head rocked on his neck as the slide of the Star pistol struck him. Bolan slammed his boot up between the young man's legs and Del Carpio crumpled.

He leveled the Star and squeezed two rounds into Daniil's throat. He turned and shot the man next to him in the temple. Brognola shot another as he leveled his weapon. The remaining two Russians held the cut-down M-79 grenade launchers.

Both of the single-shot weapons were empty.

"Freeze!" Brognola roared.

They didn't freeze. They blurred into motion with the speed of trained special forces troops. They dropped their spent launchers and went for their handguns. They were extremely fast. They cleared leather as Bolan and Brognola fired together.

Both Russians fell with a bullet between their eyes.

Bolan knelt and ripped away Del Carpio's radio. The young man gasped and blinked up in shock at the bloody face of the Executioner.

The soldier took a ragged breath as the house began to burn in earnest behind them. "We have to talk."

"Wh-why?" Del Carpio swallowed with difficulty. "Why did you—"

"We don't have much time. Listen, the Iceman? The Club? They've killed federal agents. They've killed United States marshals. They killed cops, Del Carpio, and they did it for no other reason than money. The man standing beside me is the man you came to kill tonight. He's a friend of mine, and this is their second attempt on him. The Club is going down."

Del Carpio's bruised face screwed up with anger and confusion.

Bolan was relentless. "Either you're with me, or I cap you right here. I can't afford to let you be arrested. The Iceman has all kinds of contacts I have no idea about. I can't afford to be compromised. You said you wanted to use your skills. You wanted to fight the good fight, to serve your country, to be righteous. This is your one and only chance. You come back with me and back up my story about how this went down, or I put you to sleep, here and now."

Bolan lowered the smoking muzzle to point at the young man's forehead.

Del Carpio stared up in unblinking determination. "They killed cops?"

"I saw it on video." Bolan locked his gaze with the young man and held it. "And I've seen it with my own eyes."

Del Carpio didn't blink as he met the Executioner's gaze. "Can you prove it?"

"Not right this second, but I can. You'll just have to trust me until then." The muzzle of Bolan's pistol didn't move. "Are you down for this?"

The young man let out a breath between his teeth. "Yeah."

"You going to trust him?" Brognola asked. "Just like that?"

"I've got a feeling." Bolan grabbed Del Carpio, and the young man winced as he was yanked to his feet. Bolan shoved his submachine gun in his hand.

Del Carpio's swollen face was tight as he stared at the loaded weapon in his hand and then at Bolan. "I'm down with this unless I find out you're lying to me. Then I cap your ass."

Bolan nodded. "Fair enough."

He bent and examined the Russians. Most had holes in their skulls. Daniil lay in the dirt with his throat torn open. Bolan pulled out his bandanna and packed it into the wound.

Del Carpio stared. "What are you doing?"

"Using props. Grab his other arm." Bolan and Del Carpio suspended the dead man between them. Bolan turned to Brognola. "Hal, I've got everything on these guys and nothing. The Iceman comes and goes like a ghost. All I've got on them is a houseboat address in San Diego and the name Michael Brand. I think we'll be headed back to California, but I can't be sure. I'll try to make contact any way I can, as soon as I can."

The big Fed nodded. "What do you want me to do on my end?"

"Listen, these guys are as tough as they come. I also get the feeling they have something big planned. I intend to find out what it is and who's involved. Get Able Team and Phoenix Force assembled and ready. Keep Jack hot on the pad 24-7. When I go active on these guys, I am going to need every bit of backup I can get, and I'll need it ASAP."

"You've got it."

Bolan glanced at the burning house. "Hal, they knew you were here. They've gotten to someone in the Justice Department, someone high up enough to know about your comings and goings outside of the Farm."

"Yeah, I figured that."

"Where's your family?"

"Out of country." He looked at Del Carpio and didn't elaborate further.

Weakness washed across Bolan as he felt the blood leaking out of his body. He yawned and blinked again. "I've got to move."

"I've got to make some phone calls. We'll be waiting for your signal." The head Fed turned and stopped. "One other thing."

"Make it quick."

"There's an ATF agent named Kip Smalls. We think he's connected somehow to the D.C. raid, probably as an informant. We have an audio tape that was sent to his family. It's him being tortured in some kind of dungeon. It took him eight hours to die. See if you can connect him to the Iceman without blowing your cover."

"I'll see what I can dig up."

Bolan jerked his head at Del Carpio. "Come on."

The two of them began moving through the thin woodlands toward the river. The dead Russian grew heavier with every step. They quickly lost the light of the burning house and stumbled on through the dark. Bolan wearily consulted his mental map and kept them moving toward the water.

The river shimmered slick and dark as they came out of the trees. A pair of motorboats lay beached in the gritty sand and gravel. A deep voice spoke from the darkness. "Freeze."

Bolan gasped wearily. He didn't need to put on an act. "It's Belasko and Del Carpio and Daniil."

Bolan's legs failed him and he fell. He recoiled as the bright beam of a flashlight blinded him. He squinted into the glare. The light was fixed beneath the barrel of a semiautomatic shotgun.

"Jesus, buddy." Brand's voice was a quiet rumble. "You are chewed up."

"Daniil...he's hit, bad." Bolan pushed himself up to one knee. "He needs a doctor or he's going to die."

Brand knelt beside the Russian and pulled away the blood-soaked bandana. He pressed his hand into the wound and then checked for a pulse on the other side of his neck. He shook his head. "Daniil didn't make it."

"Jesus..." Bolan put a hand to his face.

Brand eyed Bolan critically. "It ain't just your face. You're bleeding all over. Del Carpio, get him in a boat. There's medical kits in the lockers."

Del Carpio helped Bolan to his feet and got him into one of the motorboats. Brand and a Russian joined them. "If it's just us, we'll leave the other boat." The big man's voice went grim. "You see what happened to C.T.?"

Bolan sighed as the boat's motor rumbled into life. "He took it in the face. Same almost happened to me. Right as the door opened. I tried to pick him up, but his skull was blown open."

Brand's massive fists creaked. "Sokolov, give me a hand. We're out of here."

Brand and the Russian pushed the boat out into the water. Bolan's eyes closed. It was a warm night, but he felt cold from blood loss. He wondered if Del Carpio would betray him. He wondered if he would wake up alive. Brand slid behind the wheel and shoved the throttle forward. He shook his head grimly as the boat surged down the river.

"Ice isn't going to like this."

**15**

*Gary, Indiana*

Bolan opened his eyes.

It was swelteringly hot. He couldn't quite open his right eye completely. He was on a table in an operating room. He was naked except for the sheet covering him up to his torso. An IV unit hung to one side with its needle taped to the inside of his left elbow. The warm syrupy feeling surrounding his head and the dull, faraway feel of his wounds told him he was being administered morphine. Despite the drugs Bolan heard a sharp-pitched ringing, and his entire head ached and throbbed. He looked around his surroundings. He wasn't in an operating room; he was in a warehouse. The operating table he lay upon and the modern medical equipment surrounding it formed a little brightly lit island in the cavernous gloom. The color of the sky was purple in the skylights high above.

The beautiful shape of Anggun's face eclipsed the operating lights above Bolan. Her black hair fell around his face like a jasmine-scented curtain. In the dripping heat, she wore only a turquoise sarong and a bikini top. Her face was upside down to his as she leaned over him. Her lips turned up into a smile. "Good morning."

Bolan attempted to smile. Dull pain radiated out from his temple to his jaw. Whatever local he had been shot up with was fading. He spoke out of the left side of his mouth. "Morning."

"How are you?"

Bolan swallowed. His mouth was on fire and tasted like something was nesting in it. "A little thirsty."

The woman nodded and went to a wheeled table and picked up a sports bottle. She put a hand around Bolan's neck and helped him prop himself up a bit. She tilted his head to the left and gently squeezed some water into his mouth. Dull pain throbbed to life in his right side and shoulder with the movement. His face flared in pain, but he took several long swallows.

"Not too much," she warned. "You lost a lot of blood and went into shock. You don't want to throw up after the beating you've taken, trust me."

It was good advice. Bolan lay back down. "Where are we?"

"Gary, Indiana." She gestured at the equipment surrounding them. "We have a medical setup here and a couple of doctors who owe us favors. You remember the flight?"

"I don't remember much after getting in the boat to extract." Bolan nodded for a little more water. "How many of us made it out?"

"You, Del Carpio, Sokolov and Michael. Of course, they were part of the extraction team. They say you and Del Carpio brought one of the wounded Russians in with you, but he was DOA at the extraction site, and you were a mess."

"I remember." Bolan stared up into the lights. "How bad is it?"

"You took a burst from an automatic weapon. You lost a lot of blood before they got field dressings on you in the boat. They shot you full of morphine and pumped you up with blood expander once you were on the plane." Anggun held up a hand mirror and tilted it to show Bolan his right side. His ribs were taped. Along his right side there was a seven-inch line of bloodstained bandaging. "It took about seventy stitches to close. The rib bone is scored but not broken. You took one across the shoulder, too." She held up the mirror. Bolan's shoulder was swollen to the size of a melon. "It's like the one in your side, shallow, but messy. No bones broken or nerves cut."

Bolan looked up meaningfully at the mirror. "How's my face?"

Her eyebrows rose questioningly. "You sure you want to know?"

"I don't know. Will it affect my Handsome Boy modeling school scholarship?"

She rolled her eyes. "It's been eight hours since you got hit. It looks bad now, and it will only get worse looking for the next forty-eight hours or so." She reluctantly held the mirror over Bolan's face. "I wouldn't quit your day job anytime soon."

Bolan stared up at his reflection.

He looked like a horror movie.

His right eye was swollen. His right brow and cheek were lumped with blisters. What wasn't blistered was blackened and bruised from the unburned propellant that had been driven into his face. What wasn't bruised or blistered was an angry red.

"Cheer up," Anggun said, smiling. "Most of it is flash burns. You'll look like a mess for a while but you should be fine. You got lucky. The doctor said your eardrum should have been shattered, if not perforated. The earpiece of your tac-com got shattered instead. As it is, you got your bell rung. You may have some balance problems and headaches for a while. Don't expect the ringing to go away anytime soon.

Bolan peered up at her. "Do you still love me?"

"No." She shook her head. "Sorry."

Bolan closed his eyes and sighed. "Damn it."

"Don't worry." She made a show of puckering her lips in sympathy. "In a few weeks you'll be fine."

"How's Del Carpio?"

"He took a blow to the face, but he looks a hell of a lot better than you."

"He's a tough kid." Bolan looked up at her pointedly. "Did we get that Brognola asshole?"

"You guys nuked the place. But then, we tried to burn him up once before and missed him. Until we actually have his head on a stick, we're just going to assume he's healthy."

Bolan let out a long breath. "How's Ice taking all this?"

"C.T. was a good friend of his." Her smile fell. "He's not happy." She regarded Bolan frankly. "He's going to want to talk to you about what happened. Extensively."

"I figured." Bolan used his good eye to look around the warehouse. "Where's Del Carpio?"

"The doctor took a look at him and cleared him for duty. I suspect he's in California already."

Bolan kept his poker face. The way it was mangled at the moment it wasn't hard. Inside him a cold wind was blowing. If Del Carpio was in California, the Iceman would be grilling him. Bolan had faith. The young man was much smarter than his boyish earnestness gave off at first glance. If he weren't, he would never have made Green Beret. But they'd had almost no time to coordinate any kind of alibi out in the field, and Bolan had no doubt the Iceman would debrief them separately and compare stories. Without a doctor's note saying he had a concussion, an amnesia routine wasn't going to fly.

Bolan raised his good eyebrow hopefully. "Do I have a concussion?"

"No." She shrugged elegantly. "You're just ugly."

Bolan sighed.

He was going to have to ad-lib the whole thing, and one wrong statement would get him and Del Carpio killed.

"Where's my gun?"

"I don't know." Anggun dismissed the matter with a shake of her head. "Michael or Del Carpio must have it."

Her eyes revealed nothing, but Bolan knew he wasn't going to be shooting his way out of Indiana. He wasn't strapped down with restraints, but in his current condition, he had every faith that she could beat him into oblivion if he tried to hobble off and make a break for it.

He was going to have to ride it out.

Bolan made a mental note of the shining rack of stainless-steel scalpels on the instrument tray a few feet from his right hand. "When do we move?"

Anggun examined Bolan's face critically. "The doctor wants to keep you for observation for at least another twenty-four hours. Though that probably has more to do with forcing you to rest than anything else."

Bolan nodded slightly. He had one day to figure out what he was going to do.

Meantime he would have to build up his local loyalty base as much as possible. Bolan grinned up at her crookedly. "You know, you look sexy upside down."

"You look hideous, but I'd be lying if I said it didn't kind of turn me on."

"You're a very sick little girl." Bolan reached up with his left hand. Anggun's bikini top fastened in the front. He was pleased that his hand didn't shake. The bikini top popped open with a deft twist of his fingers.

"You know something, Tiger?" Her smile grew predatory. "I don't think you have enough blood left in your body."

"Actually—" Bolan's hand trailed up to caress her face "—I'm full of blood expander."

Her eyes trailed down the sheet covering his lower torso. Her eyebrows rose appreciatively. "You know, I believe you are."

She smiled as his finger traced the sensuous shape of her mouth. Her lips parted and slowly engulfed his finger.

Bolan grinned with the good half of his face.

## The Clubhouse

THE ICEMAN TURNED as Brand and another man entered the study.

The second individual was shorter than the big man by a head, but his shoulders were as wide as an ax handle. The sleeves of his flannel shirt were rolled up, and forearms like bowling pins crawled with twisting veins. Every bone and tendon in his oversized hands stood out in high relief. Years of free-climbing the nastiest rock faces in the most desolate spots on Earth had forged hands that could rip telephone books in two and break a grown man's bones simply by squeezing. C.T. had been one of the most dangerous martial artists the Iceman had ever met, and even he was leery of locking horns with Lawrence. The ex-Green Beret had the power to simply reach out his hand and kill people. When Lawrence wasn't rock climbing, he was hunting. After his stint in the Green Berets, the two activities had become the consuming passions of his life. Long ago, Lawrence's hunting had graduated beyond firearms.

The Iceman smiled.

Other than elephants, the only things on the planet that Lawrence didn't hunt with a bow or a spear were humans.

"Hello, Lawrence."

"Hey, Ice." The man from the backwoods of Michigan spoke with a slight drawl. "I hear you've run into a few hitches."

"Hitches, hell." Brand's face was an angry mask. "We got stopped."

Lawrence nodded understandingly at the Iceman. "Well, maybe you should have sent me." He rolled his eyes over at Brand. "Instead of fatman, here."

"You can suck my fat one, nature boy," Brand said as he dropped his mass into a chair and glared out the panoramic window at the Pacific.

Lawrence ignored the big man. "So what can I do for you, Ice?"

"Well, I just want you around for a while. Things have gone wrong that shouldn't have. I want your instincts on this one."

Lawrence accepted the statement with a nod. "I hear you've got some new recruits."

"Yeah, we do." The Iceman's face grew unreadable. "What do you think of them now, Michael?"

The big man stared at the sea. "Belasko came back a mess. He was shot to shit, but he was still carrying Daniil. Except the Russian had massive throat wounds. He'd bled out by the time they got him to the boat."

"Yes. I know the facts." The Iceman looked at the big man intently. "But what's your opinion?"

"Well, shit, Ice. The man's a stone-cold fighting machine. He's the goddamn Hammer of the Gods against our enemies." Brand pointed a massive finger. "And with his buddies? He's one of those 'everyone goes home' types. He came back looking like hamburger. He was lying there bleeding to death in the bottom of the boat, and he's asking about the rest of his team."

The big man leaned back in his chair. "You want my opinion? I'll give it to you. I want him on every mission I go on. I'll sleep better at night knowing he's on my team."

The Iceman nodded. "What about Del Carpio?"

"He was limping a bit, and his face was messed up." Brand frowned. "But he wasn't really injured."

"And?"

"And, I don't know. I just don't know. I like him. He's a hard charger, and he seems kosher."

The Iceman's eyes narrowed slightly as Brand's frown deepened. "And?"

"And I don't know." The big man looked back out at the sea. "He came back looking beat up, rather than shot up like Belasko.

That struck me as kind of odd, since Del Carpio was assaulting with grenades from the tree line with Daniil's team."

The Iceman regarded Brand's opinion rather highly. It was jibing exactly with his own.

"You know," Lawrence said conversationally as he stared up at the massive boar's head mounted on the wall of the study, "maybe I should eyeball these boys for you."

"You know, Lawrence?" The Iceman poured a round of whiskey. "I was hoping you might say that."

Lawrence smiled lazily as he took a glass. "Michael, you say this boy Belasko is shot up?"

"Yeah, it wasn't fatal." The big man took the glass Lawrence handed him. "So we flew him into Gary. We have some secure surgeons with a nice little setup there."

Lawrence turned to the Iceman. "You want me to go talk to him?"

"You know, that's not a bad idea," said Ice, "but I think I'd like to debrief him myself, and then I'd like you to give me your first impression."

"You the man." Lawrence turned and eyed the head of the pig again. "What about this guy, Del Carpio?"

"Him?" The Iceman sipped his whiskey. "He's an ex-Green Beanie like you. Him, I think I might like you to have a talk with."

"You want us to have a friendly little chat?" Lawrence's oversized hand closed into a fist. His knuckles popped and cracked like he was crushing a handful of marbles. "Or do you want me to have a Come to Jesus with the boy?"

"I'd be tempted to say the first." The Iceman joined Lawrence in admiring the pig. "But use your best judgment."

**16**

*Gary, Indiana*

Bolan opened his eyes to find the Iceman standing over him.

He kept the grimace from his face. The wounds, the painkillers and not least of all Anggun's ministrations had taken their toll on him. The Iceman could have executed him in his sleep if he'd wished.

Bolan grinned up at the man. Beneath the bedsheet he laid his thumb on the back edge of the surgical scalpel he had liberated when Anggun had gone to the bathroom. "Hey, Ice, how's it hanging?"

"Hello." The Iceman peered at Bolan's face critically. "Damn, you are ugly."

"No, I ain't ugly. I got uglified. There's a difference." Bolan felt the heat of the wound in his face and let his grin fade. "You pissed?"

"Yeah." The Iceman nodded. "You could say that."

Bolan widened his good eye warily. "At me?"

"I don't know." The Iceman was as cool as his name. "Should I be?"

"I would." Bolan let his voice drop angrily. "We got violated,

Ice. Heinously." He raised his empty hand to his face. "I came one inch from having my head blown off. Good men died."

"So, you're saying you're pissed off?"

"Damn right, I'm pissed off. They knew we were coming. Somehow they got tipped off."

"More to the point, someone tipped them off." Iceman cocked his head slightly. "Any idea who?"

It hurt, but Bolan let his lips curl into a snarl. "You saying it's me?"

"If I had decided it was you, you'd be—"

"Dead." Bolan kept his face angry. "Yeah, I know."

"No." Ice smiled. "You'd be in the Boneyard."

Bolan sagged back onto the bed wearily. "What's that supposed to mean?"

"You'll find out."

Bolan gripped the inch and a half of surgically sharp steel he held concealed and calculated the distance between himself and the Iceman. "Oh, really."

"Really." The smile stayed on the Iceman's face. "As soon as I find our Judas, you'll get an up close personal view of what that's supposed to mean. Sooner or later, everyone who works for me does."

Bolan frowned. "So what is it?"

"It's educational," the Iceman said. "It lets everyone know where they stand."

"Okay, so until then, what happens?"

"Get dressed." The Iceman nodded toward the door. "Let's go for a drive."

"Is this one of those offers I can't refuse?"

"In a way."

"You know I've heard of those." Bolan shook his head slowly. "It doesn't sound promising."

"Actually," the Iceman said, "I think you'll find it very intriguing."

"Well, I like intriguing." Bolan rolled the scalpel under his thigh, getting ready to sit up. "Let me take a leak and get dressed."

The Iceman motioned toward the office in the corner of the warehouse. A blond man built like an athlete came forward holding a clipboard. The Iceman spoke over his shoulder as he turned and walked away. "Twenty minutes."

"Okay." The doctor glanced at Bolan's chart. "Let's take a look at your face."

Bolan sat up on the table.

The doctor smiled. "So how do you fee—"

Bolan groaned as his elbows buckled. His eyes rolled, and he started to slide off the table. The Doctor grabbed Bolan's shoulders and shoved him back up on the table with effort.

The doctor peered into both of Bolan's eyes critically. "You okay?"

"Sorry, Doc." He took a few breaths and steadied himself. "I got woozy there for a second when I sat up."

"Not a problem. Don't worry. That's normal." The doctor looked deeply into both of Bolan's eyes again and then examined his face. "How does your face feel?"

"It hurts." Bolan shrugged. "When it doesn't hurt, it itches."

"That's good." The doctor checked Bolan's shoulder and side. "Good. Very good. I don't see any sign of infection. The flash burns should heal in a week or so. The blisters and bruising maybe the same, the powder wounds will take a little longer. The shoulder and side will take longer, but you seem to heal fast, and I think you're healing clean. Don't push it, but I'm clearing you to leave. Wherever Ice takes you, stay in bed for a day or two. Keep an eye on the ringing in the ears, and let me know if you start developing new and interesting headaches. I'll fly out by the end of the week and look at you again."

"Thanks, Doc. Thanks a lot." Bolan looked around. "Where're my clothes?"

"You just sit a moment and catch your breath. I'll get them for you." The doctor turned and went to a small bank of metal lockers. Bolan sat up straight. He took a deep breath and listened to his ribs protest. He did feel woozy, but that wasn't why he fell. What he had needed was a physical distraction and moment of contact.

Bolan slid the doctor's cell phone beneath the bed sheet.

*At 1,000 feet*

THE NORTH AMERICAN F-86 Sabre jet screamed over Indiana at 700 hundred miles per hour. It was a beautiful plane. The Korean War-era fighter bomber had been civilianized. It had been stripped of its original internal armament of six .50-caliber machine guns, and the rocket and bomb hardpoints in the wings had been removed. It made an already beautiful design even smoother and faster. The swept-wing F-86 was one of the cleanest aircraft ever built. It was sheer joy to fly and beloved by any pilot who'd had the privilege to sit behind the stick. Jack Grimaldi gushed about them and took every opportunity to fly one. The Sabre's sweet handling characteristics had kept it competitive for decades against faster, more sophisticated and more heavily armed opponents. The plane was painted a blue as deep as the sky. Bolan sat in the front of the twin-seat trainer as the Iceman brought the Sabre out of a barrel roll and nosed it over into a steep dive.

Bolan was shoved back in his seat as the fighter screamed down upon the plains of Indiana like a hawk. Blood pulsed in his cheek as it flooded with blood and a screw tightened in his right ear and bored into his skull.

"How do you like her?" the Iceman asked.

Bolan watched a cornfield rush up at the nose of the plane with startling speed. "She hurts my face."

"Sorry." The plane leveled off and cruised beneath the rising sun.

Bolan felt the ache of the wounds in his side and shoulder and the flaring in his face. The painkillers and antibiotics sent their outriders of nausea into his stomach and the taste of copper behind his teeth. He was pretty certain the Iceman knew it and was not sorry at all.

"You fly?" Ice asked.

"A little." Bolan watched a long finger lake pass underneath them. The plane was a two-seat trainer and had been retrofitted for racing with ejection seats. Stray thoughts of explosive bolts going off and hurtling up in the air strapped to a steel chair without a packed parachute passed through Bolan's mind.

He dismissed the idea of squirming around in his seat and trying to deploy the scalpel blade hidden in his boot just as quickly.

"You want to take her?"

"Sure." Bolan took the stick. Both of them were slammed back in their seats as Bolan shoved the throttle forward and cranked the flaps up as hard as he could. The engine roared as the afterburner lit.

The Sabre went vertical.

"You know," the Iceman said conversationally, "this baby only has about nine thousand pounds of thrust."

Bolan ignored him and rammed the throttle all the way to its stop. The engine screamed into full emergency war power.

The Iceman's voice showed no concern whatsoever. "This should be interesting."

The Sabre clawed its way into the sun. The airspeed dial whirled backward as they dumped velocity. The engine shuddered and roared as the plane swiftly approached the limit of its thrust. The entire airframe shook with strain as it struggled ever upward. Lights began blinking in panic on the controls. The plane could go no higher. At sixty thousand feet, the Sabre had reached its vertical limit. The jet could produce no more thrust, and the thin air conspired to strangle the engine.

Turbojets were totally unsuitable for the hammerhead maneuver. In 1945, the North American design team had never dreamed of anyone doing something so stupid in the plane they had envisioned.

The joystick remained free in the soldier's hand. The Iceman sat in the instructor's seat and could override anything Bolan did. He was waiting to see what Bolan would do next.

The airspeed dial froze at zero. For a split second, the Sabre jet hung suspended in the cloudless azure sky. Bolan's stomach dropped as the fighter began its tail slide and began to fall backward. The soldier kicked the rudder and the plane's nose swung down and around like an ax falling. The engine thudded and groaned as it went into overpressure.

The airframe thumped as the engine promptly flamed out.

The world fell into a silence broken only by air hissing over the airframe. The Sabre slowly spun as it began to fall toward the ground without power. Bolan ignored his gorge as it rose. He stopped the spin and watched the altimeter begin to whirl as crazily as the airspeed indicator had but a moment before. He slid the throttle into flight idle as he felt the nausea begin to rise again in his stomach. Bolan ignored the pressure in his face and turned his attention to the airspeed indicator. It quickly spun as the plane fell like an arrowhead at the earth.

At two hundred knots, Bolan punched the igniters.

Nothing happened.

The arc of the earth rose to meet them.

Bolan waited for the airspeed indicator to hit 250 and punched the igniters again.

The engine thumped as the can lit. The airframe rumbled with renewed power. Bolan shoved the throttle forward, and the resurrected engine roared into life. He leveled out the plane and took a deep breath.

"Nice." The Iceman sounded genuinely pleased.

Bolan craned his head around and grinned out of his pulsing face. "Well, it's a nice plane you got here, Ice."

"Where did you learn to fly?"

"Here, there." Bolan released the joystick as he felt the Iceman take it behind him. "I got a real good friend who's as crackerjack a pilot as they come."

"Really." The Iceman seemed to be filing that away. "What else can you fly?"

"Multiengines, a chopper, but only in a pinch." Bolan shrugged. "A MiG-29 might present problems."

"No, not at all. They're sweet machines."

Bolan craned his head around again. "Sounds like you're speaking from experience."

"I am."

Bolan put disbelief into his voice. "Yeah, and who let you fly one of those?"

"Oh, you know. Some Russians." The Iceman's voice brightened. "Tell me, Belasko, what would you think an F-22 is worth?"

"A stealth fighter?" Bolan snorted. "Hell, they're barely out of the prototype stage. I don't think we're selling them to anybody."

"I know that. But what do you think one is worth?"

Bolan shook his head. "To who?"

"The Russians. Or the Chinese."

"I don't know." Bolan looked back and smiled at the idea. "Billions?"

"The Russians are offering thirty billion." The Iceman turned the jet into a long slow banking maneuver. "The Chinese offered thirty-five. I'm thinking I can talk them both up to forty. Particularly if I can deliver one to each of them without the other knowing it."

Bolan was silent for a moment. "You're talking about eighty billion dollars."

"Well, a billion here, a billion there. Pretty soon it adds up to real money. You know, a man's got to think about his retirement."

"You know, you're talking conspiracy to commit treason."

"You and I served the same master." The Iceman threw Bolan's own words back at him. "And he is insane and ungrateful."

"Okay, forget treason." Bolan turned back around. "You're talking suicide."

"Do I seem suicidal to you?" The Iceman spoke as if he were asking Bolan if he liked his tie.

"I think you're about as cool a customer as they come, Ice." Bolan watched Indiana pass by beneath them. "But the idea of eighty billion can do funny things to any man's thinking."

"That's a good point," the Iceman conceded, "but tell me, with everything you know and everything you've ever done, are you saying it's impossible?"

"No." Bolan shook his head. "Nothing is impossible. I learned that a long time ago."

"You're right. Nothing is impossible. It could be done. No one would expect a combat team to come into the facility and take the planes by force. It's inconceivable. Their security is built around defending the technology. Keeping people from finding out the specs or getting close enough to take photographs of the interior or hacking into the computer files. They make sure the pilots flying them are red, white and blue to the bone. I mean who the hell would want to live in Russia or China? No pilot in his right mind would defect. Even if he did, the CIA would move heaven and earth to assassinate him as a warning to the next rube with ideas. For that matter, the planes are right in the middle of a high security air base. No one would dare assault it."

"How would you do it? If you had to?"

Bolan knew exactly how he would do it. He'd done similar things before. "You go in hard. You get into the hangar, get two of the planes fueled and ready, and you go. But let's assume you have people who can fly them, and you actually take off without getting blown up. What about the assault team you're leaving behind, Ice? If you think I'm going to be on the tarmac waving a hanky at your afterburners while the Air Police tactical response teams surround the hangar with their armored vehicles, you have another think coming."

"Would I do that to you?"

"Would you?"

"I don't know." The Iceman laughed. "What would you do with your assault team?"

"You leave them behind, and they're going to roll over on you." Bolan sighed. "You'd have to kill them before you took off."

"Or?" Ice prompted.

Bolan turned in his seat again. The plane was heading west, away from the airfield they'd taken off from. "Or I'd put them in the internal weapons bays. With oxygen bottles. F-22s have supercruise. You could give the men parachutes so they could bail out over Mexico before their air ran out and link up later. No air-defense system south of the Rio Grande could detect the planes in flight, but you'd have to have your own bases somewhere south of the border. You couldn't get to Asia without aerial refueling. If I did it, I'd land them in South America, pack them in a freighter and ship them by boat. No satellite would ever know what was in the hold."

"You know, Michael was right about you. I'll sleep better knowing you're on our team. Now, tell me what you really think."

"Are you serious?"

The Iceman shrugged. "It's just an idea."

"Piloting is the main problem." Bolan frowned. "Who has any experience flying an F-22?"

"I know someone."

"That's a real limited line-up. They'd deduce him in a second." The Iceman's smile stayed fixed. "What if he's dead?"

"You mean what if everyone already thinks he's dead." Bolan shook his head. "You are one twisted son of a bitch."

"And you can fly high-performance aircraft. I didn't know that about you." The Iceman's eyes narrowed slightly. "You said you had a friend who taught you to fly like that."

"I did." Bolan nodded very slowly. "And I do."

"Listen, we're going to refuel in Utah and then head out to California. I want you to lean back, enjoy the ride, and think about this hypothetical situation very carefully."

"And then?" Bolan asked.

"And then I'm going to show you something." The Iceman laughed. Once more Bolan detected genuine amusement in the Iceman's voice. "And then we'll talk more."

**17**

*Cedar City Airstrip, Cedar City, Utah*

Bolan stood in a men's room stall in the flight shack of the civilian aviation park. He had stolen a roll of tape from the flight desk and had finished taping the stolen scalpel to the inside of his left wrist. He pulled his jacket back on and punched a number into the doctor's phone. After being verified by security and redirected, Barbara Price answered the phone. "Striker!"

"Yeah, I'm all right."

"Where are you?"

"I'm in Utah. Cedar City, with the Iceman."

"You want us to pick you both up?"

"No." Bolan leaned against the stall wearily. "We're leaving in five minutes. If I stall at all, he'll know something is wrong. I don't have much in the way of armament, and in my condition I doubt I can take him down."

"What are you going to do?"

Bolan considered that. "I could be wrong. This guy earned his nickname in more ways than one. I can't read him, but he's making noises like he's going to give me the keys to the kingdom. I think we're going to Club Central."

"What do you mean keys to the kingdom?"

"I think he's planning one final big score, and then he's going to either go legit or drop of the face off the planet."

The Farm's mission controller reviewed what little she knew about the Iceman, and the idea bothered her. "What kind of big score are we talking about?"

"He's talking like he intends to rip off a couple of F-22s and sell one to the Russians and one to the Chinese."

There was a moment of silence on the phone. "That's ridiculous, if not suicidal."

"Barbara," Bolan said quietly, "I think the Iceman has done every single thing he's ever set out to do, and succeeded. This guy's a force unto himself."

"You're not kidding about the F-22s, are you?"

"Tell Hal to talk to the President. Have every base flying F-22s put on full alert until we have this situation bottled up. Tell him to beef up the muscle on the base. If the Iceman goes in, he's going in hard. It's going to be an assault. Not an infiltration."

"I'm on it."

Bolan kept his eye on the door of the shack. "What have you got for me?"

"Michael Brand, former Navy SEAL. He took an honorable discharge and at least outwardly is an honest tax-paying citizen."

"How is he affording palatial houseboats?"

Bolan could hear her fingers whipping on the keyboard. "He's a military consultant to the movie industry. He's been involved in some big budget movies in the past ten years."

Bolan thought about the big man. "You know, I can't prove it, but I think when the Iceman formed his little club, Brand was the first man he contacted. My instincts say they served together. See if you can find any kind of SEAL reference on an 'Iceman,' and see if you can get a list of every SEAL that has ever been on the same team or on an operation with Brand."

"Done."

"Get Able and Phoenix out to California. Full war load."

"Okay." Price paused. "Where do you want them?"

Bolan mentally flipped a coin. "South. That's where all the action has been so far. Brand works in Hollywood and has a houseboat in San Diego. I'm betting the inner circle of the Club hangs pretty tight."

"Both teams are assembled here at the Farm. I'm deploying them now to Los Angeles. They should be there in five hours. Jack is already there and hot on the pad."

"Good. I'm out of here. I'll contact you again as soon as I can."

Bolan clicked off the phone. For one moment he considered trying to hold on to it, but he knew if they found it on him it would mean a bullet in the back of the head. The Executioner hated giving up his one lifeline, but he would have to wing it.

Bolan dropped the phone into the toilet and left the stall.

Outside the shack the Iceman stood by his plane. "Ready?"

"Where to?"

The Iceman pointed west. "The Clubhouse."

*Mendocino, California*

BOLAN WATCHED the morning fog creep through the towering redwoods. The breakers boomed off the cliffs in the distance. He took a long breath and smelled the ocean air, then let the breath out long and slow. He had guessed wrong. The Club had its headquarters in Northern California, not the south.

The Land Rover wound its way up a one-lane road on the mountainside. At the bottom of the mountain, they had passed a golf course in the predawn gloom, and then the road had gone steep. They came around a bend, and Bolan shook his head.

The Iceman lived large.

In the twilight, a house seemed to hang from the mountainside, defying gravity. The multilevel mansion followed the folds of the mountainside with beautiful symmetry. Parts of it were built around the towering redwoods and seemed to merge with them. As they came around a bend in the road, Bolan could see a long gravel drive terraced into the mountainside. Below the house was an open area that had been manicured into a small lawn and garden area. Beyond that was a clearing with a concrete pad just large enough to land the helicopter currently resting on it.

A pair of men in navy blue polo shirts and matching caps stood before the iron gate to the drive. Both men carried stainless-steel Mini-14 carbines slung over their shoulders. Bolan's eyes narrowed. The Iceman had his own guards. Bolan had to give the Iceman credit. What he really had was his own Stony Man Farm, only run for profit. The armed security guards waved at the Iceman, and the automatic gate swung open. A Porsche 911, a Jeep and a convertible Mustang 5.0 were already parked on the drive.

The Iceman parked the Land Rover, and the two of them got out. "Let's go talk in the study."

Bolan followed the Iceman inside. The interior of the house was as beautifully designed as the exterior. A pair of guards with rifles were stationed inside the door, and another pair stood out on the hanging patio. The Iceman shrugged as he led Bolan up a flight of stairs. "Security is always tight when we're having a big meeting."

"We're having a big meeting?"

The Iceman nodded as they went down the hall to the last door. It opened on a large study with a panoramic view of the forest, the golf course below and the Pacific Ocean beyond. Eight other men were in the room. Several of the men Bolan recognized from the firing range and the party on the houseboat. Others were new to him. Brand turned and grinned. "Hey, Ice! Bout time you got here." He looked at Bolan's face and shook his head in mock sympathy. "You look like shit."

"Yeah, my movie career is on hold."

"Oh, I could probably get you in a movie," the big man replied, smiling. "Of course, with that face, it would probably be as an extra in *Zombie Island Massacre Part V*, but I could get you in something."

Bolan laughed. "I'll keep that in mind for my retirement plan."

The Iceman took a seat and motioned Bolan to the chair at his left hand. "Let's talk about your retirement."

"You were talking about snatching F-22s," Bolan stated.

"Yes, I was," Ice agreed. He gestured at the men around them. "You know Michael. The rest of them you'll get to know very quickly during your training. All of them can fly high-performance jets. We need redundancy in case anyone gets wounded or killed."

"Makes sense."

Iceman pointed at a tall man with brown hair beside Brand. "This is Mark Parish. He's flown the prototype F-22s. Unfortunately he had a tragic accident and was killed in a car wreck two years ago. He's our golden goose. Protect him with your life."

Parish smiled easily and waved his drink. "Nice to meet you. Michael has told me good things about you."

"Thanks," Bolan said. He thought Parish had the unmistakable attitude about him that screamed fighter jock. "I guess this job makes you the man."

"Oh, I am the man," Parish agreed.

The Iceman took the whiskey that Brand offered him. "For the next month, Parish is going to be your drill instructor, along with everyone else in this room. He's going to put you in the know on every nuance of the F-22 that he can without actually getting you behind the stick. You're going to learn that bird, forward and back. After that, you and the rest of the team will be going to Russia. Contacts I have there are going to let you get flying time on MiG-29s and SU-30s. They won't be the same as the planes we'll be snatching, but it will be valuable practice with high mach numbers. From there—"

"No, wait." Bolan shook his head as he interrupted. "Hold on a minute."

The temperature of the room seemed to drop several degrees as the rest of the men stared at him. Bolan ignored the sudden sense of danger. "You were talking about a potential eighty-billion-dollar haul."

"Yes," the Iceman said. "And?"

"And so what's my cut?" Bolan let his brutalized face go hard. "I've got expenses."

The men in the study laughed at Bolan's boldness.

The Iceman snorted. "What if I said one percent?"

"One percent of the take?" Bolan frowned. "Sounds kind of cheap, Ice."

"Jeez, Belasko." Brand grinned. "Do the math."

"Okay." Bolan did the math. "That would be, what? Eight...hundred...million dollars?"

"That's right. Eight hundred million dollars." The Iceman smiled like a shark. "But, since I like you, I might be willing to make it two percent."

Bolan stared.

"Plus expenses." The Iceman shrugged carelessly. "You in?"

"Can I think about it?"

"You need a beer to think about it?" Brand held out a can of beer. "You need a pen?"

The men who had been at the firing range laughed.

"Naw. My face hurts too much, and I don't need to think about it." Bolan nodded. "Cut me in for two percent, and I'm your man."

The big man pounded Bolan on the shoulder. "I told Ice we could count on you."

"And you know, I believed him." The Iceman swirled his drink. "You said you had a friend who taught you to fly like that. Would he be interested? With C.T. and Hertzog dead we still have an opening available on the assault team."

Bolan took the beer from Brand and cracked it. "He'd definitely be interested."

The Iceman leaned forward in his chair. "Would he be willing to go through the same sort of screening you did?"

"Well, he ain't an operator. He's a pilot first and foremost, but he's done some covert crap for the government. He's been in the shit, and he can shoot. Tell you what. You tell me when and how you want me to put you two in touch, then I'll get out of the way and let you two work it out between you. If it doesn't work out, you get no hard feelings from me."

"Fair enough." The Iceman gestured at the man sitting next to Bolan. "Belasko, this is Lawrence. Assuming everything works out, he's going to be your partner on game day."

Lawrence and the Executioner regarded each other. The Iceman was a cipher. He was absolutely unreadable. Lawrence was a different matter. It took Bolan all of a second to read him.

Lawrence was a sociopath and a stone-cold killer of men.

The man smiled in friendly fashion and held out his hand. "Nice to meet you, Belasko."

"Likewise." Bolan took the hand and shook it. Lawrence's oversized hand closed to a certain degree and stopped. It was like shaking hands with a piece of iron. The strength the man held back during the handshake was inhuman. Bolan grinned. "Hope you don't mind hanging out with a two-percenter."

Lawrence laughed. "If you're half as good as Brand says, I'll see about getting you bucked up to three and a half."

The Iceman stood. "Let's get down to the next order of business."

Everyone around the study rose to their feet. Bolan glanced around the circle of extremely dangerous men. "What's up?"

"I promised to show you something back in Gary."

Bolan rose. "What's that?"

The Iceman smiled. "I promised you a visit to the Boneyard."

The Club fell into a phalanx around Bolan as he rose.

## *The Boneyard*

BOLAN STARED STONE-FACED at the hole in the ground.

The cemetery was discreetly located behind the golf course at the base of the mountain. A bit of path behind the Clubhouse led down to it through the woods. The sun was just beginning to throw some pink light over the top of the mountain as the nine men stood in a circle around an open grave.

Del Carpio lay shackled in an open casket six feet down. He was alive.

The Iceman had put him in the Boneyard.

Bolan knew exactly what had happened to the late ATF Agent Kip Smalls. The scalpel taped against the inside of Bolan's arm burned to be drawn.

All eight of the other men openly wore handguns on their belts or in shoulder holsters. All were watching him for his reaction. Bolan stood with his arms folded across his chest. He could have the little blade out in an eye blink. He was fairly certain he could kill two, perhaps three before he was gunned down.

He was absolutely certain he would join Del Carpio in the hole.

Del Carpio looked to have taken a severe beating. Blood covered him, and his face was lumped and swollen. Bolan spoke coldly. "This is our leak?"

All eyes turned upon the man in the grave. Del Carpio stared up at Bolan out of eyes nearly shut by swelling. Bolan's eyes flicked around the circle of men. For one second everyone was glaring at Del Carpio. The soldier met his bruised stare and held it. The Executioner silently and with great exaggeration mouthed two words.

*Semper fi*

Del Carpio made no sign he had seen or understood the Marine Corps motto. The Iceman spoke. "All right, one more time, George. Then things are going to start getting ugly. Now, who do you work for, and how did you get yourself inserted into The Club without my knowing it? I want to know about your organization."

Del Carpio smiled out his mashed lips. "You can blow me. Then I'll tell you."

"He sure is feisty." Brand laughed unpleasantly. The big man reached into his pocket and pulled out a jelly jar. Small brown shapes crawled within it.

"You have a choice," the Iceman said very quietly. "You tell me everything I want to know right now and I cap you and cover you over. I'll even let your mama and your sisters keep the money you've already sent them. If you don't...." The Iceman jerked his head at Brand.

The big man unscrewed the lid of the jar and slowly swirled the contents over the open grave. The spiders within darted and fought with one another as they were agitated.

The Iceman shrugged. "The spiders bite your face off. I bury you alive. Then me and the boys go pick up your mama and your sisters. We bring them back here, and we have ourselves a party."

Brand grabbed his crotch and laughed. Lawrence produced a long hunting knife and let the setting sun glint off of it.

The Iceman's tone stayed fixed. "A very private party, George. A real weekend fling. All the boys will be invited, and when everyone's had their fun, when your womenfolk are busted like piñatas, when they can't even moan anymore, then we put them down with the spiders, alive, right next to you."

"You bastard!" Del Carpio thrashed in his chains with rage.

The Iceman jerked his head.

Brand emptied the jar over the grave.

The Iceman nodded. "Bury him."

The big man grabbed a spade. He squatted on his heels over the grave while Del Carpio flailed and roared obscenities as the spiders had at him. Brand watched a moment and flipped the lid of the casket closed.

The other Club members picked up shovels and joined the big man.

"So, Belasko." The Iceman regarded Bolan expressionlessly. "What's on your mind?"

Bolan met his gaze. "I'm starting to see how you earned your name."

"And?"

"And he's a snitch. He got a lot of good men killed." Bolan put a hand to to the flash burns on his face. "I hope the spiders have fun."

The Iceman nodded. "Lawrence, Jeremy, come with me." He turned and spoke over his shoulder. "Belasko, don't get too comfortable. You have a flight to catch."

## 18

*The Clubhouse*

The Iceman and Lawrence sat in the study. The Iceman peered at the sociopath sitting across from him. "What do you think?"

"About what?"

"This morning." The Iceman waved his drink meaningfully. "Del Carpio."

Lawrence stared into the middle distance and frowned. "I didn't like it."

"Me, neither." The Iceman stared at Lawrence intently. "What problem did you have with it?"

"I've dropped some Special Forces spics, shit like that in South and Central America." Lawrence shrugged. "They're tough. Ruthless when they're winning, and when the shit hits the fan and all is lost, they're positively suicidal. They got hearts as big as mountains."

"And?"

"But you got one chained in a hole, and you start talking about his family, hell, anyone, except maybe you and me, they're gonna fold. They're gonna start singing. Any tune you care to call."

"And?" the Iceman repeated.

"This De Carpio guy didn't sing. He went down tough as nails."

"Some people are." The Iceman didn't blink. "He was a Green Beret. Just like you."

"If you say so." Lawrence shrugged indifferently. "But you said you wanted my instinct on things."

"I do." The Iceman smiled.

"And you put that asshole in the Boneyard with spiders on his face and covered him over, and he was still salty."

"And?"

"And my instincts tell me that asshole still has hope." Lawrence leaned back in his chair. "Kind of odd."

The Iceman leaned back in his chair and regarded Lawrence frankly. "It is sort of disturbing."

"Positively anomalous."

"What about Belasko?"

Lawrence smiled. "Well, he kind of reminds me of you, Ice. I can't read him. Cept that he's a killer of men and has been in the shit, I have no idea what he's about."

The Iceman was silent for a moment. "Have they taken off yet?"

"Yeah, Brand, Cleveland and Belasko took off for the training area about half an hour ago. Parish was flying the chopper."

Both men looked up as there was a rapid knock on the door. The Iceman pushed a button on his desk and unlocked the door. "Come in, Jeremy."

Jeremy and Anggun came in. Jeremy's face was ashen.

The Iceman looked at the manila folder he held. "What is it?"

"You better look at this, Ice." Jeremy opened the folder and put it on the Iceman's desk. The first sheet on top was a copy of a ballistics report. Comparison photos of mushroomed hollow-point bullets and notes on rifling filled the page. "It took me a few days to get it, but that's the ballistic report of the bullets taken out of C.T.'s head."

The Iceman radiated cold. "And?"

"And they're Winchester 147-grain 9 mm subsonic hollow-points. Straight out of Belasko's gun. Most of the Russians had

Belasko's bullets in them as well. And look at this." Jeremy flipped the page.

There was a charcoal sketch of a man's face. The Iceman stared long and hard at the drawing. Take away the bruises, blister and burns and it was the man they had just made a member of the Club that very morning.

The Iceman stared at the sketch. "This is the composite sketch of the Russian colonel from the hospital?"

"The same." Jeremy scowled. "The sketches from the D.C. cops and the eyewitnesses in the hospital all come up with the same guy."

The Iceman looked up from the picture. "What do you have on Del Carpio?"

"He's clean." Jeremy pondered. "I don't know what his deal is. Should we dig him up and ask him again?"

"No. Even if he's clean, I think he's lost that lovin' feeling for us. Leave him where he lies. Monitor the recorder on him for the next few hours. If he starts singing about names or organizations, we exhume him. If not, let him rot."

Lawrence grinned at the Iceman. "You think Belasko got to him."

"I'm sure of it. Del Carpio is down there right now with the spiders on his face, and he's betting that Belasko is going to rescue him."

Jeremy unconsciously put his hand on his HK-4 pistol. "This Belasko guy penetrated our organization. He went number one with a bullet, and we just made him a member. We could be compromised right now and not even know it."

"No, I don't think so." The Iceman steepled his fingers on the desk. "If we were, FBI fast-reaction teams would be blitzing us right now. I think all he has is Brand and possibly Pooky. He wants me, you and the whole organization. The minute the chopper touches down he's going to try and break loose and make contact with his people. They'll mount a rescue operation for Del Carpio, followed by a seek and destroy on us."

Lawrence seemed remarkably unconcerned. "So how do you want to play it?"

"Scramble everybody. I want the Clubhouse on full alert. I want everyone ready to bug out if necessary." The Iceman turned to the communications rig mounted into his desk. "The only place that chopper touches down is back here."

*Redwood Empire Mountain Range, 800 feet*

THE IMMENSE SEQUOIAS rolled by beneath the skids of the OH-6 Cayuse helicopter. Bolan sat in the rear passenger seat and Brand sat next to him drinking beer. Parish flew the helicopter over the redwood forest. A former Green Beret named Cleveland sat in the copilot seat.

The compass in Bolan's watch told him they were flying south by southwest. Back in Mendocino, Del Carpio was slowly asphyxiating six feet underground. He'd maintained his cover and kept Bolan's while the dirt had been shoveled over him. The words *Semper Fi* echoed in Bolan's head.

The young Green Beret had kept the faith.

It was a debt Bolan had to pay.

He had to rescue the young man. Failing that, he had to avenge him.

Bolan glanced at his watch. Del Carpio had been buried for over an hour, and with each second they flew farther and farther away. The soldier looked around the cramped cabin of the four-seat helicopter. A folding stock Mini-14 was racked both in the front and the back of the helicopter. Both were out of reach and required going through Brand or Cleveland to get to them.

Bolan leaned back in his seat. "Can I get my gun back? I feel kind of naked without it."

Brand laughed. "Buddy-boy, when we get to where we're going, you're going to have access to firepower like you've never dreamed of."

"Well, how about a beer, then? I feel kind of naked without one of them, too."

"Good man." Brand reached down to the stainless-steel ice chest between his boots and handed Bolan a beer.

Cleveland spoke over the rotor noise. "Shame about Del Carpio. I liked the kid. Hate to see a fellow Green Beret go down in the Boneyard like that."

"Screw the Judas son of a bitch." An unpleasant gleam came

into the big man's eyes. "I'm looking forward to meeting his sisters."

Parish put a hand to his headset and listened for long moments. He craned his head around and handed the headset to Brand. "Ice is on the line. We've got trouble with a shipment. He wants to talk to you." Parish shook his head. "I think you screwed up, big man."

"What? Gimme that." Brand took the headset and adjusted it to his massive skull. "Ice! What's up?"

Bolan leaned back in his seat. Brand nodded as he listened. "Yeah, well, who could have known. Yeah, I can make it good. Not a problem."

The Executioner's instincts suddenly began speaking to him. He glanced out the window at the two hundred foot giants below and then looked at the compass in his watch. The arrow was very slowly and steadily creeping eastward. Bolan watched it for several seconds.

They were very slowly and subtly turning.

"Okay, Ice. You've got it." Brand smiled at Bolan jovially. "Me and the boys can handle it. You just—"

Bolan shook the beer in his hand and opened it into the big man's eyes.

"What the—"

The soldier sent the spraying beer tumbling end over end into the cockpit.

"You son of a—" Brand's head snapped backward as his nose broke under Bolan's elbow. The soldier rammed his elbow into Brand's face a second and third time. The big man's head bounced off his headrest with every blow. As Brand lolled forward, stunned, Bolan drove his elbow into his temple with bone-cracking force.

Brand went limp against the back of the pilot's seat.

"Kill him!" Parish roared.

Bolan ripped the scalpel free from under his arm.

Cleveland twisted in the copilot's seat and pointed a Browning Hi-Power pistol at Bolan's head. The soldier seized the pistol by the slide and shoved it toward the cabin roof. The pistol fired once, and a bullet tore into the roof. The pistol's slide squirmed in Bolan's hand and short-stroked as the Executioner held it in a death grip. The pistol jammed as it failed to eject the spent shell.

Cleveland screamed as Bolan drew the surgical steel blade of the scalpel down diagonally across the veins in his wrist.

The pistol fell from Cleveland's hand to the floor of the cockpit. Bolan slid the scalpel's handle between his second and third fingers and made a fist. The scalpel blade protruded from his hand like a push dagger as he swung his fist in a wicked straight right.

The scalpel punched through Cleveland's left eye and entered his brain. The ex-Green Beret sagged sideways in his seat against Parish as Bolan yanked the scalpel free. The pilot took the joystick in his left hand and struggled to control the yawing helicopter. Velcro tore as he produced a .357 Magnum pistol from his shoulder holster and shoved it toward Bolan.

The sound of the muzzle-blast was deafening in the enclosed confines of the cockpit. Flame and burning powder singed Bolan's brow as he yanked his head out of the way. The window in the passenger door blew outward, and the wind of the helicopter's passage vortexed into the cockpit. The gun went off again as Bolan seized the pilot's wrist, and he and Parish struggled. The soldier leaned his weight forward and pinned his adversary's forearm against the back of the copilot's seat.

The Executioner pistoned the scalpel into Parish's throat three times in rapid succession.

Arterial blood sprayed across the cockpit. The pistol fell against Bolan's knee and hit the floor. The helicopter dropped sickeningly as Parish lost control. Bolan took the scalpel in his hand like a carving knife. He yanked back Parish's head and finished cutting his throat.

The pilot went limp and the engine began to lose power. Bolan rose out of his seat and struggled to yank Parish out of the pilot's seat as the helicopter slowly began to spin on its axis as it lost altitude.

"Come on asshole!" A forearm as thick as a fire hose snaked around Bolan's throat and vised down. "Let's get it on!"

Bolan grit his teeth and tried to jam his chin down, but it was already too late. The big man's massive biceps and forearm had clamped down on his carotid arteries like a python. Blood immediately began to pound in Bolan's temples. The soldier tried to bring the scalpel around and stab, but the big man used his weight to shove Bolan across the passenger compartment. Brand put his massive left hand against the side of Bolan's head and shoved the Executioner's throat deeper into the strangle lock.

Bolan's head and shoulders were shoved right out of the shattered window.

The soldier flailed his arms in empty air as the rotor wash whipped across him. The horizon spun crazily as the helicopter went into autorotation. The spinning canopy of the forest below began to blacken around the edges as Bolan's brain starved for oxygen. The big man roared above the sound of the falling helicopter's rotors. "You go to hell, asshole! You go to hell and you die!"

Bolan still held the scalpel. He punched it into the top of the big man's hand and it grated on bone. Brand's forearm opened like a letter as Bolan ripped the blade all the way up his arm to the elbow.

The man roared and his grip loosened. Bolan dropped the scalpel on the floor. He grabbed the frame of the door in both hands and heaved himself backward. Bits of glass broke as Bolan shoved himself and Brand back inside the helicopter. Bolan torqued around. He drew his fist back and his hand opened into a blunt spear aimed at the man's throat.

Brand's fist crashed into Bolan's chest like a truck.

Bolan's lungs caved in as he was smashed to the floor of the cockpit. The big man seized the headrests of the seats to steady himself in the spinning helicopter. He lifted his right boot and stomped down at Bolan's face.

The soldier caught the boot in both hands and slowed its impact, but Brand used all of his weight to force his boot against Bolan's neck. The Executioner released the boot with his right hand. Agony flared in his skull as Brand's heel pressed into the side of his neck with all of his near 280 pounds behind it.

Bolan accepted the sacrifice as his right hand scrabbled and closed around the grips of the fallen .357 Magnum pistol. The big man's eyes flew wide in sudden terror as Bolan shoved the pistol up between Brand's legs. The pressure on Bolan's neck disappeared as the big man desperately heaved himself aside.

Bolan squeezed the trigger.

A great hand smashed the helicopter upside down, and the cockpit glass shattered inward. Metal screamed and failed, and the engine howled as the rotors snapped away. The helicopter went nose down, and the cockpit crumpled inward as the top of a tree erupted into it. Branches snapped and flew like shrapnel inside the cockpit, and the big man fell on top of Bolan. Bolan grunted under the weight and grabbed the bottom of the co-pilot's seat. He jammed himself against the floor as the helicopter tumbled onto its side. The chopper turned tail down and rolled, and Brand's weight was gone. The tail caught on something, and the helicopter suddenly righted itself.

Every bone in Bolan's body attempted to flee his flesh and slam through the floor of the helicopter as the fuselage hit something that didn't yield.

All motion ceased.

Above him Bolan could hear the crippled engine clanking and moaning as it tried to keep its rotorless turbines moving. Something spattered his face. The burns on his face stung like fire, and his nose filled with the choking stench of fuel. Bolan coughed and gagged and pushed himself up. Pain flared in his left hand. He felt the telltale nausea behind his teeth and knew his hand was broken.

The Executioner sat up and leaned against the seat. The door on Brand's side of the chopper had been ripped away in the tumbling crash and so had the big man. Bolan pushed the door open on his side and eased himself onto the crumpled skid of the helicopter. He reached into his pocket and took out the bottle of painkillers and antiinflammatories the doctor had given him. He popped a handful of the pills.

Bolan looked around. The stricken helicopter sat on the edge of a long slope. Shattered redwood limbs lay all about. The massive giants surrounding the chopper were scored and stripped by the dying helicopter's plunge down among them. Bolan reached back and found the pistol and scalpel again. He rose and found that he could stand.

For the most part, he had the use of his limbs and he could walk. God only knew how black and blue he would be in a few hours. If he was bleeding internally, he would find that out soon enough as well. He was somewhere in the Redwood Empire. He knew there were a number of small towns dotting the vast redwood forest, but they could be hundreds of miles apart and he could wander for days without seeing any sign of them.

He had to get away from the crash as quickly as possible.

Bolan clambered back painfully into the crumpled fuselage and began looting the helicopter.

He found the Mini-14 carbine in the front of the cockpit and slung it. The one that had been racked in the back was gone. Cleveland's and Parish's bodies had been brutalized by the tree trunk that had violated the cockpit. Bolan searched Cleveland's pulverized corpse and found a tiny Kel-Tec .32-caliber pistol and a Bali-Song butterfly knife in his pockets. He put the second pistol in his pocket and slid the folded knife down into his boot. Bolan took Cleveland's bloody bandanna and tied the broken fingers of his left hand together. Cleveland also had a pair of energy bars in his pocket, and he liberated them. There was no water aboard, but Bolan found beer cans rolling around on the floor from the broken open ice chest. Bolan filled his jacket pockets with cans.

The radio was smashed. He needed a phone.

Brand always had a cell phone with him. Perhaps Parish had one, as well. Bolan leaned into the front of the cockpit and began rummaging through Parish's pockets

Sparks flew from the fuselage by Bolan's head as an automatic weapon ripped into a long burst.

"Come on!" Brand roared.

Bolan jerked back as Parish's head came apart with a second burst.

Bolan caught sight of a bloody face in the trees and the yellow muzzle-blast of Brand's carbine. Bolan dropped low and rolled out of the helicopter. He put the fuselage between himself and Brand, then scooted himself downslope. He unslung his own Mini-14 and locked the folding stock open.

"You're dead, asshole!" The big man's voice was a bellow of rage. "Do you hear me? I've already dropped the dime on you! I'm through playing with you, asshole! We're turning Lawrence loose on your skinny ass! You hear me? He's going to hunt you down and bring you back to the Boneyard! You're going down with the spiders! You hear me?"

Bolan pushed himself farther down the slope and checked his watch. It wasn't even 10:00 a.m. yet. He had sensed the vague fear the other members of the Club felt around Lawrence. It appeared he was the Club's troubleshooter, and Brand was drawing him like a gun. If the big man really had called the Clubhouse, he could have Lawrence and his hunting party here within and hour to an hour and a half.

That gave them a good seven hours of daylight to hunt him.

**19**

*The Clubhouse*

The Iceman hung up his cell phone. His eyes revealed no emotion. "The chopper is down."

"Down?" Jeremy sat upright. "What do you mean?"

"I mean down."

"What?" Jeremy shook his head in disbelief. "You mean they had an accident?"

"No, I mean Belasko brought down the helicopter."

Jeremy went white.

Anggun's usual inscrutability failed her. "What about Parish and—"

"Parish is dead. So is Cleveland. Brand says he's smashed up pretty bad, and cut up worse, but he can walk. He's taken some high ground and is holding down the crash site. He's called for reinforcements."

Jeremy's worst fears as the intelligence officer of the Club were swiftly becoming a hideous reality. "But Belasko—"

"Is armed and at large in the redwoods." The Iceman rose from his chair and turned to his gun cabinet. He removed his boxed set of .44 Magnum Mateba semiautomatic revolvers. He broke open the action of first one pistol and then the other and checked the loads. "The crash site is about an hour and a half east of here. Michael has his GPS on him. He's hanging tight. Get everyone to the airstrip. I want two full strike teams ready in twenty minutes."

Lawrence walked into the study with two other men. He held a large gear bag over his shoulder and a cell phone to his ear. He nodded as he listened. Brand's voice could be heard bellowing through the receiver. "Okay, okay, stay on the line."

Lawrence shrugged at the Iceman. "He called me as soon as he got off the line with you. Man, is he pissed."

"So am I." The Iceman turned to the man next to Lawrence. He was a tall dark complected Indian with a mustache and perfect posture. He carried an FN assault rifle with an electro-optical sight slung from his shoulder. On his belt hung a massive khukri fighting knife. Suresh Panikhar had been a former officer of Gurkha riflemen in the Indian army before he went on to become a paracommando.

Panikhar spoke his English with a distinctly British accent.

"So, Ice, what are we to do about Belasko?"

"We're splitting into two teams. I'm leading one. Suresh, you're leading the other. Lawrence will be calling the shots during the hunt. I'll be taking most of the Club. You take Armstrong and Grey and as many guards as you need to fill out your team."

"We'll be assembled in five minutes. I'll meet you out front." Panikhar turned and left the room. His voice boomed as he called out to assemble his team.

Jeremy's face set. "What about me?"

"What about you?"

"I want in on this."

The Iceman cocked his head slightly and smiled. "And I thought you didn't like wet work."

"I suddenly find myself attracted to the idea." Jeremy nodded at the gun cabinet. "I want a shotgun."

"Okay. You stick close to me." The Iceman took a 12-gauge riot gun from his gun cabinet and tossed it to Jeremy. He reached back into the cabinet and pulled out a Steyr scout rifle. He clicked in a 10-round magazine of .308-caliber partitioned bullets and flicked the bolt.

Lawrence smiled appreciatively at the precision weapon. "You want Belasko alive, right?"

"I want him alive or dead by sundown. Alive preferred, but I don't want to be dicking around playing Boy Scout with this guy once it gets dark. I want him in the Boneyard, one way or the other."

Lawrence smiled innocently. "Okay."

The Iceman knew the smile well. "What are you thinking, Lawrence?"

"Well, I'm wondering how many NBC suits you have around the house."

"A few." The Iceman raised an eyebrow. "Why?"

"Well, here's how I want to play it." The hunter smiled again as he warmed up to his idea. "Once we get there, I'm going to pull a fade. When your teams have Belasko spotted and occupied, I'm going to work my way up real close to him."

"And then?"

"Then I bring him down with this." Lawrence reached into the bag and pulled out a compound hunting bow. A brace of wickedly barbed broad-head hunting arrows were clipped to the bow stave. Lawrence set the bag on the floor and lifted out one of several gray metal canisters. He held it up to the light.

"Jesus!" Jeremy took an involuntary step back.

The Iceman regarded the grenade. "What's that for?"

Lawrence was grinning from ear to ear. "Why, this is to make him come along quietly."

*Redwood Empire*

THE EXECUTIONER RAISED his rifle. He flicked off the safety on the Mini-14 as he crouched behind the massive stump of a fallen giant. The Redwood forest was not an ideal killing ground for him. It was an ideal hunting ground for the enemy. The towering redwoods soared upward of three hundred feet in the air, choking out all other trees. Beneath the canopy there was almost no underbrush other than occasional clumps of ferns. The forest floor was like a vast empty cathedral with little natural cover except the vast pillars of the trees themselves, and they were widely spaced leaving long clear lanes for firing and observation. There was no stony ground to mask his trail. The ground beneath

Bolan's feet was a thick, even carpet of red dust and mulch that took his every footprint. The soldier frowned as an almost subliminal sound grew loud enough to identify as the beating of multiple helicopter rotors.

They were coming.

"You hear that, boy?" Brand's voice boomed through the trees. "We're coming for you! Gonna bleed you good!"

Bolan had one only choice. He had given up on running the moment he'd gotten out of Brand's line of fire. He couldn't mask his trail in the redwood forest, and he was too injured and weary to evade the enemy for hours until the sun fell. Even if he did, he had every reason to suspect the Iceman and his men would have night-vision equipment with them, and he would have no counter for that. His every instinct told him that once he became prey on the run he would be in Lawrence's backyard.

The only choice was to attack. He had to kill a Club member and take his phone or radio, and then try to live long enough to use it. Bolan counted the rotors. Two helicopters changed the odds significantly, but that no longer mattered. The Executioner had to attack. He had a few slim advantages. As far as he knew, there was no good place to land a helicopter close by. His enemies were facing a rope insertion of anywhere from two hundred to three hundred feet.

That was a lot of hang-time.

Bolan rose as the first gunner rappelled out of the canopy like a spider. The Executioner shouldered his rife and squeezed off three quick rounds of semiautomatic fire. The guard jerked and twisted his rifle as two rounds hit him in the chest. His head snapped back as Bolan's third shot hit him in the head. His grip relaxed, and his harness rope hissed with friction as he rappelled out of control. A second guard one hundred feet up locked his handbrake and braced his feet against the trunk of a giant sequoia as he aimed.

Bolan flicked his selector to full-auto and squeezed off a burst. Sparks flew on the man's torso. Something in his harness failed, and he fell screaming headfirst to the forest floor.

A third man hung suspended in midair, squeezing off rounds. His gunfire halted as he was abruptly yanked back up through the canopy like a yo-yo. The helicopter above rose away from the treetops.

The soldier ran forward and knelt by one of the fallen gunners.

Bolan's burned and brutalized face split into a snarl.

The man had a tactical radio, but no cell phone or communication device that would reach up out of the redwoods. He didn't have a canteen, either. Bolan stripped him of his five spare magazines. He rose and swiftly looted the second corpse of its ammunition as well.

They hadn't known it, but the two gunners had been a calculated sacrifice.

The Iceman had expended them like pawns in a chess game. He had read Bolan like a book, and now Ice knew Bolan's basic position. The Executioner stuffed spare magazines into his pockets and began walking upslope toward Brand's position. He could hear the helicopters hovering higher up the hillside. He knew they were deploying around Brand's strongpoint.

Bolan's plan had gone to hell in a handbasket.

He'd just have to kill every last one of them.

He dropped into a prone rifleman's position among a clump of ferns and waited. Shapes began running downslope from tree to tree to meet him. Bolan put his front sight blade on a running figure and began to take up slack on the trigger. The man was big, but he wasn't Brand. Bolan's eyes narrowed. The enemy was wearing armor. It was another advantage they had over him. Del Carpio was dying in the ground and the enemy was swarming.

It was time to play rough.

Bolan lowered his aim. The carbine cracked.

The man cried out and stumbled downhill out of control as Bolan shot his leg out from under him. The large man lost his rifle as his arms flailed. He went face first into the trunk of a redwood and bounced off. He fell stunned to the ground.

"Armstrong!" someone shouted from out of sight higher up the slope. "Armstrong!"

"Don't move!" An English-sounding voice boomed from the higher ground. "Hold your positions!"

Bolan couldn't allow them to hold their positions. He knew instinctively that he was already being flanked.

He kept his sight on Armstrong. The big six-footer was trying to drag himself behind the tree he had bounced off. Bolan slowly squeezed his trigger.

Armstrong screamed as the bullet took him through the other leg.

"Armstrong!" roared a voice.

"Hold your positions!"

Bolan waited a moment for the shouting to die down and shot Armstrong through his first leg again.

"God!" Armstrong screamed. "Help me!"

"Bastard! You bastard!" A man burst out from the trees firing an M-16 from the hip-assault position. Two gunners followed him, spraying the landscape with their carbines. Bolan waited in the ferns.

"Grey!" roared the commander. "Grey! Hold your bloody position!"

Grey came for his comrade. He sprayed his rifle through the trees one-handed as he seized Armstrong by his belt.

Grey screamed and fell as Bolan put a bullet through his knee.

Armstrong screamed again as Grey collapsed on top of him. The two hardmen stopped short and began shooting in all directions in wild panic. Bolan put his front sight on the chest of one of them and walked a short burst up his neck and face. The man spasmed and fell. The other turned and ran for the closest tree.

Bolan put a bullet in the back of each of his legs, and he fell screaming into the mulch.

Armstrong, Grey and the surviving guard lay thrashing on the forest floor screaming for help.

"Hold your bloody positions!" the commander roared.

Bolan shot Grey through the shoulder as he attempted to drag himself away.

Chaos reigned at the top of the hill as men all shouted at once demanding to help their comrades.

The man in command's voice boomed at parade-ground decibels. "I'll shoot the next one who moves without an order!"

Bolan rolled out of the ferns. The hideous trick of the sniper's-draw wouldn't work a second time. He left Armstrong, Grey and the other man alive and howling to cover the sound of his own movement. The gunners were better than retired cops, but they were still security men, and weren't up to the caliber of the Club members. They were the brush beaters who were supposed to drive Bolan down the hillside while the real badasses moved in on both flanks. They were force multipliers and cannon fodder.

Bolan hoped they were starting to realize this. A little dissension in the ranks never hurt. He looked up as the thunder of rotors grew louder. The skids of a commercial Bell JetRanger helicopter were skimming the treetops. A man stood on a skid and leaned from the passenger compartment by chicken straps. An M-60 machine gun hung in his hands as he scanned the forest.

Bolan stepped directly into a break between the trees.

The machine gunner pointed down at Bolan wildly and swiveled his weapon.

The soldier raised his rifle to his shoulder. He ignored the machine gunner and put his front sight on the pilot's-side observation window beneath the chin of the helicopter. The Mini-14 tore into full-auto in his hands. The helicopter lurched as the 10-round burst erupted upward into the cockpit. Bolan snapped in a fresh magazine and put his front sight onto the copilot's window. The chin window spiderwebbed and pocked with bullet strikes as Bolan burned all twenty rounds in his magazine.

The helicopter dipped backward, and its tail rotor hacked into the treetops and broke apart. The crippled aircraft nosed down, and its main rotors snapped apart in great flying shards as they chopped into the thick redwood trunks. The scream of the machine gunner was lost as he was scraped from the side of the helicopter by the trunk of a 150-foot sequoia.

The rotorless helicopter plummeted between the great trees like a stone. Its fuselage snapped in two as it landed across the trunk of a fallen giant. Jet fuel puffed out in orange blossoms from the shattered windows as the stricken helicopter ignited. Black smoke began to belch forth from the burning airframe.

Bolan moved forward.

He couldn't outrun the flanking teams.

The only way to avoid the jaws of the trap was to go down its throat before they closed.


"BLOODY BASTARD." Suresh Panikhar watched the helicopter burn.

"Suresh." The Iceman's voice spoke in his earpiece. "What just happened?"

"He shot down our second helicopter." Panikhar continued to sweep the trees with his optical sight. The afternoon breeze was spreading the black smoke of the burning helicopter into an ugly, obscuring smog. "Grey and Armstrong are badly wounded, and I can't get to them. Healer is downslope with them in the same condition, maybe dead. I'm down to five men. All guards."

The guard next to Panikhar looked up from his carbine and stared at him reproachfully. Panikhar ignored him. "Listen to me, Ice. This guy is good, he's not going along with the game plan, we need to—"

"I know. I'm sending you reinforcements. He isn't running. He'll be coming forward. You need to—"

"Bloody hell!"

The head of the gunner next to him snapped back and forth as he took multiple hits in the forehead. Panikher saw the yellow flash of muzzle-blast through the smoke forty yards away. The big battle rifle in his hand hammered into life on full-auto. The figure in the smoke ducked behind the trunk of a redwood. Bark flew in great strips as the rifle rounds tore into it. The rifle clacked open on empty, and Panikhar slid in a fresh magazine with fluid efficiency. His crosshairs never left the target.

The figure suddenly stood square in his optical sight.

The muzzle of his rifle was pointing directly at Panikhar's right eye.

"Bloody—" Panikhar pulled his trigger and threw himself backward. He squeezed his eyes shut as his optical sight exploded and bits of glass and armored plastic were driven into his face. Tears flooded his eyes, but he could see out of both as he opened them. Bark flew from bullet strikes inches from his head along the fallen tree trunk he was using for cover. His battered rifle lay in the dirt outside of his cover. Panikhar drew his .40-caliber SIG pistol.

"Dickens!" Panikhar stabbed his finger down the hillside. "Cover me! I'm going to—"

Dickens fell forward over his rifle as a bullet blew out the back of his head. The rifle in the smoke seemed to fire every two or three seconds. Every time it fired, it killed a man or kept someone pinned behind cover.

Panikhar snarled.

His team was being slaughtered.

Panikhar rolled out of cover and raised his pistol. He began squeezing his trigger. The SIG bucked in rapid fire and was suddenly smashed from his hand in a shower of sparks. Panikhar rolled back behind cover. His hand buzzed from the bullet impact. He still had all of his fingers, but his pistol was gone.

His hand went to the khukri sheathed on his belt. He whipped his head about frantically.

All of his men were dead.

"Ice!" Panikhar shouted.

He could hear his executioner walking up to his position.

"Iceman! I need reinforcements! I need it now!"

An immense pistol began booming ten yards behind Panikhar. Brand's huge voice filled the forest. "Eat this, asshole!"

A shotgun roared, and a rifle joined it in a crescendo of concentrated firepower. Panikhar jerked as a 9 mm Glock pistol thudded into the dirt beside him. He snatched up the handgun and rolled back out of cover with the weapon barking in his hand. He ceased fire as he swept his front sight through the trees.

The killer had disappeared into the black smoke drifting through the trees.

Rifle shots began cracking farther down the hill.

"Suresh." The Iceman's voice spoke in Panikhar's ear. "We have him in sight. Join Brand and follow."

THE EXECUTIONER scrambled down a culvert. Rifle fire sought him out. His own rifle was empty. He had almost pushed through the trap and turned it inside out, but the sudden reinforcement and counterattack by the enemy had caught him out in the open and forced him to retreat into the smoke. The flanking teams had closed in on him. He'd killed two more, but he'd expended nearly all of his ammunition and been forced to run. He was being driven like a fox before the hounds. He'd found a small creek that cut down the mountainside and taken it at a dead sprint. He was playing into the enemy's hands, and there was nothing he could do about it except turn and die.

The creek had dried to a trickle in the summer heat. Slimed pebbles and river rocks slid under his boots as he took the steep descent at a pounding run. He yanked the empty rifle from his back and opened his stride. He'd heard the remaining helicopter fly over a few moments ago. The Iceman had leapfrogged men ahead of him.

Bolan filled his hand with the Ruger. He was exhausted, and he knew it. He hit a near vertical patch of creek and sat on his heels as he slid downward. His legs splayed out before him as he came to a halt at the bottom in a puddle of muck.

Bolan sat back into the blissfully cool trickle of the tiny waterfall and breathed.

He was done.

Brand's voice boomed across the mountainside behind him. "You're dead, asshole!"

Bolan nodded wearily.

They were going to bring him down.

The Executioner closed his eyes. Tilting his head, he opened his eyes and stared up at the sky. The vault of heaven was an incredible azure blue above the redwoods. A single snow-white cloud sustained itself motionlessly directly above him.

It was a beautiful day.

Bolan closed his eyes again and let the little rivulet of water wash over the top of his head. The cold clear water of the tiny mountain stream poured in a sweet chill down his face.

The soldier took a deep breath and opened his eyes again. He took stock of his weapons.

He had a Ruger with four rounds in it, a scalpel, a Bali-Song butterfly knife in his boot, and a .32-caliber Kel-Tec automatic pocket pistol with seven rounds in the clip.

He also had a surgical scalpel.

A plan began to materialize in Bolan's mind.

He took out the tiny Kel-Tec pistol and shoved it down the front of his pants. He left the Bali-Song knife where it lay concealed against his ankle. He picked up the scalpel in his left hand and rose. The culvert forked before him. At the bottom of the mountainside the culvert left a cleft that was too small for the redwoods to root and take hold. The tiny, well-watered double valley it presented was choked with scrub oak and brush that took advantage of the break in the redwood forest to exploit the exposed water and sunlight.

It was a fine place to make his final stand.

Bolan heard movement behind him.

He stuck his head up out of the cleft formed by the creek bed and shot a gunner between the clavicles where his armored vest stopped. Dirt flew as an automatic rifle sent a burst near his position. Bolan fired back two rounds.

A huge handgun boomed at him.

"You're dead!" Brand bellowed.

"Do it!" roared Bolan. He fired the Ruger in retaliation, and Brand's massive form ducked behind a tree trunk for cover.

Bolan could hear men moving swiftly downslope toward him on either side of the creek. The soldier took a half second and waited. When the big man stuck his pistol around the tree, Bolan pulled his trigger twice.

The click of the empty revolver sounded very loud in the sudden silence.

Brand's rumbling voice spoke low and very clear. "You are one dead asshole."

The big man appeared from behind the redwood with a 10 mm Glock pistol in his hand. His nose was smashed flat on his bloodied face, and his lacerated left arm hung bandaged and bound in a hasty sling across his chest. The Glock leveled at Bolan's head.

Bolan grinned like a wolf out of his smoke blackened and brutalized face. He dropped the empty revolver and held up the scalpel to the light. "Let's finish it."

"No way." Brand shook his head as he began to walk forward. The pistol never wavered. "You don't go down that easy. You go down with the spiders."

Bolan turned the scalpel in his hand so it glittered. "Come and try it."

The big pistol boomed as Bolan dropped back into the culvert.

THE ICEMAN STARED at the twin entrances to the culvert. He wore a closely fitting gray plastic coverall with gathers at the knees, wrists, ankles and elbows. Anggun stood beside him, cradling an M-16 rifle. Jeremy held his shotgun grimly. The Iceman turned to Brand. He had lost eleven men and five members of the Club in the past hour. "He went in there?"

"Yeah," Brand said, nodding. "He's in there somewhere."

The Iceman examined the two tangled thickets cut by the diverging streamlet. "Which fork?"

"Don't know." Brand shrugged as he kept his pistol leveled. "He popped down out of sight. I didn't see which way he scampered. I don't think he's gone anywhere far or fast, though. Our boy looks pretty done in to me."

The Iceman wasn't willing to bet on his quarry collapsing anytime soon. "Any wounds?"

"He was covered with smoke and shit. There was blood. His left hand was wrapped up." The big man glowered. "But he was still talkin' sass."

"You see what kind of armament he has left?"

"Oh, yeah!" Brand laughed. "I got a real good look."

"And?"

"He had Parish's Magnum." The big man's smile was horrific to behold. "And I watched him fire it dry. And I know for a personal fact Parish didn't have any reloads on him."

Panikhar stepped into the arc of armed men. "We found the carbine he took from the helicopter. It was empty. All other weapons are accounted for."

The Iceman kept his eyes on the fork in the creek. "So he's unarmed?"

"Oh, I wouldn't say that." Brand shook his head ruefully.

"What does that mean?"

Brand raised his wounded left arm. The field dressing had soaked through and the sling was dark with crusted blood. "It means he's still got that goddamn scalpel. I think the asshole has gone into last-act-of-defiance mode."

"A scalpel, then?" Panikhar drew the heavy, thirteen-inch steel crescent of his Assam rifle regiment khukri fighting knife and turned to Ice. He held up the massive recurved chopping blade so that it glittered in a shaft of sunlight. "Shall I go and get him?"

"No." The Iceman shook his head. "I want him alive, and you, too."

Brand examined the fresh blood dripping down his arm. "So what are you going to do?"

Two of the remaining guards came forward in suits that matched the Iceman's. Both held high-pressure garden sprayers with yellow plastic tanks.

The Iceman began to gather up the hood of his coverall and arrange it over his head. "I think I'm going to let Lawrence handle it."

"Yeah?" The big man looked about. "And where the hell is Lawrence?"

The Iceman pulled the goggled hood over his face and gestured at the choked culvert with a gloved hand. "He's in there."

THE EXECUTIONER HELD the scalpel low against his side. He could hear men moving down the culvert, and men down the opposite fork as well. They were coming for him. Bolan knelt in the thicket and considered his dwindling options. He considered the little plastic-framed .32 pistol concealed in his crotch.

If there were even the faintest shred of a chance he could survive to rescue Del Carpio, or at least to somehow get out a message, then whatever happened would have to be borne. Bolan had been to the Boneyard. He knew the price of failure. The Executioner's hand tightened around the steel handle of the scalpel.

Bolan began to slowly move backward through the thicket. He kept the enemy hunting line within earshot but out of sight. It wasn't difficult. The enemy made no pretense of stealth. They had no ambitions of sneaking up on him. They were moving forward slowly, steadily and cautiously. He was injured and exhausted prey. The enemy would take no chances.

They were flushing him out.

Bolan crept backward, looking for the right spot to lurk. He knew that in reality he was committing slow and painful suicide. He stood no chance at all. When they took him down, they would do it hard. These men were all Special Forces operatives. His concealed weapons wouldn't stay hidden. After the incident with the scalpel they would strip him and take his weapons within seconds. There would be no surprise point-blank head shots with the little pistol. He would never get his hands on the butterfly knife tucked down his boot.

He would just die, horribly, after every shred of information about Hal Brognola and the Farm was extracted from him.

None of that mattered.

Del Carpio lay in a grave with spiders on his face, slowly asphyxiating. Bolan's knuckles went white around the scalpel.

He froze. His instincts told him he was being watched. The Executioner's eyes flicked about the thicket looking for the eyes that observed him. Nothing moved. There was no sound except the noise of the men coming down the twin creeks to kill him. But there was someone else. Someone right on top of him. Every hair on back of Bolan's neck told him so.

He dropped to one knee at a slight plastic rasp from above. The scalpel flipped into the unbroken fingers of his left hand as his right hand seized up a fist-sized river stone. Bolan heard the snap and hiss of bow. He staggered as an arrow punched into his thigh.

Bolan snarled and stood.

A bizarre figure hung from the trunk of a redwood sapling twenty yards above. The hunter was clad in a dull gray, body-hugging hooded coverall. The perforated silver disk of an air filter covered his mouth, and the mirrored lenses of his goggles made him look like a giant insect. Climbing spikes shod his feet, and he leaned out from the trunk on a rope harness. He was already laying a second arrow across his bow.

Bolan wound up and flung the stone with all of his fading strength.

The rock thudded into the man's side just below his armpit. The hunter's arrow flew wide into the thicket, and he dropped his bow. Bolan took a half second to kneel. A wickedly barbed broad-head arrow stuck out of the side of his leg. He was lucky. His leg was much thinner than the torso of a deer. The powerful bow had driven the arrow all the way through his leg rather than leaving the barbs imbedded. Bolan snapped off the head and withdrew the shaft transfixing his flesh.

He could hear the men up the creek breaking into a run.

An object clanked to the rocks at Bolan's feet.

A gray cylinder lay in the creek bed between the soldier's boots. It hissed, but nothing appeared to be coming out of it. Bolan read his epitaph in the bold block writing on the side of the grenade.

It read V-55.

It was nerve gas.

He stared up at the hunter in the tree. The masked man raised his gloved hand to Bolan and waved goodbye.

The Executioner hobbled away from the grenade and went for the fallen bow and arrows.

Bolan felt the saliva flooding his mouth, but he couldn't spit enough to keep the sudden flood of froth from spilling down his chin and hanging in viscous streamers. His vision doubled, tripled and blurred. Sweat broke out across his body in a chill wave as his every pore compressed of its own volition. Bolan's lungs spasmed, and the tightening in his chest clamped down like an iron fist. He wheezed and drooled. Weakness washed through him like a wave and left him with joints that felt like rubber and wouldn't obey him. His whole body began shaking like a leaf in the wind. Bolan's knees buckled as he threw up on himself. He fell onto his hands and threw up again. Bolan collapsed. He involuntarily rolled onto his side as his body folded up.

The last thing Bolan saw before he went into blind convulsions were the men in protective suits walking down the creek toward him.

**20**

*The Boneyard*

The nerve gas hadn't been the end. It had been only the beginning. The Iceman had stuck Bolan with a syringe full of atropine, and then he'd been bound and hoisted up into the surviving helicopter and they had returned to the Clubhouse.

Bolan lay twitching and staring up at the sky.

He dully wished he could move his hands but they were bound tight in front of him. His feet were also tied up. The folded Bali-Song butterfly knife was still thrust all the way down his boot, and the tiny Kel-Tec .32 pistol still lay concealed in his crotch.

Bolan lay in the grass collecting his will. He concentrated every last vestige of strength he could still summon into the pit of his belly. Bolan sent his will through the war-torn battlefield of his body. Every ounce of his personality coalesced into his right hand. Bolan willed his hand to move towards his waistband and draw the hidden pocket pistol.

The Executioner collapsed within himself and floated in the fugue of pain.

He couldn't reach the little pistol. He was finished.

"Shall we put him down, now, Ice?" Panikhar stood over Bolan, looking at the vomit on Bolan's clothing and wrinkled his nose. "He's getting a bit ripe."

"In a minute." The Iceman rose from his chair and knelt beside Bolan. He took Bolan's chin in his hand and turned his head to the side. A freshly dug grave lay open a few feet away.

"You know where you're going, don't you?"

"He's going to hell," Brand said, sneering.

"Now you have a choice," continued the Iceman. "You can go to sleep with a bullet in your brain, or you can sleep down into the dark, all Halloween horror-show, with the spiders."

Bolan's head rolled back, and he stared up into the sky.

The Iceman nodded as he measured the brutalized body lying before him. He judged him to be just about ready. "Now, once more." The Iceman's voice was pleasantly conversational. "Who are you, and how did you get inside the Club?"

If he was going down, he might as well tell them that they weren't as covert or invincible as they'd thought. Bolan's voice was a broken slur. "I work with Hal Brognola."

"Yeah, and?"

"You killed Federal marshals. You pissed off Hal. He called me in as a favor."

"How did you figure out we were Special Forces?"

"I saw the video of the D.C. hit. One of your men in the morgue was wearing a Ukrainian cross. We put it together."

"Jee-sus Christ!" Brand snarled. "Damn Russkies! I am gonna beat Yuri's ass next time we link up!"

"That's unimportant, for now." The Iceman's eyes never left Bolan. "You were the Russian colonel in the hospital."

"Yeah."

"You were the second man with Brognola in the house on Jug Bay."

"Yeah."

"How did you know about Hook, much less compromise him?"

"I know some SEALs."

"Calvin James?"

"Yeah, he checked around and got us an interview. We didn't compromise Hook. We just got lucky."

"You know something? I believe you." Ice nodded. "Now, I want you to give me every phone number and access code to Brognola."

Bolan closed his eyes wearily. "I'm only an operative. I haven't reported back in days. Everything I was issued will have been changed already. Damage control is already underway."

"Fair enough." The Iceman prodded Bolan's head with his finger until his eyes opened. "Who's been compromised in our organization?"

"We know Brand was a Navy SEAL."

"Shit!" The big man raised a boot to stomp Bolan, but the Iceman waved him off.

"And?"

"We're looking for connections to an Iceman. We suspect Cisasthmi was a Dutch agent in Indonesia."

The Iceman looked down at Bolan for long moments without blinking and then rose. "All right."

He unsnapped his holster and filled his right hand with the art-deco lines of his massive Mateba semiautomatic revolver. The cold black muzzle of the .44 Magnum pistol stared Bolan between the eyes. The cylinder turned as he cocked back the hammer.

"Say good night."

Bolan calmly watched the tendons in the Iceman's finger as he started to pull the trigger. He was very tired. Except for Del Carpio, it was all right that his War Everlasting finally ended.

The hammer dropped with a click.

The Iceman smiled. "Oops."

The Club members burst out laughing.

"I told you, asshole," Brand taunted. "You don't go down that easily."

"Wow." Panikhar nodded respectfully. "He didn't even blink."

"Yeah, he's pretty cool." The Iceman smiled and looked around the group. "Tell me, anyone have any more spiders?"

"I think we used them up on Del Carpio." Lawrence

shrugged. "You want me to go and hunt up some critters in the woods?"

"No, don't worry about it." The Iceman holstered his pistol. "Just bury him."

*Travis Air Force Base, California*

HAL BROGNOLA CHOMPED manically on his unlit cigar. He sat in a briefing room. A laptop sat open on the desk in front of him. His cell phone sat on the table next to it. He took turns willing each device to do something.

Both sat still and silent.

The hours continued to mount. In the very pit of his gut, the big Fed knew something had gone terribly wrong. The members of Phoenix Force sat in chairs around the table in stony silence. Brognola had split his forces. California was a big state. Able Team was in L.A. waiting for the signal to move.

Brognola had FBI fast-reaction teams waiting in a dozen major cities up and down the state.

Every man in the room bolted upright as Brognola's phone rang. He seized the cell. "Striker!"

"No," Barbara Price's voice answered, "but I have something."

"What have you got?"

"I'm transmitting." The laptop in front of Brognola chimed. "It should be coming through now."

Brognola looked at a face. The man had blond hair and a short blond beard and mustache. Cold blue eyes stared out of the screen. "Who's this?"

"Charlton 'The Iceman' Eischen." Information began to scroll across the computer. "Former Navy SEAL lieutenant-commander. Congressional Medal of Honor winner in the Gulf War. Olympic level swimmer at UC Santa Barbara before joining the Navy."

"What else do you have?"

"We know Michael Brand served on the same SEAL team Eischen did. After the Gulf War, Eischen served two tours with Delta Force and brought Brand in with him. What they did with Delta starts getting classified real fast. We're trying to cut through the red tape here at the Farm right now."

"Forget that for now." Brognola glared at the face on the screen. "Then what happened?"

"Both men resigned their commissions at approximately the same time. Brand took some high-profile security jobs in L.A. that led to his work as a technical adviser in Hollywood. What the Iceman did to keep busy gets shadowy. From what little we can find out so far, we know he travels all over the world. He owns a lot of things. Several import-export companies, golf courses, a graveyard, restaurants, nightclubs, a regular laundry list of small businesses. All of which he acquired at least ostensibly with the help of foreign investors."

Brognola chomped his cigar as he read the screen.

Laundry list was right. It was how Eischen was laundering the money from his operations. His foreign investors would be the special forces operatives in other countries he made contact with during his service in the SEALs and with Delta. "How many residences does he have?"

"In the United States? That we know about? Dozens."

"Narrow it down to California."

Price's voice was a study in frustration. "In California, at least half a dozen. The stakeout has turned up nothing on Brand's houseboat. No one has come back."

"I want local law and FBI in each city where he has a house to pay a visit."

"Hal, we don't have anything on him yet without Mack confirming the—"

"Make it happen!" the head Fed roared. "I don't care how!"

Brognola sagged back in his chair.

Something in his bones told him time was running out.

*The Grave*

THE EXECUTIONER AWOKE in pitch-blackness. His body ached as if it had rained hammers in his sleep. His face was on fire. The air was thick with his own vomit stench and suffocatingly thin of oxygen. Bolan groaned as he tried to rise.

His head bumped into rough wood.

Blind panic shot down Bolan's spine with realization.

He'd been buried alive.

Bolan's bound hands clawed at the rough unyielding wood.

A roar tore out of his mangled face as he shoved with all of his might. The lid of the coffin didn't move. It didn't even flex or creak.

Six feet of soil entombed the coffin in the dark unyielding womb of the earth.

The wound in Bolan's thigh screamed as he kicked his tied feet. He could get no leverage. The confines of the coffin were much too close to bring his knees into his chest. He could hardly move his elbows. Bolan felt panic rise within him as the coffin seemed to constrict around him. The Executioner exerted his will and barely managed to crush down the scream before it reached his throat.

The Executioner lay quietly in his grave. Claustrophobia caused the coffin to close around him like a vise. He willed his heart to slow its beating. He found himself panting and forced himself to breathe shallow and slow breaths to conserve air.

There was only one way out.

Bringing his hands to his mouth, he used his teeth to untie his hands. Several minutes later Bolan reached his right hand down the front of his pants. His fingers closed around the grips of the tiny .32-caliber Kel-Tec pistol. He withdrew the gun and laid his hand upon his chest. Despite the suffocating stench, he forced himself to take several long slow deep breaths. The soldier put himself into the vortex of his pain. From the very center of his impending death he found he could coolly observe it. Bolan took a long breath and then another one. This terrible eye of the hurricane was a place he had been before. His death was something he'd been forced to contemplate untold times in his one-man war against the Mafia and again in his work with Stony Man Farm.

Bolan held the pistol in his hand as he waited for his heart to slow and his breathing to normalize.

He wouldn't panic.

Del Carpio lay interred a few yards away. He had gone down into his grave with spiders on his face, knowing that Bolan would come to save him. They were debts that had to be paid.

He pushed the muzzle of the little pistol against the lid of the coffin and fired.

The muzzle-blast of the little pistol was a thunderbolt in the confines of the coffin. Bolan squeezed his dark-adapted eyes shut against the flash of the gun as he fired three more shots to draw the shape of a box the size of his hand. He punched two holes inside the box and stopped. There was a single round left.

Bolan's face drew back into a snarl and he fired the last round into the lid.

He dropped the pistol against his chest and heaved his shoulder against the side of the coffin for leverage. He bent his beaten body as much as he could as the fingers of his right hand strained for his bound feet. After finally untying them he focused on the laces of his right boot. The knot came undone and he strained down again and yanked on the tongue.

The very tips of his fingers brushed the butterfly knife's handle.

With sweat starting to roll down his face. Bolan groaned as he contorted himself. The nail of his index finger caught on the knife's safety catch. The nail bent back as he pulled but the knife slid up slightly. The safety catch popped open as his fingernail bent back again and failed.

Bolan's fingertips closed around the latch of the double-handled knife.

He drew the knife up to his chest and slid the latch between his thumb and forefinger. Bolan snapped his wrist and the knife clacked open. His left hand traced the pattern of bullet holes he had made.

The Executioner stabbed the knife upward into one of the holes. He twisted his wrist and wood splintered. He stabbed upward again and shoved on the handles. A sliver of wood fell on his chest as he worked the thick lid. Bolan stabbed and pried and worked the damaged wood from bullet hole to bullet hole.

Wood cracked as he leaned on the handle.

Bolan spit as dirt fell in his face. He stabbed upward again and pried. A large shard broke away, and a fist of soil fell in his face. Bolan put the knife on his chest. He reached into his pocket awkwardly and found his handkerchief. It took him many long moments to get it over his face and tied behind his head. He reached up again and his fingers pushed through soil and closed around the top of the coffin lid.

Bolan braced his body against the sides of the coffin and heaved.

The board cracked downward. An immense, suffocating weight of dirt covered his face. Panic surged, and he fought it and lay still until he was calm. He reached up his left hand and began scooping the dirt away from his chest and face and shoving it down toward his feet. He freed his right hand and began working the boards again.

The vision of the Iceman's smiling face filled his mind.

His tortured body screamed with each effort. The dirt pushing against his face was the dirt of the grave, and resolution filled his exhausted mind. Dirt fell against him and packed hard as he tried to move his arm. He moved his left hand very carefully to shove dirt away. His every move threatened to pack the dirt around him and trap his body like a fly in amber. Exhaustion and defeat fought within Bolan's breast. His muscles ached. His brutalized lungs couldn't suck enough air through the dirt packing against the handkerchief across his face.

Bolan felt his will ebbing.

He reached for the last source of strength he could summon.

Bolan thought once more of the Iceman and summoned hate.

He gave himself over to it. He centered himself with it. Hatred turned the black depths of the grave into a bloody red haze behind the Executioner's eyes.

Bolan burned hatred for fuel as he dug upward out of his grave.

**21**

*The Clubhouse*

The Iceman loaded shells into his revolver and holstered it. He spun the dial on his wall safe and began taking out thick stacks of bearer bonds and hundred-dollar bills.

Jeremy walked into the study. His mouth was grinning, but his eyes looked concerned. "So, we're bugging out?"

"Yeah." The Iceman began piling the cash and bonds into a briefcase. "Spread the word. I don't want a panic, but have everyone gather up any personals that they may want to hold on to and then prepare to take their assigned extraction routes out of the country. We'll meet up in Mexico. The house in Cabo should do. Make sure everyone has sufficient pocket money. Meantime, tell Panikhar to gather up every weapon around the Clubhouse that isn't California legal and dump them down the old Spanish cistern on the hillside, and then cover it over."

Jeremy's face tightened. "You expecting a raid?"

"No, more like a visit. I don't think anyone has anything on me, but if they've identified me, they might start playing fast and loose with the law to search the place. Get on the horn. See if there's a warrant out for the arrest of any members of the Club. Pooky has diplomatic immunity, she can skate, but Michael may be in some real shit. I want him out of sight if the Feds come by before we leave, and I want him out of the country ASAP."

Jeremy stared at the massive pistol in the Iceman's hand. "What's that for if you're just expecting the Feds or cops?"

"Just a feeling."

"What kind of feeling?"

"This Belasko asshole. He went to Mexico and shot Eddie. He took down C.T. and the Russians. He doesn't play by cop or Fed rules. If he has pals, they may show up for some payback. I'm thinking the kind of friends he has won't show up with warrants in their hands, and they won't play by the rules, either. I just don't want us caught with our pants down before we can extract."

"I'm on it." Jeremy nodded. "Anything else?"

"Yeah, call Jebediah down at the Boneyard."

"It's still four hours until dawn." Jeremy checked his watch. "He's probably asleep. Hell, he slept through Belasko going down."

"Wake him up anyway," the Iceman ordered. "Tell him I want those headstones on the new graves by morning."

"Okay, but he's gonna be cranky and asking questions." Jeremy frowned. "What do you want me to tell him?"

"I don't care. Tell him the families are flying out this morning, special. Make up something up, but get the skinny old bastard moving."

"I'm on it."

"One other thing."

"What's that?"

"When you're done with that, go to the rec room and give the sound system a listen." The Iceman smiled. "I want to know if Belasko has woken up and started screaming yet."

*Redwood Valley Cemetery*

JEBEDIAH HOEK PUTTED his lawn tractor across the cemetery grounds. A small wagon hitched to the back of the tractor contained a pair of marble grave markers. He checked his plot numbers and turned down a long lane of headstones. He had seen his seventieth birthday a month ago. He didn't like the phone ringing in the late hours of the night.

However, he'd run the cemetery for the past forty years. He took his job seriously, and he liked the new owner. The man had doubled his salary and for the most part had left the running of the establishment to him.

Hoek had learned not to ask questions when new graves appeared that he had not been informed of. The new owner had taken him aside and explained things to him. He had clients. Clients with unusual needs. Sometimes things happened between these clients, and the families didn't want public burials. They also wanted to be able to visit the gravesites in private. The new owner had bought Hoek the tractor, hired him a pair of assistants in town and installed a large-screen television with full cable in the caretaker's cottage.

It didn't strike him as odd at all that the headstones on the "unusual" or "unexpected" graves that occasionally cropped up all had Italian names. Hoek understood. The owner had thanked him for his understanding. The caretaker occasionally got a call from the house up on the mountain to do a late-night job. It was irksome at his age, but he liked his freedom, he liked cable TV and he particularly liked the way his paycheck fluctuated when he received one of these late-night calls.

Hoek brought his little tractor to a halt beside a pair of new graves.

He sat back in the seat and reached for his thermos. He would have to wait for the boys to arrive from town to help him, but he had brewed fresh coffee and he enjoyed watching the sun come over the mountains.

He unscrewed the cap of his thermos and poured himself a cup of coffee. He looked at the two recent graves and back at the markers in his trailer. Maria Rosa Pia Colari and Vicencia Antonini were engraved on them. He absently wondered what feud or family misfortune had befallen the two Italian girls.

A bloody hand holding a knife punched upward from the fresh topsoil of the grave.

His chest seized. His coffee spilled in his lap as he toppled out of his seat and fell against the trailer. He clawed for the metal pillbox in the front pocket of his overall bib that contained his nitroglycerine tablets.

The hand released the knife. Hoek watched frozen in horror

as the hand clawed about the top of the grave a moment. The fingers tore into the earth. A moment later another hand bound in a bloody rag thrust upward. The two hands flailed for purchase and then bunched and heaved. The soil between them sifted and rose like a volcano.

Hoek felt a scream rising within him.

Something was coming up out of the hole. A veil of filth fell away from the head-sized lump.

The caretaker screamed as the dead rose before him.

The old man's shriek caught in his throat as the head craned around and peered at him. Hoek went white. His hammering heart threatened to burst from the cage of his ribs like a frightened bird as the dead spoke.

"Give me a hand."

Hoek shook uncontrollably.

"Help me, please."

The old man's spell of frozen fear broke. Terror filled every pore in his body with a new realization. The thing before him was a living human being.

A human being whom his employer had buried alive.

"I..." Hoek stuttered. "I..."

"Damn it." The brutalized thing reached out its hand. "Just...help me."

He knelt and began scooping dirt away from the man. It took him ten minutes to finish disinterring him. He hooked his arms beneath the man's shoulders and heaved him forth from the earth. The two of them flopped on the ground and panted in the fresh air. The man smelled worse than any dead man Jebediah had been exposed to in forty years of funerals.

"The grave...the new one...one plot over."

Hoek sat exhausted and shaking. "What about it?"

The man turned to regard him with burning eyes. "Help me dig it up."

*Travis Air Force Base*

"GRAVEYARD!" Hal Brognola's fist crashed down on the tabletop. "The bastard owns his own graveyard!"

The men of Phoenix Force shot to their feet.

"Smalls didn't die in some torture tomb! He was asphyxiating!" The head Fed's face was terrible as he rose. "The bastard buried him alive!"

He punched the preset on his cell. Barbara Price answered in half a ring.

"Hal! What is it?"

"What's the name of that graveyard, and where is it?"

"Redwood Valley Cemetery." Price paused for a half second. "Mendocino County, Mendocino. About ten miles outside of town."

"Hal?" Calvin James's hands flattened the map of California before him. "That's barely a hundred miles from here."

Brognola nodded. "What about our Iceman, Barbara? Does he have a house nearby?"

He could hear her fingers flying across the keyboard. "Yes. About a mile or so up the mountain from it. He owns the golf course nearby, as well."

"We're moving. Get local law involved, now. I don't care how, but get them to the Iceman's house and get paramedics into the cemetery. Any fresh graves are to be dug up immediately. I take full responsibility. I want the Northern California FBI fast-reaction team airborne. Use my line and wake up the President if you have to, but make it happen."

The line clicked off as the mission controller began making it happen.

Brognola seized his shotgun and grabbed his body armor from the back of his chair. In the time it had taken to call Price, Phoenix Force had already armored up.

The big Fed punched a second preset number in his phone.

Jack Grimaldi answered from the cockpit of his helicopter out on the airfield. "Are we a go?"

"Yes!" Brognola and Phoenix Force swept from the room. Air Force personnel hurled themselves out of the way of the heavily armed phalanx of grim-faced warriors. "Get your rotors turning, and download the following location!"

*The Boneyard*

DEL CARPIO'S SCREAM was muffled beneath the lid of the coffin. "I'm here! I'm here!" His frenzied hands scrabbled and clawed at the wood. "I'm alive!"

Bolan nodded to Hoek as he bent wearily to the lid. It took them a moment to dig away at the soil at the side of the coffin concealing the latches. They flicked them open and heaved back the upper lid. Del Carpio had a nice coffin. The wood was well finished. The silk lining the interior was shredded and stained with the blood of the young man's clawing hands.

Hoek turned green and made a gagging noise as he looked at the man in the coffin.

The Club had beaten Del Carpio's face into hamburger. The swollen, superating wounds of the spider bites on top of that left little that looked human. His features were almost completely obscured. His eyes were swollen slits. Del Carpio's lips opened and took a great gasp of air. "Belasko! Is that you?"

"Yeah, it's me. Hold on. Don't move." Bolan opened the second lid and straddled the coffin. He wrapped his hand in his handkerchief and methodically crushed the spiders on the young man's chest and in his hair. Bolan's eye flicked to a small microphone taped to the lip of the coffin behind Del Carpio's head. Bolan ripped it out and hurled it away. He and Hoek lifted the young man out of his grave.

Bolan leaned back against the wall of the reopened grave. "You all right?"

"No." Del Carpio shook his misshapen head. "I can't see."

Both of the young man's eyes were swollen closed into slits surrounded by angry red flesh.

"What..." Hoek spoke shakily. "What happened to you fellas?"

The old man flinched as Bolan turned his horrible gaze upon him. "You have a phone?"

"Yeah, but..." The old man cringed. "It doesn't dial out."

"It doesn't dial out." Bolan blinked. "You have a gun?"

"Yeah, but...I don't keep it loaded."

"You have a car?"

Hoek looked toward his lawn tractor.

Bolan closed his eyes. "How far is it into town?"

"'Bout ten miles, give or take." The old man swallowed. "I'll take you, if you like."

Bolan shook his head. The Club would be getting out of Dodge and dispersing. Bolan didn't want to meet any of them on the road into town in the wagon of a lawn tractor.

Del Carpio spoke. "I know where there's a phone."

"Yeah." Bolan nodded slowly and looked up toward the Clubhouse hanging on the mountainside. "And I know where we can find guns and a car."

Del Carpio turned his blind face toward Bolan. "I can't see."

"I know."

"You have a knife?"

Bolan withdrew the butterfly knife from his pocket and clacked it open. "Yeah."

Del Carpio took a shaky breath. "Cut me."

"Jesus, Joseph and Mary!" Hoek backed away as far as he could in the pit.

Bolan froze the panicking man in place with his gaze as he raised the knife to the lumped flesh swelling Del Carpio's eyes shut.

"Hold him."

**22**

*The Clubhouse*

Jeremy's face was white as the Iceman and Lawrence walked into the rec room. Jeremy sat at the desk with his chair swiveled toward the massive sound system. He held a headphone against his ear. The Iceman noted the look on his face. "What is it, Jeremy?"

"I think you'd better listen to this." Jeremy pulled the headphones and turned up the volume on the stereo. For long moments there was no sound at all. The Iceman raised an eyebrow as a distant hoo-hooing noise came through the gigantic German speakers. "Jeremy, what channel are you on?"

Jeremy swallowed uncomfortably. "Belasko's grave."

The Iceman turned and looked at Lawrence dryly. "Tell me, Lawrence. You didn't go and bury an owl down there with him, did you?"

"Umm." It was the first time the Iceman had ever seen Lawrence look startled. "No, Ice. That would be a negative."

The Iceman drew his revolver. "Jeremy, what do you have on Del Carpio's channel?"

Jeremy flicked a switch. Nothing but a few crackles of static came through the speaker. "I got nothing at all." Jeremy's shook his head in mounting horror as he looked at the sound system's controls. "Del Carpio's line is...dead."

Anggun strode into the room. Her hair was still wet from a shower, and all she wore was a sarong. She cradled a 9 mm Heckler & Koch VP-70 machine pistol with its shoulder stock attached. A laser sight had been custom-fitted beneath the slide. Her beautiful lips curled back in consternation. "I paged that idiot Tomlinson to carry my bags down to the car. He's not responding." Her dark eyes flicked across the stern faces of the men in the room. "What's happening?"

"Tell me." The Iceman checked the load in his pistol. "Where are Panikhar and Brand?"

"Suresh is in his room finishing packing. I think Michael is outside loading his car." The woman unconsciously cradled her machine pistol closer. "What's happening?"

Everyone in the room jumped except the Iceman as a human scream split the dawn out on the grounds. The scream ended abruptly as if something had interrupted it. The Iceman nodded. "Everyone, get your weapons. Get tactical communication gear on."

Anggun's voice rose. "What's happening?"

The Iceman went to the gun cabinet and withdrew a second massive revolver. "He's here."

THE EXECUTIONER put his foot into the chest of the guard. Neck bones splintered as he pulled the shovel blade free from the corpse's cervical spine. Bolan took a deep breath. His reactions were slow. Too slow. Despite his best effort, the hardman had managed to turn. If the man had gone for his gun rather than screaming in horror, Bolan would probably be dead.

When the enemy lived next door to a cemetery, looking like the living dead had tactical advantages.

Bolan knew that one panicked guard was as far as that card would take him. He'd lost the element of surprise, and the Club members wouldn't hesitate to blow their disfigured faces off.

Lights were blinking on all over the Clubhouse.

Bolan tossed aside the shovel and relieved the dead security man of his carbine. He took his spare magazines and handed Del Carpio the man's side arm. Del Carpio's face was a mask of blood from the eyebrows down. Bolan had lanced the horrific swelling above and below his eyes. Blood and spider venom still leaked down his face. The young man would be horribly scarred, but at least he could open his eyes.

Del Carpio took the .45-caliber Smith & Wesson pistol and checked the loads.

Bolan took the dead man's tactical radio and punched the transmit button. "Hey, Iceman."

There was a long pause. The Iceman's voice came back. "You sound tired."

Bolan ignored the remark. "Why don't you come outside?"

"No." The Clubhouse plunged into sudden darkness from within. "Why don't you come in?"

"All right." Bolan clicked off the radio and clipped it to his belt. He put in the earpiece and nodded at Del Carpio.

They had stopped off at the caretaker's cottage to get cleaned up and gather weapons. Hoek had not lied. He didn't have a car, and his rotary phone no longer dialed out. His medical kit consisted of a tin of Band-Aid strips and an ancient squeeze bottle of bactine. The action of his single-shot shotgun was rusted shut. However, the old man's favorite evening "constitutional" appeared to be a screwdriver. He kept a lot of vodka around the house, and his freezer was well stocked with orange juice concentrate.

Hoek also kept a full of can of gasoline outside for his tractor.

Bolan would have preferred detergent for a gelling agent, but it seemed the caretaker didn't do a lot of washing.

After changing into some clothes left by the previous—and thankfully larger—caretaker, Bolan took one of the four glass Smirnoff bottles from the tool bag they had liberated from the cottage. He shook the bottle to agitate the watery orange sludge within. "Light it."

Del Carpio took out Hoek's lighter and lit the oily rag Bolan had stuffed down the neck of the bottle. Bolan took aim at the vast panoramic window of the Clubhouse rec room and heaved the bottle like a javelin.

The Molotov cocktail flew through the air trailing blue flame and sailed through the window with a crash of breaking glass. There was a slight thump and whoosh sound as shards of shattered window fell and broke. The darkened interior of the rec room suddenly lit up in lurid hues of Halloween orange and chimney red.

The plaintive shriek of a smoke alarm began pulsing.

A high-caliber handgun roared, and Del Carpio staggered backward and fell.

Bolan caught him by one arm and dragged him back behind the massive trunk of a redwood as he sprayed his carbine on full-auto.

The pistol hammered three more times and bark flew from the trunk.

"I've got them pinned behind the bog tree! By the lawn!" The big man's voice bellowed across the grounds. "Suresh! Lawrence! Flank them!"

Bolan peered around the tree and nearly had his head blown off as Brand fired his 10 mm Glock to keep them pinned down. The big man had a very firm firing position behind a massive brickwork barbecue ten yards away. Bolan turned to Del Carpio. The huge bullet had holed the young man through the left shoulder and shattered his collarbone.

"Can you shoot?"

"Sure." Del Carpio took a gasping breath. "Kinda."

"Empty your gun at him on three." Bolan took out another bottle and lit the rag. "One, two, three."

Del Carpio stuck his arm around the tree and began methodically firing toward the barbecue.

Bolan rose and went around the other side of the tree and tossed the Molotov cocktail in a high underhanded lob.

Brand popped up from behind cover with his pistol held in both hands as Del Carpio ran dry. He put his front sight on Bolan. His head jerked up as he caught sight of the flaming object falling down at him. The big man instinctively swatted the object way with the slide of his pistol. Glass shattered and the viscous fluid drenched him.

The big man screamed in agony as the jellied gasoline ignited and flame rose up in a consuming sheet over his head and shoulders and arms.

Anggun screamed from a window up in the Clubhouse.

Three quick bursts from a small automatic weapon stabbed into the tree trunk. Bolan kept the tree between himself and the house. Brand went up like a torch. The big man flailed and jerked across the lawn like a flaming marionette, screaming in inhuman torment.

Bolan raised his carbine.

The single shot snapped back Brand's burning head and dropped him prone to the lawn. The big man lay motionless in the grass and burned. The stench of charring flesh was sickening.

The automatic weapon up in the house tore into the tree again. Anggun was screaming obscenities in a language Bolan didn't understand as she hysterically fired burst after burst. Two more weapons joined it, and bullets swarmed angrily into the trunk of the tree. Bolan knelt by Del Carpio "Can you walk?"

The young man looked up at Bolan with infinite weariness. "You have any more of those painkillers?"

"You ate the last of them in the cottage."

"Damn it." Del Carpio groaned as he pushed himself to his feet. The slide of his pistol was racked open on an empty chamber. He dropped the spent gun and nodded. "Let's go."

Bolan and Del Carpio kept the tree before them as they faded backward from the edge of the lawn and crouched out of sight on the steeply falling hillside. Bolan jerked his head. "Let's try the driveway."

"All right."

Del Carpio gasped and staggered as they worked their way around. Bolan's own feet felt like clay beneath him. The arrow wound in his thigh and the half-healed bullet wounds in his shoulder pulsed, and his ribs ached.

The Iceman's Porsche, two Jeeps and Brand's Mustang were parked in the gravel drive. Bolan's eyes narrowed. The trunk of the Mustang was open.

The big man had been packing to leave when the attack had begun.

Bolan handed Del Carpio the carbine. "Shoot at anything."

The Executioner lit the third firebomb and hurled it at the front door of the house. The entryway smeared with the homemade napalm and flame sheeted upward toward the eaves.

Bolan moved for the Mustang.

Glass shattered in the upstairs window overlooking the drive. Bullets struck the gravel by Bolan's boot. Del Carpio raised his carbine and burned an entire magazine at the window. Bolan ducked to a halt behind the Mustang and pulled forth a pair of black cordurra gear bags out of the trunk. He was pleased with their weight as he hunkered down behind the car. More bullets struck the Mustang from the window upstairs overlooking the drive.

Del Carpio responded with short bursts from the tree line.

Bolan unzipped the longer bag and withdrew the folding stock shotgun inside and the bandolier of shells. He smiled as his hand closed around the familiar grips of the Star machine pistol. He thrust the pistol in the front of his waistband and stuffed the four loaded spare magazines into his pockets. Bolan opened the other bag.

Inside was a coiled set of tactical communications gear, another 10 mm Glock, several thick wads of hundred-dollar bills and a pair of Vietnam-vintage M-9 offensive hand grenades.

Del Carpio hissed from his position a few yards back. "I'm down to my last magazine!"

Bolan took the grenades and slung the bag with the Glock back toward Del Carpio.

Renewed fire came from the window. Bolan could hear Jeremy and Anggun shouting to somebody. The woman ripped burst after burst into Bolan's position as Jeremy rapidly pumped and fired a shotgun. Del Carpio kept to a thick tree trunk and sprayed his carbine at the window to drive them back. Bolan lit his last firebomb. He rose from behind the Mustang and hurled it.

Jeremy shouted in alarm. He and Pooky leaped back as the flaming bottle sailed end over end and shattered against the windowpane. Flame spewed into the upstairs room and framed the window in fire.

The burning front door burst open on its hinges, and Panikhar and Lawrence came out with guns blazing in their hands like Butch Cassidy and the Sundance Kid.

Del Carpio lowered his aim and his carbine snarled as he held down the trigger. Lawrence's M-16 spun out of his hands and his feet skidded from beneath him as the rifle burst tracked his body. The hunter-killer went down in a tangle of limbs beside one of the Jeeps and lay unmoving. Panikhar staggered with bullet strikes. He struggled to raise his rifle and track the muzzle onto Del Carpio. Del Carpio stood forth from cover and held the carbine outstretched in one hand like a massive pistol as he kept his trigger down. Flame shot from both men's rifles simultaneously.

Panikhar's head rocked back as his skull split, and he fell face first into the gravel.

Del Carpio dropped to one knee in exhaustion. He had to use the smoking muzzle of his empty carbine as a crutch to shove himself up again.

Bolan scooped up the shotgun and unlocked the folding stock. "Del Carpio, are you all ri—"

The Mustang's chassis groaned as it took Lawrence's weight. The killer vaulted the convertible's front and rear seats and the trunk lid slammed shut and buckled beneath his boots. Bolan raised the shotgun, but Lawrence was already on top of him.

The Executioner was borne backward as Lawrence's inhumanly strong hands closed around his throat. The air blasted out of Bolan's lungs as his adversary fell on top of him. His knee rammed into Bolan's guts, and the shotgun was pinned between them. Lawrence's pupils were pinpoints of insane rage in the lurid light of the burning house.

"Now, you just goddamn die!"

Lawrence's fingers sank into Bolan's throat.

The Executioner twisted the shotgun between Lawrence's arms to break the hold, but he had no leverage. Lawrence's knee pinned the machine pistol. Bolan torqued the shotgun against Lawrence's elbows with all of his strength to no avail.

The strength in the sociopath's hands was sickening.

Bolan's vision began to blacken.

Del Carpio staggered forward into the firelight. His left arm hung at a terrible angle. He held his spent carbine by the barrel and swung it at Lawrence's head like a cricket bat.

Lawrence's huge left hand released Bolan's throat and caught the carbine with ease. His fist clenched around the pistol grip and ripped the rifle from Del Carpio's hand. Lawrence rose to his feet. The vise of his right hand took Bolan up with him by the throat. He backhanded Del Carpio across the face with the barrel of the empty carbine and smashed the young man to the ground. Lawrence tossed the carbine away and dropped back down on Bolan with all of his weight. His left hand joined his right again around the soldier's throat.

"Now, where were we?" Lawrence's thumbs vised down on Bolan's trachea to crack it. "Oh, that's right, why don't you just goddamn—"

Lawrence's eyes flared as he felt the muzzle of the Star machine pistol pressed into his abdomen.

Bolan clamped down on the trigger and held it. Lawrence let out an explosive gasp as the machine pistol hammered back and forth on full-auto. The killer shuddered and went limp as all nine rounds tore through his guts and out his spine in the space of a second.

The Executioner shoved off Lawrence's corpse and lay wheezing for air in the gravel. He ejected his spent magazine and used the unbroken thumb and forefinger of his left hand to fish a fresh magazine from his pocket. Bolan slid the reload into the smoking pistol and released the slide into battery.

Del Carpio's voice was a broken whisper a few feet away. "I hate these guys."

Bolan pushed himself up slowly and stumbled over to Panikhar's body. He stripped the dead paracommando of his armored vest and awkwardly pulled it on. It was a size or two too small, but Bolan cinched the straining straps with effort. He pulled the pin on one of the hand grenades and wrapped the unbroken fingers of his left hand around the safety lever. "You ready?"

"Yeah." Del Carpio spit out broken teeth as he reached down with his good arm for the Glock in the bag. The two men stood with pistols in their hands and faced the Clubhouse. The open front door was framed in crawling fire.

It looked like the door to hell.

The two of them maneuvered their way into the house through the flaming portal.

They crossed the marble foyer and peered carefully around the corner into the spacious living room. Clouds of oozing smoke hung around the ceiling fan and light fixtures from the spreading inferno upstairs. The house was dark except for the flickering orange glow of the spreading fires. Bolan did some quick math. "Iceman, Jeremy, Pooky. I make it three, unless there are guards left we don't know about."

"Okay. Fine." Del Carpio leaned against the wall and closed his eyes. "Let's kill them."

Bolan eyed the young Green Beret. Del Carpio was in terrible shape. The Executioner didn't dare consider himself. Only will kept him standing. Bolan heaved a deep breath and choked on smoke. "Okay. Cover me."

Del Carpio leaned out of the foyer. The Glock shook in his hand.

Bolan stepped into the living room. Nothing moved other than the shifting shadows as the flames rose and fell behind them and glowed from the landing upstairs. Bolan peered at the darkness of the open kitchen door across the room.

"Look out!" Del Carpio shouted.

The huge glass panel of the sliding patio door shattered inward as a 3-round burst pounded into Bolan's side and shoved him down against a couch. Del Carpio's gun barked twice. A second burst of autofire from the darkened patio ripped chunks out of the wall in answer as Del Carpio reeled back behind cover.

Bolan struggled to rise from the couch.

Anggun stood outside on the patio deck. She held a stocked machine pistol mounted at her shoulder. A ruby red light gleamed beneath the barrel.

Bolan raised the Star as a red dot appeared squarely on his chest. Flame spit from the woman's weapon, and the burst patterned itself around the red dot. The trip-hammer blows shoved Bolan back and sat him down on the couch again. He yanked himself aside as he fell. Two bullets punched into the top of his shoulder armor, and the third ripped into the cushion beside his ear as Anggun went for the head shot.

Bolan thrust out the Star again and fired.

The ancient pistol snarled on full-auto. The woman staggered backward, shuddering and jerking across the patio as the rounds drew a line up her body from her belly to her brain. She tumbled back and plunged through the plastic cover of the hot tub.

Flame strobed from the kitchen doorway.

Stuffing tore from the top of the couch as Bolan dropped low and reloaded. Del Carpio's pistol boomed and bits of the kitchen door frame shattered away. Jeremy stood in the entry, holding a small pistol in a two-hand combat stance. The pistol snapped spitefully in his hand on rapid semiauto. He swung his pistol up from the couch without pause and continued firing at Del Carpio.

Del Carpio sat on the steps as a bullet hit him in his shattered shoulder.

Bolan shot the slide home on his reload and ripped the pin from his grenade. He lurched up and lay his gun arm across the back of the couch.

Jeremy swiveled and lowered his aim.

Bolan raised his front sight above Jeremy's armored vest and pulled the trigger.

Jeremy's arms flapped spastically as the machine pistol hammered his head apart.

"Uhhh." Del Carpio groaned as he struggled to stand. "I'm—"

The young man flew back heels over head as a pair of thunderclaps boomed from the top of the stairs.

The Iceman stood upon the burning landing.

He swung a pair of smoking revolvers the size of hand cannons on Bolan. The Star was locked open on empty in Bolan's right hand.

The Executioner's broken fingers opened as he lobbed his grenade left-handed at the Iceman.

The massive revolvers roared in the Iceman's hands. Twin thunderbolts smashed Bolan back from the couch and sledgehammered him down across the coffee table. The glass top shattered as Bolan fell through and collapsed into the chrome frame beneath in a tangle.

Yellow fire flashed on the upstairs landing. The whip-crack sound of the grenade's detonation sent shreds of razor-sharp shrapnel hissing at head level through the living room. The light fixtures and ceiling fan broke apart under the onslaught and rained down in pieces.

Bolan lay collapsed in the twisted frame of the coffee table, too stunned to do anything except breathe. He ran a palsied left hand over the torn fabric on the front of his armor. His vest was cratered with bullet strikes. Bolan's body was so bruised and beaten he couldn't tell if his armor had held or not. He lay crumpled where he was and struggled for breath.

Over the sound of crackling flame, he could hear Del Carpio wheezing.

Bolan ejected the Star's spent magazine and fumbled for a reload. He didn't have one. He dropped the pistol and heaved himself up. It took him three tries to extricate himself from the tangle of glass and chrome. He was too tired to stand. Bolan slowly crawled across the floor and sat on the steps beside Del Carpio.

The young man lay spread-eagled on the marble floor of the foyer.

Between Brandt, Jeremy and the Iceman, Del Carpio had taken three bullets through the same shoulder. They had ground the joint into hamburger. That was the least of Del Carpio's concerns. The Iceman had put two .44 Magnum rounds into Del Carpio, and the second one had hit him on the right side lower down. Bolan could tell by the young man's breathing that his right lung had collapsed.

Bolan leaned against the wall and stripped away the twisted bandanna holding his broken hand together. He packed the filthy wad of fabric down into Del Carpio's chest wound with his finger.

"There." Bolan groaned and used the wall to push himself up. "Don't die."

Del Carpio's gun lay on the tiles. The pistol lay locked open on empty.

Bolan leaned back against the wall and closed his eyes.

He opened them again at a strange sound. He looked down and found the earpiece of the tactical radio he had taken from the guard was hanging against his chest. Tiny sounds were coming out of it. Bolan screwed the earpiece into his ear and listened.

The sound was a methodical gasp for breath and then a groan of effort.

It sounded like someone crawling under great duress.

Bolan pushed himself away from the wall and stumbled across the living room. He went to the kitchen and flicked on the light. Jeremy lay on the linoleum with very little left of his head. Bolan knelt and picked up the little black pistol that lay near the dishwasher. It was a .22-caliber HK-4. Bolan pushed the magazine release and wearily examined the magazine.

There were two hollowpoint rounds left, plus the one in the chamber.

Bolan slid the magazine back in and limped toward the stairs. He put his elbow on the rail and his hand on his wounded thigh. Bolan grunted and shoved himself up each step. He coughed as he reached the thickening smoke at the top of the stairs. The wall and door frame around the landing were scored with the passage of grenade shrapnel. A huge black revolver lay at the top of the landing. A second one lay a few feet away. Blood stained both of their wooden grips.

There were bloody handprints on the wall. One smeared down

to the floor. From there, swaths of blood discolored the carpet in a clear trail down the smoke-filled hallway.

Bolan wheezed and choked as he breathed smoke. The heat of the fire channeled itself down the hallway and seared his face. He put his arm across his eyes and kept his head down as he followed the trail of blood down the hall. He passed the rec room. The door was blackened and radiated heat like an oven. Bolan flinched as the door ignited and flame rose in a slow-motion sheet toward the ceiling. The smoke alarm in the ceiling shrieked endlessly.

Bolan moved toward the open door of the study at the end of the hall.

He gasped in exhaustion and leaned heavily against the doorjamb.

The Iceman stood behind his desk. Flames from the burning eaves outside lit him up in lurid red light. His hands and face were covered in blood where his armor hadn't protected him from grenade shrapnel. Blood dripped from his torn arms and scored legs. He was fumbling with bloody fingers that didn't obey him at the glass doors of the gun cabinet.

Bolan extended a shaking hand.

The little .22 spit, and one of the gun cabinet's glass panels shattered beside the Iceman's head. The Iceman turned and glanced back at Bolan in vague surprise. The Executioner steadied his arm on the door frame and fired again. The Iceman jerked and flinched as the bullet struck the Kevlar collar of his vest and snapped it back against his throat.

Bolan took a deep breath and steadied himself. He took a moment to cradle the butt of his pistol in the palm of his broken left hand. He put the white dot of the front sight on the Iceman's forehead. The Iceman raised his bloody hands before his face as Bolan squeezed the trigger.

Blood blossomed in the palm of the Iceman's right hand, and it flapped like a broken bird as the little .22-caliber lead hollowpoint round mushroomed and broke apart against the bones in his hand.

Jeremy's pistol clacked open on a smoking empty chamber.

The Iceman stared at the bloody hole in his palm. He looked once at Bolan and then turned and shoved his left hand through the shattered panel of the gun cabinet. Metal rattled as he seized something.

Bolan staggered forward a step and flung Jeremy's pistol.

The gun bounced off the side of the Iceman's head. His temple slammed forward and spiderwebbed the glass of the other cabinet panel, then his eyes rolled back in his head. Whatever he held fell with a clatter inside the cabinet. His empty hand slithered out of the jagged glass as he slid to the floor.

Blood rolled down the Iceman's jaw. Blood bubbled over his lips and into his blond beard as he raised his head. His eyes focused on Bolan. "Fuck...you."

Bolan's mouth fell open in a demonic grin. It pleased him to hear something so uncharacteristic come out of the Iceman's mouth. The two men glared each other. Their blue eyes burned bloody murder as they panted for every breath and choked on smoke. The Iceman spit bloody froth.

"Well?"

Bolan reached into his pocket and pulled forth the Bali-Song. His thumb popped the catch. He twisted his wrist mechanically and the blood-crusted butterfly knife clacked open in his hand.

The Executioner shambled forward.

The Iceman shoved his elbows back against the gun cabinet. His eyes squeezed shut, and he groaned with the effort of shoving himself erect.

Bolan took the knife in an ice-pick grip and raised it up over his head. The Iceman raised his arms in a crippled cross to defend himself. Bolan stabbed downward, and the knife sank to the hilt into the Iceman's arm. He tore the knife from the Iceman's flesh and raised it again. The Iceman fell back against the gun cabinet as he tried to keep his hands up. Bolan drove the knife down. It sliced across the Iceman's forearm and chopped into the chest of his armored vest. Bolan ripped the knife free from the Kevlar fibers. He stabbed down again in another hammer blow. The blade punched through the bullet hole in the Iceman's hand and came out the other side.

The Iceman's hand closed reflexively around Bolan's fist. The two men yanked back and forth exhaustedly for control of the blade.

Blood spattered Bolan's face as a shout of effort exploded out of his adversary's lungs. The Iceman whipped his elbow around and drove the joint into Bolan's jaw. The knob of bone crashed into the soldier's mouth. Bolan saw stars as his head rocked back on his shoulders. Fresh blood filled his mouth as he toppled backward across the Iceman's desk and tumbled to the floor.

The Iceman sagged back and fumbled at the knife transfixing his hand. He stumbled a few steps forward and leaned heavily on the desktop. Shoving the handle of the knife under his armpit, he pinned it with his biceps. He yanked his right hand, and the bloody knife fell to the carpet. The Iceman went to his knees from the effort of pulling the blade free of his bones.

Bolan's vision swam and he tried to sit up.

The Iceman put his elbows on the desk and shoved himself standing. He staggered forward and raised his foot to kick Bolan's face. The Executioner heaved his head aside as the foot stamped down. The Iceman gagged as Bolan drove his fist up between his legs.

The Iceman fell on top of him. Bolan's right hand was pinned. He tried to punch the Iceman in the side of the head, but his broken left fingers wouldn't form a fist. The Iceman shoved his lacerated forearms into Bolan's face and wept with effort as he pushed himself up. He shoved his left thumb into the soldier's mouth, trying to rip it open.

The bones in the Iceman's thumb cracked as Bolan bit down.

The Iceman tried to yank his thumb free, and he let out a scream as Bolan's teeth met in the middle and the thumb parted at the second joint.

The Iceman reared up as Bolan spit out his thumb.

Bolan's vision exploded into a black field broken by purple pinpricks of light as the Iceman drove his forehead down into Bolan's with bone-cracking force.

The Iceman sat on his opponent's chest and reached out across the carpet. He managed to get the fallen butterfly knife into his hand, but he couldn't close his fingers around it. He took the handles between his palms like a prayer and raised the blade over his head.

Bolan reached up and pawed at the Iceman's wrists as the man struggled to drive the knife downward.

The Executioner's right hand seized the Iceman's ear. He closed his hand into a fist and heaved. Flesh parted as the ear tore halfway down his head. The knife fell from the Iceman's hands as he toppled over in agony. Bolan rolled over and leaned his elbow into the Iceman's chest for leverage. He climbed on top of his opponent as if he were climbing a mountain.

Bolan jerked his head aside as the Iceman clawed at his face. He climbed blindly on top of him and straddled his chest. He shoved his broken hand down into the Iceman's throat and pinned him. The Iceman gagged as his throat compressed under Bolan's weight.

The Executioner heaved a ragged breath and rammed his right elbow down into his tormentor's face. He reared back, and the Iceman's cheek cracked as he drove his elbow down a second time. The man went limp with the third blow. Bolan's elbow rose and fell into the Iceman's skull again and again.

His right hand closed around the twin handles of the Bali-Song. The Iceman lay unmoving in bloody ruin beneath him. Bolan reeled as he sat back and raised the knife overhead.

"Freeze, asshole!"

Bolan drove the knife down with all of his strength.

The knife plunged into the floor beside the Iceman's head as Bolan was bowled over. Bodies piled on top of him. Hands seized his wrist, and the knife was wrenched from his hand. Arms locked around Bolan's shoulders and arms. He struggled to reach the Iceman's unmoving form.

"I'll kill you! You hear me?" Bolan surged with insane strength against the men restraining him. The world turned bloodred behind his eyes as he shouted at the Iceman and the men holding him.

"Striker!" The voice was familiar, but only the most distant part of Bolan's mind recognized Hal Brognola's voice. The world was a maelstrom of men in dark blue windbreakers and body armor. Bolan's muscles contracted as he sought to hurl off his assailants.

"Hold him, damn it! Hold him!"

"He's getting loose! Get the Taser! Hold him! Hold—"

Calvin James appeared before Bolan. His eyes flared in horror as he looked into Bolan's face. He hesitated one second and then cocked his open hand back behind his ear.

The edge of James's hand sliced down into Bolan's temple.

The Executioner's world went black.

# Epilogue

*Costa Rica*

Mack Bolan lay on the floor of a hut with his arms outstretched in a cross. He took a deep breath as he lifted his legs up to vertical. The ocean breeze played across him as he slowly let his breath out and he twisted his hips to his left. He kept his legs poker stiff as he slowly lowered his feet to the palm of his right hand. Bolan took long slow breaths as he relaxed into the lying twist. His ribs had healed to the point where the twisting of the yoga poses no longer bothered him. Bolan looked out over his left shoulder, and his eyes rested on his hand. It was healing nicely.

"Awesome! Perfect!" Kimmy beamed down at Bolan. "You know, you have a beautiful body."

Kimmy was half Hawaiian and half Irish. Her huge dark eyes and raven hair reminded Bolan of Anggun, but the resemblance ended there. There was nothing inscrutable in her shining eyes or the huge smile she was almost incapable of turning off. Her swimsuit model's body radiated happy health rather than cool and jaded sensuality. Kimmy was twenty-five. She had been studying yoga for ten years and teaching for five.

She had taken on his physical rehabilitation as her Karmic mission in life.

"No, *you* have a beautiful body." Bolan grinned up at her and felt the tight pull of the healing wounds in his shoulder and side.

Kimmy blushed.

The bruising his body had taken had gone all the way down to his bones and internal organs. He had lost a good fifteen pounds of muscle mass, but his strength was swiftly returning. His thigh no longer bothered him, and his five-mile morning jogs on the beach were getting easier. He had to be careful how he positioned his hand, but his bench press had climbed back up over the three-hundred-pound mark. The neurosurgeon had proclaimed him recovered from the concussions. There had been no bleeding in his brain. He was expected to make a full recovery.

It had been a week since he'd awakened in a cold sweat, yelling and clawing for his gun from nightmares of the grave.

The bamboo of the veranda creaked under the weight of someone climbing the stairs. The hut had no phone. Bolan had a satellite link in a suitcase under the bed, but he had not touched it in the month he'd been living on the beach.

Bolan rolled to his feet. Kimmy gasped as he drew the sound-suppressed Star machine pistol from beneath the cushion by his feet in the same motion. The pistol was set on full-auto. The safety flicked off beneath his thumb.

Bolan leveled the pistol as someone knocked on the thin rattan slats of the door.

"Striker?"

The soldier lowered the pistol. "Come in, Hal."

Brognola walked in. His dark blue suit looked totally out of place in the tropical hut. "It's hot out there."

"You need to invest in a sarong." Bolan put the pistol on a low table. The big Fed took off his sunglasses and stared at Kimmy in grudging awe.

Kimmy had no qualms about public nudity, and the secluded strip of coastline was clothing optional. Bolan smiled. "Kimmy. Could you get some cold beers? Hal is looking kind of parched."

Kimmy nodded happily. "Okay."

Brognola shook his head as he watched Kimmy's yoga-trained body walk down the stairs to the beach. "My God..."

"What's up, Hal?"

"Just seeing how you're doing. We haven't heard from you in a while."

Bolan sighed. They both knew Brognola was lying. "How's Del Carpio?"

"He still might lose the arm. There wasn't a lot left to attach it to. It will take a couple of more surgeries, but he should get his face back. He was having some problems making adjustments, and with nightmares. He's on some pretty heavy antidepressants, but his therapist doesn't think he'll have to stay on them. But the initial 'rough patch' he's going through is pretty rough." Brognola shook his head. "He's a tough son of a bitch, though. I think he's going to be all right."

"He was a Green Beret."

"Yeah, they don't come much tougher than that. We'll take care of him. All the way."

The two men were silent as the unspoken lay between them. Bolan let out a long breath. "So?"

The big Fed looked away. "He's alive."

"I know."

Brognola didn't ask how Bolan knew. The subject hadn't been mentioned since they had brought Bolan unconscious from the Clubhouse. He hadn't spoken of it during his surgeries or asked in his convalescence. Bolan hadn't mentioned the Iceman before he had climbed aboard the plane for Costa Rica with Kimmy a month ago, and he had been incommunicado since.

"I'm going to kill him."

"I don't think that will be necessary."

"And just what does that mean?" Bolan bared his teeth. "He still has assets we can't even begin to imagine. You stick him in Leavenworth, under maximum security, bury him in solitary, and he's still a threat to you and your family."

"No."

"No? He's a war hero, Hal. He won the Congressional Medal of Honor in the Gulf. No matter what he's done, no prosecutor will go for the death penalty, and no judge will give it out as a sentence. This doesn't go to trial."

The head Fed flinched before Bolan's terrible gaze. "It's...not going to go to trial."

Bolan's voice went very calm. "Tell me what that means, Hal."

"Striker, he's brain dead."

Bolan stared.

"You pounded his brains out of his head. Hell, you pounded his left eye right out of his head. They reconstructed his face and wired his jaw together. They sewed his thumb back on and cemented his skull fractures. The attorney general was hoping we could put him on trial, but he's done, Mack. You cracked his skull. There was extensive bleeding within the brain. The only thing on what's left of the Iceman's mind is where his next bowl of applesauce is coming from."

Bolan stared out the window at the beach.

"Listen." Brognola shook his head in frustration. "I know what he did—"

Bolan's voice went as cold as the grave. "You have no idea what he did."

Brognola flinched.

"The only person on Earth who does is Del Carpio, and he's on happy pills." Bolan's eyes flared. "Pray to God you never get even an inkling."

The big Fed looked away.

The soldier turned and stared out the window at the ocean again. The sun was starting to sink. The afternoon breeze was cool as it whipped up whitecaps out in the breakers. The days were still warm, but the cool afternoon wind and the colder nights were delivering a message.

Summer was over.

"Striker, there's something else you should know."

"And what's that?"

Brognola cleared his throat. "He's a quad."

Bolan turned.

"You cracked two of his cervical vertebrae. You put him in a wheelchair, and he doesn't have the brains left to maneuver it with a mouth control. Forget him."

Kimmy came back in with a twelve-pack of beer and a bottle of tequila. She smiled happily.

Brognola tried to keep his eyes off of Kimmy's body. Bolan smiled, and the tension in the hut eased "Tell you what, Hal. Let's enjoy the sunset. Then tomorrow, you get your ass on a plane."

"Okay, deal. And what about you?"

"I'll be back in a week."

He looked sidelong at Bolan. "You promise?"

"Hal, I give you my word of honor. I'll be back in a week."

*Hullman House Mental Facility, Virginia,*
*six months later*

BOLAN GAZED upon the Iceman.

"Can I have a moment alone with him?"

The nurse looked up at Bolan and reexamined the pass he had pinned to his shirt and the badge he wore around his neck. "Well, it's a little irregular with a patient in his condition."

"We have history." Bolan sighed. "I know he probably can't hear me, but there are things I need to say to him." Bolan looked at the nurse an earnestly. "Can you understand that?"

"I can understand that. It's a terrible thing." The nurse nodded. "Will five minutes be enough?"

"Yes, thank you, and thank you for understanding."

The nurse turned and closed the door.

The room was a blank white cube. There was no window. A single bare fluorescent fixture lit the room. The only things inside were a bed, a rack holding two fresh gowns and a side table that held a vase with some flowers. A bedpan sat on a shelf.

The Iceman sat in a wheelchair. It had no motor. His emaciated frame sat collapsed against the chair back and his head hung to one side. A black patch covered the broken, empty socket of his left eye. Deep scars showed through the hair that was growing back from his surgery shavings. His head, face and jaw were oddly lumped from the fractures to his face and skull. His beard had grown down and almost touched his sunken chest. A thin trail of drool slid from the corner of his mouth. His remaining blue eye was rolled toward the ceiling and stared dully at nothing. There was nothing of the Iceman within it. His breath came in a steady shallow wheeze from his slack mouth.

"Hello, Ice."

The Iceman's single eye stared blankly upward. His breathing didn't change.

Bolan reached into his jacket. He pulled out a jelly jar with a dozen small, crawling brown shapes inside it. He swirled it before he set it on the little side table. The little brown spiders tried to crawl up the sides and fell back to fight among themselves.

"Ice, you're a quad. You can't move. That's a medical fact. So I want you to consider your position very carefully. If you don't answer me, I'm going to upend this jar over your head and lock the door."

The Iceman stared at the ceiling catatonically.

Bolan picked the jar up and unscrewed the cap.

"Del Carpio sends you his regards."

The Iceman's remaining eye rolled down and stared at Bolan. It was utterly cold and calculating. "You know, I've spent months trying to figure out a way to kill you and your friend, Brognola."

Bolan nodded back. "I know."

"But I just can't do it. Not like...this." The Iceman's eye trailed down his body to his withered limbs. His eye tracked back to meet Bolan's. "Kind of a catch-22. I open my mouth and I go on trial. I don't, and I sit here and drool in this little room until I go insane."

Bolan looked down upon the man who had buried him alive. "I want you to know I did everything in my power to kill you, but there were just too many of them. They pulled me off."

"So I gather." The Iceman smiled slightly. "And now you're here. You know, it's actually kind of nice to talk to someone."

"I didn't come here to talk."

"No. No, you didn't." The Iceman peered at the jar and its crawling contents. "So, you here to turn me in, or you going to put me down in the Boneyard with the spiders?"

"Your body's your Boneyard, Ice." Bolan's voice went cold. "I'm hear to give you the option that you didn't give me or Del Carpio."

The Executioner and the Iceman stared at each other for long moments. An understanding passed between the two men.

The Iceman didn't blink.

"Kill me."

The Executioner crossed the room with a single stride. He barred his forearm beneath the Iceman's chin and placed his palm against the back of his head. The Iceman's atrophied neck muscles gave almost no resistance as Bolan heaved.

The Iceman's neck broke like a rotten branch.

Bolan released the Iceman. His head fell bonelessly onto his chest. Bolan closed the jar and put it back in his pocket. He left the tiny room and closed the door behind him. The nurse looked up from her desk as Bolan walked up and signed out. "His file says he was in the Navy. They say he won the Congressional Medal of Honor."

"He did."

"I'm sorry." She nodded sadly. "It's a terrible thing."

"Yes it is."

The nurse watched as the man walked away.

Stony Man is deployed against an armed
invasion on American soil....

# ROOTS
# OF TERROR

A country held hostage by a violent military junta,
Myanmar is a land of horror and beauty. As the ruling party
struggles to maintain its stranglehold on millions of innocent
countrymen, the rally cry of freedom fighters rings on the
anniversary of slaughter. But those in power are prepared to
retaliate with stockpiles of deadly nerve gas and American
nuclear weapons. Stony Man operatives spring into action
before Myanmar's call to freedom becomes a death knell.

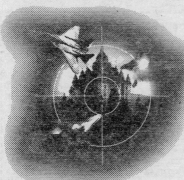

## STONY
## MAN

*Available in
April 2003
at your favorite
retail outlet.*

# Take
# 2 explosive books
# plus a
# mystery bonus
# FREE

# James Axler
# Outlanders®

## TALON AND FANG

Kane finds himself thrown twenty-five years into a parallel future, a world where the mysterious Imperator has seemingly restored civilization to America. In this alternate reality, only Kane and Grant have survived, and the spilled blood has left them estranged. Yet Kane is certain that somewhere in time lies a different path to tomorrow's reality—and his obsession may give humanity their last chance to battle past and future as a sinister madman controls the secret heart of the world.

*In the Outlands, the shocking truth is humanity's last hope.*

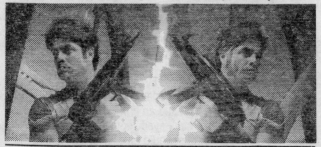

# DEATH LANDS®

## Damnation Road Show

*Available in June 2003 at your favorite retail outlet.*

Eerie remnants of preDark times linger a century after the nuclear blowout. But a traveling road show gives new meaning to the word *chilling*. Ryan and his warrior group have witnessed this carny's handiwork in the ruins and victims of unsuspecting villes. Even facing tremendous odds does nothing to deter the companions from challenging this wandering death merchant and an army of circus freaks. And no one is aware that a steel-eyed monster from the past is preparing a private act that would give Ryan star billing....